Brad fell he~~~~~~~~~~~~~~~~ out of him. As he str~~~~~~~~~~~~~~~~, Morgan found the light switch. Stunned by the fall, it took him several seconds to regain his bearings. What jolted him back to reality was Morgan's blood-curdling scream.

Morgan's face was pale, her eyes wide with fear. One of her trembling fingers pointed to something behind Brad. He pushed himself into a sitting position and turned. Then he, too, inhaled sharply.

What he'd slipped in was a pool of blood. The blood had oozed wet and sticky from its source: a man lying on his stomach, hands crudely bound behind his back. The back of his head had been split open with a heavy knife . . .

"An all-out, go-for-broke medical horror story."
—Stephen King on *The Unborn*

"Marvelous . . . the best of its kind since *Rosemary's Baby*."
—Mary Higgins Clark on *The Unborn*

"The scariest novel we've seen in years . . . lock your door . . . and start reading."
—*Cosmopolitan* on *The Unborn*

"A winner . . . Top-notch edge-of-your-seat entertainment . . . A non-stop roller-coaster ride into medical terror!"
—Michael Palmer on *The Center*

THE
PROVIDER

DAVID SHOBIN

St. Martin's Paperbacks

THE PROVIDER

Copyright © 2000 by David Shobin.
Author photo on back cover by Maureen Bahou.

ISBN: 0-312-97185-0

Printed in the United States of America

St. Martin's Paperbacks edition/February 2000

St. Martin's Paperbacks are published by St. Martin's Press, 175 Fifth Avenue, New York, N.Y. 10010.

10 9 8 7 6 5 4 3 2 1

in memory of Jack Shobin—
a kind and gentle man

ACKNOWLEDGMENTS

Heartfelt thanks to Alan Goldblatt for help with the forensic details of the manuscript. As before, thanks to Deanna Gebhart for technical computer assistance.

A thank you also goes to Joe Veltre, of St. Martin's Press, for editorial help, and especially to Linda Price, for her tireless editing, insight, and wisdom. Continued thanks to my agent, the indefatigable Henry Morrison.

Finally, an ongoing vote of appreciation for Jim Byrne, Bob Kaplan, Bob Riley, Nat Blumberg, Jerry Levin, Robert Hirsch, John Franco, and Jerry Garguilo for help with personal matters.

AUTHOR'S NOTE

University Hospital at Stony Brook is a real (and superb) tertiary care institution on Long Island. But other than for the hospital, the characters and events are products of the author's imagination and should not be construed as real. Any resemblance to actual people or events is coincidental. The characters, events, and dialogue herein are purely fictitious and are not intended to depict actual people or events.

THE PROVIDER

PROLOGUE

The beetles were quite beautiful.

Only half a centimeter long, this rare species of the order *Coleoptera* had extraordinary coloring, a spectacular combination of onyx and lavender. The hardened forewings were lustrous, gleaming like burnished shields. A pastel lavender swath cut across their wing cases like a regimental stripe, and the two menacing green dots prominent on their heads, pseudo-eyes, were prominent like iridescent buttons.

When huddled together, as they were now, the beetles were a quivering mass of color. Carrion eaters, they had an extraordinary sense of smell, and the scent of decomposition was in the air. They crowded expectantly in their box, barely moving, their wafting antennae gently probing the air, knowing on some primitive level what awaited them.

The man deposited what was left of a cadaver on the stainless steel table nearby. The corpse was nearly skeletonized, devoid of internal organs, stripped of all flesh and outer appendages. Yet bits of cartilage and ligament still remained, holding the bones together. It was for these biological fasteners that the beetles were intended. Working cautiously, the man carried the enamel beetle box to the table and gently tilted it. In a wave of ebony pellets, the beetles spilled out into the middle of what remained of the thorax.

They hadn't fed in days. The beetles immediately began swarming, scurrying toward putrefying remnants. An evolutionary miracle that hadn't changed in millions of years, the insects were ideally suited for this sort of

work. When they encountered a morsel of flesh, their
pincer-like mouthparts would firmly skewer the tissue,
and then their razor-sharp mandibles would whittle it
away. Even the toughest gristle eventually yielded to
their persistence. The hundreds of beetles fed quickly in
a wave of voracious, piranha-like consumption.

While some gorged on the ribs, others hastened up
the vertebral staircase, eventually reaching the back of
the head. In its crypts and recesses, the skull contained
a wealth of tissue. Swarms of *Coleopterae* scuttled into
the foramen magnum at the skull's base, spilling over
one another in their haste. Several dozen worked their
way into the ear canals, where choice bits of tissue clung
to the tiny bones of the inner ear. Still others rushed
crab-like along the temporal bone to reach the posterior
orbits. Although the eyes were gone, the sockets contained a richness of food, from minuscule remnants of
muscle to fine strands of ligament.

The feast lasted an hour. When the man returned, the
skeleton had a fresh and polished look, picked clean
down to the glistening bones. Having fed, the beetles
massed together in groups of ten or twenty, small coal-
like lumps on an ivory background. Here and there, a
wayward beetle would emerge from a bony orifice, hovering uncertainly on its rim.

The man turned the box on its side and placed it on
the table. It contained a cube of fetid, decomposing
meat. Within seconds, the massed beetles grew tense and
shimmering, picking up the scent. An instant later they
were on the move, spilling in undulating fashion across
the bones, an army on the march. Reaching the enamel
box, they piled onto the putrid morsel in a gluttonous
frenzy, five and six deep. When they were all inside, the
man sealed the box and returned it to its resting place.
He wasn't worried about the beetles' survival.

They would feed again before the week was out.

CHAPTER ONE

A quarter-century after its construction, University Hospital at Stony Brook remained Long Island's preeminent architectural masterpiece, a hospital in the round. County ordinance generally prohibited construction of buildings more than several stories tall, but University's twin nineteen-story circular towers soared over the sprawling campus nearby. The hospital was a marvel of concrete-and-glass construction. On its eighth floor, in the forty-bed Newborn Intensive Care Unit, Nicholas Giancola clung to life.

Born four weeks prematurely, little Nicholas weighed slightly over five and a half pounds at birth. His diminutive size, however, was not the problem. What most challenged the pediatricians' skill was his unusual combination of birth defects. In addition to suffering from a severe diaphragmatic hernia, in which his abdominal contents were inside his chest, Nicholas had an abnormality of the aorta's ductus arteriosis, a fetal vessel that normally closed after birth. From his initial breath, these two conditions severely taxed his compromised lungs. But what made an already bad situation all that much worse was the complication of meconium aspiration, where the residue in his colon had been released prematurely, only to be breathed in during the birth process. The combination of problems was a clinical recipe for disaster.

Nicholas' first few weeks of life were touch-and-go. His basic problem was pulmonary, and it became a challenge to deliver enough oxygen for him to survive. The thick, sludge-like meconium filled his bronchi, obstructing airflow. And his lungs couldn't sufficiently expand due to the upwardly displaced guts. It was a vicious catch-22 in which his condition was too unstable to allow the necessary surgery; yet, until his hernia was corrected, he'd never fully stabilize. The pediatric team soon realized it couldn't succeed without resorting to the extraordinary. Early on, it became apparent that Nicholas would need help.

The child's appearance made the problem all the more poignant. Nicholas had dark, soulful eyes and a head full of curly brown hair. In spite of all the trappings of modern medicine surrounding him, he often had a ready smile for the doctors and nurses attending him. From early in his hospitalization, he was a ward favorite.

University personnel had recently become ECMO trained and certified. ECMO, or extra-corporeal membrane oxygenation, was developed for cases just such as Nicholas'. He was to be the hospital's first patient to undergo the procedure. Basically a sophisticated pediatric bypass pump, ECMO removed oxygen-starved blood from the patient's body, delivered it to the ECMO apparatus, and then returned it to the patient. The pump replaced the lungs during a period when buying time was critical.

And buy time it did. While Nicholas' blood was being shunted, the respiratory therapists were able to thoroughly lavage his lungs, removing all the greenish particulate matter. After three such treatments, his lungs were deemed as meconium-free as they'd get. His O_2 saturation rose, and his rapid heartbeat fell to acceptable levels. Finally, after two weeks of treatment, Nicholas was considered clinically stable. It was time for the pediatric surgeons to work their magic.

Even at his tender age, little Nicholas had attracted a following. A De Mille–like entourage of scrub-suited personnel escorted him to the OR. The largest of the ORs was required to accommodate the two dozen people in attendance. The Chief of Surgery himself acted as first assistant. In a remarkable display of surgical dexterity, the complicated hernia repair was accomplished in less than an hour, skin-to-skin. Nicholas' lungs reacted almost immediately. Without the encumbering intestines, they expanded to full capacity, delivering oxygen-rich air to chronically hypoxic tissues. Nicholas was immediately returned to the Newborn Intensive Care Unit, where the NICU staff hovered about him as if in prayer. Finally, it began to look as if everything was going to be all right.

But it was not. With the meconium largely removed and the hernia repaired, the medical staff anticipated comparative smooth sailing. After the predictably rocky first-day post-op, they had expected Nickie to be weaned from the respiratory within twenty-four hours. Yet, forty-eight hours later, he was showing no sign of the long-awaited pulmonary freedom. Whenever the staff tried cutting back his assisted ventilations, Nickie's O_2 saturation plummeted precipitously. Clearly, something else was going on, something they hadn't anticipated. If the parents would give their consent, the time had come to perform a biopsy.

Sal and Donna Giancola would have given their lives for their son. They had already agreed to everything the doctors recommended, so getting permission for the biopsy was no great obstacle. Donna was only nineteen, her husband three years older. They came from large, supportive Italian families and were eager to get an early start on a family of their own. In truth, they were emotionally bludgeoned by everything that had happened. As time went by, constant attendance by their son's bedside was too much for them to bear. Shell-shocked, they sat in the nearby hall, watching from a distance.

Except in rare instances like this, newborn lung biopsies were generally performed post-mortem. The biopsy was done early the next morning, and it went surprisingly well. The NICU staff put a rush on it, and the results—which usually required two days to process—were ready that afternoon. What the pathologist found couldn't possibly have been more catastrophic. On top of all the other things that were wrong with him, Nicholas was suffering from an extremely rare condition known as alveolar capillary dysplasia.

The disease was a maldevelopment of the lungs' smallest blood vessels, a situation that severely impaired oxygen exchange. Even worse, it had never been successfully treated without the most dire intervention. Ultimately, it was fatal in all cases, and few children survived more than several months. The only hope was a lung transplant.

When they heard the diagnosis, the entire medical team was stunned. They'd been riding a collective high after the surgery, and now the wind was suddenly taken out of their sails. An oppressive cloud of helplessness hung over the NICU. Nearly an hour passed before anyone even made a concrete suggestion.

"I'll put in a call to H.U.P.," said Meg Erhardt, the evening shift head nurse.

"Nobody there now," said a colleague. "The transplant coordinator probably won't be back until tomorrow morning."

H.U.P. was Philadelphia's Hospital of the University of Pennsylvania, home of the nation's leading newborn lung transplant team.

"At least I can leave a message on their machine," Meg said. "Let them know they have a customer." ~

It was a long shot for survival, but it was the only chance they had. A pediatric lung transplant was a major undertaking that involved significant time and preparation. First, the child had to be accepted onto the transplant list. Then there was the matter of tissue and HLA typing, followed by payment prearrangements. A procedure of this magnitude would cost the insurance company tens of thousands of dollars. Moreover, the mechanics of intercity newborn transport were so intricate that its performance resembled a major military airlift. And finally, there was the not-inconsequential matter of waiting for a suitable donor to die.

Even in the most favorable circumstances, a minimum wait was two months. In Nicholas' case, it was doubtful that he'd remain alive that long. He was very weak, and he already had too many strikes against him.

A week later, Nickie was still hanging on by the barest of threads. He remained wedded to his respirator. It was all the team could do to keep his oxygen saturation up to minimum levels. He couldn't eat, and he was being fed through nasogastric and intravenous lines. Fortunately, the initial contact with the transport coordinator had gone well, and preliminary paperwork was underway. Samples were undergoing testing for a tissue match. The major obstacle was proving to be the insurance company.

Nicholas was an HMO patient, and an expenditure of

this magnitude wasn't in keeping with the company's policy of cost containment. Grudgingly, they'd sprung for the ECMO, but a transplant was more than they were willing to approve. They turned the request down. The doctors planned to appeal, and other staffers wrote letters about medical necessity—letters which, in time, might prove successful. But time was the one commodity they didn't have.

Often in the NICU, the joy of working with newborns was offset by their critical condition. But now the staff at University Hospital couldn't shrug off a heavy shroud of hopelessness. They had all been intimately involved in Nickie's care. His predicament affected each of them. Everyone was glum. Yet despite their mood, they all knew they'd give nothing less than one hundred percent. Keeping babies alive was their job, and it was what they did best. If everyone pulled together, they just might be able to keep Nickie going another month. Or two. However long it took until he got his transplant.

It happened on a weekend, shortly after the eleven P.M. shift change. No doctors were around. The departing nurses were scribbling chart notes before the incoming group made their rounds. Suddenly, the air was pierced by a shrill electronic bleating, the alarm of an oxygen sensor. Meg dropped her chart and looked up, startled. She quickly glanced around the nursery. Some thirty feet away, a flashing orange light beckoned.

Jesus, she thought. It's Nickie!

She threw down her pen and leapt from her chair, charging across the room. Nicholas' isolette was an open, flat, wide acrylic cradle bursting with high-tech gadgetry. In addition to cardiac, temperature, and urine monitors, the mattress was crisscrossed with a Medusa-like web of wires and fine-bore tubing. Meg prayed that the alarm had sounded because of a detached lead, but one look at the patient convinced her that that was not the problem.

Nickie's skin had the appearance of bluestone, a leaden, unhealthy slate-like color invariably associated with the oxygen deficit called hypoxia. A quick glance at the oxygen monitor revealed a low saturation of eighty-nine percent, and falling. Not good, not good at all. Meg whirled and barked at the nurse close on her heels.

"Page the chief resident, stat! And see if they can get someone from respiratory up here!"

Her eyes quickly darted back to the baby. His endotracheal tube was still in place, and the ventilator appeared to be properly set up. But kids just didn't go sour for no apparent reason. He'd been fine half an hour before—well, perhaps not fine, but as good as he could manage. It was probably a defective connection in the oxygen tubing, or maybe the ET tube was slightly loose. Meg quickly assessed the monitor readings. Other than for the O_2 sat, everything seemed all right, except for the expected rebound tachycardia. So what in the world was going on?

With equal suddenness, the cardiac monitor alarm went off, beeping incessantly. Meg was startled to find that the pattern that a moment ago had looked so benign was now tracing the ominous squiggles of ventricular fibrillation.

"He's in fib!" she shouted toward the nursing station. "Find out if the cardiologist's around, and get him here on the double!" Good Lord, she thought, what next?

She didn't have to wait long for an answer. After hurriedly checking to see that all the EKG leads were properly attached, she glanced up at the oscilloscope and was horrified to find that the sawtooth squiggles had been replaced by a flat line. The small, overworked heart had arrested. Trained to react, Meg promptly put her hands on each side of the sternum and began cardiac compressions with both thumbs.

"Come on, Nickie, come *on*," she prompted with a tone of rising urgency.

The tranquil scene was instantly transformed into one of frenzied activity. The NICU nurses were a well-oiled machine, trained for disaster. They quickly drew up meds, inspected all lines, and prepared for cardioversion. The baby, meanwhile, lay pathetically still and unresponsive, his skin the color of impending death. Within minutes, the sought-for help arrived, descending like reserves at the battlefront. Yet if not too late, what they brought was far, far too little.

They worked on the child for an hour, not wanting to concede defeat. No one could forget the two other similar deaths in the past few months. But shortly after midnight, the futility of their efforts became obvious. The tiny body had endured too much over the weeks to respond to resuscitation.

Little Nicholas Giancola, age four weeks, one day, was pronounced dead at twelve-thirteen A.M. He was the third child to die.

CHAPTER TWO

Jennifer Hartman was frightened. She was six months pregnant, and she'd just been discharged by her obstetrician. Well, perhaps not *discharged*; he was referring her elsewhere for care, to a specialist at University Hospital. It wasn't, he said, that he didn't want to take care of her. But she now needed the services of someone trained in high-risk obstetrics, a perinatologist. Oh, he'd delivered twins before, he said. But he was younger, then. And with malpractice and managed care the way they were, it was probably better all around . . .

Twins! She was still in shock. Jennifer grabbed the door of her car, stunned. She didn't know whether to laugh or cry. For her, just getting pregnant was a minor miracle, but never in her wildest imaginings had she entertained the fantasy of multiple birth. When she finally entered the car, she was overcome with a rush of conflicting emotions. Not the least of them was a strange sense of abandonment.

She'd been a patient of Dr. Strong's ever since she first began seeing a gynecologist at seventeen. He was getting on in years, to be sure, and some considered him old-fashioned. But he had been there for her during her three-year struggle with infertility, and he had an avuncular manner that she found reassuring. With only sixteen weeks to go in her pregnancy, she was looking forward to Strong's support and presence in the delivery room. Yet now . . . good Lord, twins! She'd call Richard in a few minutes, let him know. But first she urgently needed some medical insight. As Jennifer started the car and drove out of the parking lot, she worked the speed dial on her mobile phone.

"Dr. Morgana Robinson, please," she said into the hands-free mike. After a pause, "It's her sister." Another brief delay; then, "Morgan? It's Jen. You are absolutely not going to believe what happened."

Such sibling unburdening was not unusual. For the past five years, her older sister Morgan had been the backbone of what she called family, until Richard came along—a husband her parents disapproved of. Not that Jen didn't have other relatives; it was just that she didn't talk with them very much. A younger brother, two years her junior and a very independent sort, was finishing a degree in Hawaii.

As for her mother and father, well. . . The elder Robinsons were a socially conscious couple who couldn't tolerate their children's relationships with anyone of lesser social strata. When Jen met Richard, who came from a working class background and had dropped out of college, she was immediately shunned by her parents. The rift eventually widened into a veritable chasm once they married. After her parents moved to Arizona, she exchanged Christmas cards with them, but not much else. They weren't even aware that she was pregnant.

Once Jen stopped speaking, her sister's voice finally emerged from the dashboard speaker.

"I'm not going to get into an I-told-you-so," said her sister, "but remember how everyone kept saying you looked big? Really gargantuan. I honestly don't know what took him so long. Believe me, you're much better off without that old—"

"Morgan, give it a rest, okay? We've already been through this a thousand times, and it's over now. Just tell me what you know about this new guy."

"Sorry, Jen. I didn't mean to mouth off like that. What did you say his name was again?"

Jennifer eyed the professional card that Strong had given her. "Actually, he gave me two names. One was a Dr. Schubert—"

"Schubert? *Arnold* Schubert, the guy who does fetal reductions?"

"What's fetal reduction?"

"Never mind," said Morgan. "Who's the second?"

"Hawkins. Brad Hawkins, out at University Hospital. Do you know him?"

"Not personally," Morgan said, "but I've heard the name. He's fairly young, but he has a good reputation."

"How young is *fairly*?"

"Hold on, I'll check the directory." From the background, there came the riffling of pages. "Here we are. He's on your managed care plan. Hawkins, Bradford C. By his date of birth, he'd be thirty-eight. Got his boards six years ago in MFM—"

"What's that?"

"Maternal and Fetal Medicine," said Morgan. "After four years of OB/GYN residency, there's this two-year fellowship in perinatology, which they call MFM. Did his med school at Yale, then took his residency and fellowship in Chicago. It lists his marital status as *widowed*."

"Morgan, I'm really not interested . . ."

"Anyhow, your Dr. Hawkins has all the credentials. It says he has only one outstanding malpractice case, which for an obstetrician around here is fantastic. I'd say he's your man, Jen. University's a referral center, and with twins, I think you're better off there than in some backwater hospital. You told Richard, didn't you?"

"Not yet, but I will now." Jennifer exhaled with relief. "Thanks, Morgan. You're always there when I need you. So how does my big sister feel about becoming an aunt twice over?"

"I was just getting used to the one, but I think I can handle it."

"You don't think I'll have any problem with the AmeriCare paperwork, do you?"

"Don't give it a second thought," Morgan reassured. "I'll take care of everything personally."

Morgana Robinson, M.D., smiled to herself as she hung up the phone and shook her head in silent amusement, sending her red hair fluttering. Did Jennifer have any idea what she was in for, both before and during the delivery? As a pediatrician by training, Morgan was fully aware of the tribulations faced by mothers of multiples. But she also knew that, in Jennifer's case, it would be a labor of love. Her sister had been trying to get pregnant for three years. Once the shock wore off, the reality of two hoped-for children would no doubt double her happiness.

Jen had spunk. Most children couldn't handle their parents' rejection with the gutsy determination Jennifer had. Then there was Richard's lack of schooling. When Jen initially found herself the primary breadwinner, her relationship with Richard temporarily soured. Morgan had watched her younger sister persevere in a struggling marriage where others would have bailed out. Eventually, however, when Richard landed a job with a promising future, their relationship strengthened. Finally,

Morgan had seen Jen endure three difficult years of infertility stoically, and with a minimum of self-pity.

Morgan returned to the paperwork before her. Several neatly stacked piles of reports awaited her review. Morgan sighed. In some ways she longed for a return to the clinical chaos of two years ago, when she'd been an actively practicing pediatrician. But leaving the field had been her decision—a choice she'd made with full knowledge of what she was leaving, and what lay ahead. Now, at least, life-and-death decisions no longer had a haunting immediacy.

Still, in her new capacity, there were decisions aplenty to make. As Assistant Medical Director at AmeriCare, her primary responsibility was to review questionable requests for medical care. Initially, it had been simple, largely black-and-white: either the proposed services were covered, or they weren't. But now, two years into her tenure, Morgan was increasingly caught in complex shades of gray. Not that it would matter when it came to her sister. AmeriCare was Jennifer's provider, and Morgan would spare no effort to make sure Jen and the babies were completely covered.

Dr. Brad Hawkins was on his way to the delivery room when he bumped into Meg Erhardt outside the fifth-floor elevators. Meg's usually warm smile was missing, and there were fine, hard lines of worry about the corners of her eyes.

"Long day, Miss Meggie?" he asked. "You look a little harried."

"More like a long night," she said. "You heard about Nickie Giancola?"

"The ECMO kid?"

"Right. He died last night toward the end of my shift."

Brad was stunned. He'd been so absorbed in patient care since early that morning that he hadn't heard the hospital gossip. "From the ECMO?"

"No, that's what's so weird. It was just like the others—sudden duskiness and hypoxia. Then respiratory collapse and cardiac arrest."

"Jesus. You guys couldn't resuscitate him?"

She shook her head. "We tried for over an hour. He wouldn't respond."

"How many does that make it?"

"Three," she said dejectedly. "Each about four weeks apart. Completely different cases, but all with the same clinical presentation in the end."

Two months before, Brad had delivered a newborn that ended up in the NICU. Some time afterward, for no apparent reason, the child died after a sudden cardiopulmonary arrest. "Like my case?" he asked.

"Almost identical."

"What does Harrington have to say?" he asked. Harrington was Chief of Neonatology.

"Doesn't have a clue. Maybe something'll turn up at the post, but I doubt it. Look, I gotta run. Call me, okay?"

Brad stood deep in thought, arms crossed in front of his chest, staring at the elevator's closing doors. Nickie Giancola's mother hadn't been his patient, but he'd been in the DR when a colleague called him over for a bedside consultation. Although she was obviously scared to death, she'd greeted him with a warm smile.

For forty minutes Brad and the other attending agonized over the unborn baby's unusual fetal heart rate tracing, until Donna successfully delivered vaginally. It was only once they'd diagnosed Nicholas' multiple birth defects that the reason for the bizarre tracing became apparent.

For the past few weeks, Brad had popped into the NICU several times a day to check up on the child. He noted sadly that young Mr. and Mrs. Giancola had both grown haggard and had taken to lingering silently in the shadows, afraid even to ask about their son's condition. Yet, given everything that was wrong with him, Nickie's progress had been remarkable. On the face of it, Nickie's unexpected death was just as perplexing as the others, and every bit as demoralizing for the hospital staff.

CHAPTER THREE

At eleven A.M., Jennifer swung her Volvo wagon into the wide, circular driveway fronting the Islandia headquarters of AmeriCare. Jen had persuaded Morgan to accompany her on her first OB visit to Dr. Hawkins. As the station wagon pulled to a halt, Morgan bounced out of the building's front portico. Jen watched her sister approach. At thirty, Morgan was tall and slender, with a bounce in her step and Nicole Kidman good looks. She wore her red hair long and loose, and it always seemed to be catching the wind, like russet autumn leaves. Her long, horsey stride was midway between a slink and a canter.

"*Very* nice wheels, Sis," Morgan said, getting into the passenger side. She rubbed a palm across the upholstered dash. "Richard's concession to safety?"

Jennifer nodded. "His Bible is *Consumer Reports*, and this model's highly rated. But it's got some zip, and it's sort of sporty, don't you think?"

"Perfect for a mother of twins."

"Come on, it's not that bad! Anyway, your priorities become different when you have responsibilities. You'll see what I mean when you get pregnant one of these days."

Morgan smiled. "Thanks, but I'll take your word for it."

During the short drive, they exchanged sisterly chit-chat, but Morgan was distracted. Early that morning, a report had crossed her desk detailing yet another NICU death at University. Morgan knew the Giancola child; she'd approved his ECMO expenditure. The exact circumstances and cause of death were as yet unexplained. Morgan's reassurances to her sister notwithstanding, this was the third such newborn death at University in three calendar months. Maybe, out of earshot of her sister, she could ask Dr. Hawkins what was going on.

Hawkins' office was in a sprawling, single-story office park that housed the practices of many University faculty. They located his building, parked, and entered a spacious but unoccupied waiting room. Apparently, Jennifer had the first appointment. After she signed in, she was given a clipboard with the customary medical and insurance questionnaires. She took a seat beside Morgan, who was leafing through a copy of *People*.

"Is he in yet?" Morgan said.

"They say he is. I'm glad we came early."

Just then, the door alongside the front desk opened, and out came a man wearing a white lab coat. He was about six feet tall, with a lanky, athletic build. His coat was unbuttoned, and the tie-less plaid shirt suggested easy informality. He briefly smiled at the women as he approached the large fish tank in the corner of the waiting room.

Lifting a container of Tetraruby, he sprinkled a generous serving across the water, watching the flakes descend like snow. "Pizza man!" he called, lapsing into a lazy grin as he tapped once on the glass, softly. "Come and get it!" Inside the tank, the colorful fish darted knife-like through the water, attacking the flakes.

Across the room, the sisters turned to stare at one another, sharing a dubious look. Morgan shrugged good-naturedly. "Some doctors are very laid-back these days," she whispered. "Reassures the patients." But inside, she was wondering if the doctor was just as flaky as the fish food.

He gave them a goofy grin and sauntered toward the door. "Poor guys'd be lost without me," he said over his shoulder.

Before the interior door closed completely, the receptionist leaned their way and told them to enter. They were ushered into a well-lit consultation room whose corners were marked by dracaena and corn plants. Brad was sitting behind a teak desk. When he saw them enter, he hastily put a magazine on the shelf behind him. Then he stood up and introduced himself to the one obviously pregnant. Jennifer, in turn, introduced her sister.

"Morgana Robinson," Jen said, with a hint of pride. "*Doctor* Robinson."

"Don't think I've had the pleasure," he said with a smile. "I'm sure I would've remembered. You an M.D.?"

"Yes," Morgan replied, with unaccustomed self-consciousness. "We haven't met, but I've heard about you."

"Is that right? Anything worth repeating?"

"By and large. I work for AmeriCare."

"Ah," he said slowly, lingering on the word as his eyes narrowed.

Once again, Morgan realized that working for an HMO made her into a pariah. It was a familiar feeling. Managed care was not dear to the hearts of most practicing physicians. Still, she didn't think she deserved this frosty display. Her immediate reaction was dislike. She had a stinging comeback on the tip of her tongue. First there was his cutesy childishness with the fish, and now this superior attitude. Nevertheless, she was determined not to meddle. At least for now. After all, he was her sister's doctor. She leaned back in her chair and kept her mouth shut.

She was glad she did. For fifteen minutes, Brad spoke with her sister, asking probing, intelligent questions. His informal manner was reassuring, and Morgan could tell that Jennifer felt at ease.

Morgan glanced around the room. The décor was tasteful, and the walls sported the requisite diplomas. Looking behind Brad, her eyes fell on the magazine he'd been reading. Called *AU NATUREL*, its cover showed a naked woman tiptoeing into ocean surf. Good God, Morgan thought. The doctor's a nudist.

Above the magazine was a shelf of photos. Several showed a handsome young boy variously aged between around one and six. Next to them was a single picture of a beautiful woman in riding attire, smiling at the camera. His wife, maybe, but wasn't he listed as a widower? She glanced down at his hands. He was wearing a wedding ring.

At length, Brad put down his pen. "That about does it for now. Let's do a quick exam and a sono. Then we'll come back and see if we can agree on a treatment plan." To Morgan, "Want to join us, Doctor?"

Morgan wanted to give Jennifer privacy. "Mind if I wait here?"

"No problem. We'll be right back."

For the next fifteen minutes, Morgan squirmed restlessly. She wasn't sure what was bothering her. There was something she found flip and even sarcastic about Hawkins, but it certainly had nothing to do with his doctoring. His boyish breeziness notwithstanding, he seemed completely professional.

Jennifer was smiling broadly when she re-entered the room. "I know what they are!" she announced excitedly.

Morgan was amused by her sister's glee. "What, pray?"

"One of each! Isn't that wild?"

"That's terrific, Jen."

Brad interrupted. "Let's get that blood work before we talk, okay?" He buzzed the intercom and spoke briefly to his nurse. Seconds later, a white-uniformed woman led Jennifer from the room.

"Everything look okay, Dr. Hawkins?"

"Pretty much. I realize you just do managed care, Dr. Robinson, but do you know anything about twins?"

She glared at him. "I may have a nine-to-five desk job, but that doesn't make me the village idiot!"

His smile was cool, at best. "I'm sorry. It's just that I've had a lot of grief from HMOs these days. I'm sure you've had some medical experience with twins."

"Enough," she said, calming herself with a deep breath. "I did peds in the city before I moved over to AmeriCare. And call me Morgan, okay?"

His smile turned boyish. "Deal. And I'm Brad. Anyway, baby B—that's the boy—is a little on the small side. I don't think we have a growth problem, but he's kind of at the edge of the curve, so we'll have to watch him closely. And your sister's systolic's a little elevated, mid one-thirties. I'm drawing chemistries, coags, and anticardiolopins."

"Are you talking IUGR," she said, referring to growth retardation, "and pre-eclampsia?"

"No to both," he replied. "At least, not yet. But you might recall we find those things a lot more frequently with multiples, so I'm going to see her often. Possibly every week."

Morgan nodded in satisfaction. "Before Jen comes

back, I want to ask you something, Doctor—*Brad*. About the NICU at University. I didn't see any publicity about those two newborn deaths recently, but I did get reports about them. I haven't mentioned anything to Jennifer yet, but I understand there was recently a third. So I have to ask: is everything okay over there? Is there something we should worry about?"

The affability Brad had worn as easily as a loose suit disappeared, replaced by a worried look. His brooding gaze focused on her, and his narrowed eyes were troubled. "What do you know about those deaths?"

"Just that they were all NICU patients. What's going on? From your expression, I suspect you've got a problem."

Brad averted his eyes and took a deep breath. The attractive woman across the desk from him was sharp. Had other outsiders come to the same conclusion? He pushed back from his chair, got up, and walked toward the window, where he toyed with the blinds. "I honestly don't know if there's a problem or not. And I'd appreciate it if what I say doesn't leave this room."

"Done."

"Officially," he began, "there *is* no problem. Just a streak of bad luck. NICU babies do die from time to time, right? After all, it's not the regular nursery, is it? But *not* so officially, I did some chart reviewing last night. I was up there late with a delivery, and I had some time to kill."

"And . . . ?"

"On the face of it," he said, "the cases weren't all that similar. Two girls and a boy, Nicholas. The first kid was a straight preemie, who I delivered at twenty-six weeks. She had a rocky first month but finally seemed to be straightening out, okay?"

She nodded and said, "And the little girl a month later

was a thirty-two-weeker with Listeria sepsis."

"You *have* done your homework, haven't you?" he said.

Morgan shrugged. "I try."

"That brings us to Nickie," he continued. He went on to describe the child's initial condition and subsequent course, much of which Morgan already knew. "But in a particular way, all three cases were identical, at least in the way they died."

"Meaning?"

"Meaning that they all seemed to follow the same script. First, they all survived a major crisis—antibiotics, surgery, ECMO, or sometimes a combination of things. Second, they were all doing reasonably well clinically. Third, they were probably going to remain in the NICU for another couple of months, because their level of care demanded it. And finally, just when the nurses started to relax their guard, the kids went sour, straight downhill. They all died within an hour or two."

"From what?"

"Ah," he said, raising a finger, "that's where it gets interesting. According to the nurses' notes, they initially developed this acute, profound hypoxia. O_2 saturation under ninety, and plummeting."

Morgan frowned. "An embolus?"

"That occurred to them, but they could never document it. No evidence of obstruction or infarction. Those poor kids just sank. They all turned dusky, gases acidotic as hell, and then arrested. Couldn't bring 'em out of it."

"No pneumonia, equipment screw-up, or drug error?"

"No, none of the usual suspects, and they ruled out a dozen more exotic things."

"Then what was it?"

Brad returned to his desk and bent toward her, leaning on his forearms. "That's the big question, isn't it?"

Looking up, she read the concern and fear in his expression. "Tell me I'm overreacting, but could this be the start of an epidemic?"

"The God's honest truth is, I don't know *what* the heck they're dealing with, and neither do they. But because I was involved with two of the cases, I'm worried as hell."

Back in her office, Morgan glanced at her desk, groaning at the sight of the paperwork awaiting her. When she'd enrolled in med school, she never dreamed this was the way she'd be spending her medical career. Still, she had no one to blame but herself. With a sigh, Morgan sat down and leafed through the pile of incoming mail.

"Managed Care Increases the Costs of Preterm Delivery Care," one journal headline read. She put that aside. "S.C. Hospitals Vie for High-Risk Preemies," read another. She separated the journals into three piles: today's reading, future interest, and discards. When she was finished, Morgan moved on to in-house correspondence. The Giancola file was on top.

After learning about Nickie's death, she'd asked Janice, her secretary, to get her the entire folder. And now that she'd spoken with Dr. Hawkins, she wanted to reread everything. Morgan sat back in her chair and studied the file closely, evaluating the data as if it were pieces of a clinical jigsaw puzzle. On the fourth page, a memo caught her eye.

She read it over and over, growing more incredulous each time. According to this, the Giancolas' pediatrician's request for a lung transplant had been denied by AmeriCare. Morgan was furious. Here, she'd been instrumental in getting the ECMO approval, and she fully expected similar approval of further legitimate requests.

The memo was signed by the Medical Director, Martin Hunt, M.D.

Morgan jumped up and stormed down the hall to Hunt's office. She stalked past his secretary and barged unannounced into his room, where she found him on the phone. Undeterred, she demanded an answer.

"Why did you deny the Giancola lung transplant?"

Hunt placed his hand over the receiver. "Be with you in a minute, Morgan. I'm—"

"This can't wait!" she snapped, glaring at him, fists clenched.

"I'll call you right back," said Hunt, putting down the phone. "All right, Morgan. What's so important that—"

"The Giancola kid's lung transplant! A memo with your signature says you denied it!"

Hunt met her gaze. "That's right, I did. We've never approved one before, so why would I want to set a six-figure precedent?"

"Christ, Marty, how could you?" There was distress in her tone. "The poor kid, he'd never survive without it!"

"A moot point, now. He just died, didn't you hear? Way before he would have had the surgery."

Morgan sank heavily into the chair in front of his desk. "Yeah, I heard. It's just that . . . he was a little special. He'd already had successful ECMO—"

"Which I opposed, if you remember. And I was obviously proved correct. Cases like that rarely have a happy ending."

"So what does that mean?" she asked. "Just because something's unusual, or difficult, or is very expensive, we should automatically deny it?"

Hunt frowned. "What's gotten into you? We're not a philanthropy here. AmeriCare's a business, and what we do is *manage care*. God knows, if we can't control costs on experimental stuff, we'll soon be out of business! Is this a news flash to you?"

She sighed. "No, it's just that he was so helpless."

"Look, Morgan. You can't afford that kind of sentimentality when you work here. In one way or another, they're *all* helpless. I know you were a pediatrician, but for God's sake, don't overdo the Mother Teresa routine. It'll only get you in more trouble."

Her eyes narrowed. "What're you talking about, 'more trouble'?"

"You're a good worker, Morgan. But I got word from the Board to keep an eye on you. In the past few months, you've approved some items that are *way* above and beyond. You're not operating in a vacuum here, for God's sake. When you go out on a financial limb with the company's money, you draw attention to yourself. You're getting a reputation as a bleeding heart."

"What's so bad about that? Aren't we supposed to be sensitive to real-life issues?"

"No, we're not. We're supposed to be *practical* about them. And if you can't see it that way, I guarantee you, the Board will be more than happy to find someone who will."

Chastened but still annoyed, Morgan left Hunt's office in a huff, unaware of the medical director's gaze riveted on her back.

As Morgan returned to her office, Janice raised her eyebrows in a "now what?" look and followed her boss inside. In recent months, Janice had become a confidante. Needing little prodding, Morgan readily revealed what had just happened.

"I'm really up to here with their money-grubbing attitude," Morgan said, gesturing to her chin. "One of these days I'm going to tell them just what they can do with their precious job. That child needed a transplant, period. It's infuriating."

"You know your problem, Morgan?" said Janice. "You've got too much heart for this work. Dr. Hunt's right, you know. This isn't about medicine. It's about money."

"Maybe, but eliminate the financial angle, and I'm right, too."

"Then you better watch your back, boss. In this business, being right and staying employed don't go together."

The NICU staff had too many practical distractions to dwell on the Giancola tragedy. Caring for newborns was demanding. Within two weeks, Nicholas was relegated to communal memory. The staff's attention was turned to a recently admitted set of twins.

During the night, the twins had been helicoptered in from their South Shore hospital of birth. The doctor who delivered them had known that his patient was carrying twins, and even contemplated a vaginal delivery, despite their prematurity. But after an adequate trial of labor, the first twin wouldn't descend into the pelvis at all, and a cesarean section was performed. It was during surgery that the doctors discovered the reason for the problem: the babies were joined at the pelvis.

Both babies were born alive and, initially, in good condition, in spite of their size. But no one at the local hospital had ever seen Siamese twins, much less taken care of them. Thus the decision was quickly made, without dissent or discussion, to transfer the children to University Hospital.

Immediately after the pre-dawn admission, preliminary X rays were taken. More sophisticated imaging studies, such as sonography and CT scans, would have to await the arrival of the day shift radiologists. The X rays revealed that the twins were nominally joined at the *ischium*, or pelvic bone. But other than a small bony island at the iliac crest, they appeared to share little bony architecture.

The infants faced one another at a slightly oblique angle, belly-to-belly. A wide, tense bridge of tissue connected their abdomens. Through it, they were certain to share some blood supply, and probably several major organs, the extent of which was yet to be determined. Fortunately, this would not include the heart or lungs. But unfortunately, the degree of organ-sharing was not the problem at hand.

Of greater immediacy was the twins' prematurity. They were born at thirty-three weeks, seven weeks before full term. While this gestational age barely presented a challenge for singletons, seemingly minor problems were magnified in twins, a phenomenon made worse when the twins were developmentally abnormal. Within an hour of their arrival on the unit, the conjoined twins developed severe respiratory distress.

Getting them both successfully intubated proved a technical challenge. Placing the tubes was comparatively easy, but positioning two respirators so close together, almost side-by-side, was not. Finally, after some mechanical improvisations, the ventilators were up and running. It took another several hours, however, before the twins' oxygenation was satisfactory. And that was the easy part.

The NICU staff soon understood that they were beginning a long, complicated process. This particular variety was the most stable of conjoined twins. Unlike those joined at the head or chest, where separation could prove fatal to one child, twins connected at the hip were the most amenable to surgical separation. And while the physical process of separation could ultimately prove both challenging and rewarding, even getting to that point was problematic. The babies were small, maldeveloped, and in critical condition. It would take weeks, and probably months, to get them ready for operation.

The long vigil was beginning.

For Nelda Nieves, the babies' mother, the vigil proved far too long. Extended waits under the eyes of the authorities made her nervous, and when she was nervous, she couldn't think straight. Twenty-four-year-old Nelda was one of the millions of illegal immigrants who had traveled north across the Rio Grande during the nineties. It was a brutal trip of unspeakable hardships, not the least of which was the death of two close friends. Nelda had a strong religious background. She truly believed that one brought misfortune upon oneself, either through one's own actions, or from improper upbringing. She was certain that her friends had died because of their sexual relationship with their guide, *El Coyote*. It was the will of God.

She was determined that nothing of the kind befall her. Thus she was discreet, cautious, and for the most part, chaste. She eventually worked her way to New York where, after several months, she was able to get a black market ID and fake papers. Finally, she heard about a job in a *fabrica* on Long Island. The pay was adequate, few questions were asked, she had ample benefits, and she could live within the Salvadoran community. Everything went well until she met Arturo.

He, too, was an illegal. But he was also a big talker and something of a con man. Nelda knew that she ought to steer clear of him, but his bright smile and laughing eyes got the best of her. He promised her the world, and for a while, she believed him. She was four months pregnant when he left.

She knew this was a message from God—both to obey His word, and to bring a child into the world. After several weeks of self-pity, she found a doctor well known in her community. When she found out she was carrying *gemelos*, she was overjoyed. Everything was finally going well for her until the night she went into labor. From there, it all seemed to go downhill.

She was awake for the operation, having had an epidural. From the moment the twins were born, the staff didn't have to say anything for her to know something was wrong. At first, when they showed her the babies, like any new mother, her heart went out to them. But when they were unwrapped, she nearly recoiled in fright.

It was *un maldicion*, a curse on her actions. From that moment on, she withdrew into a shell. While she was recuperating in the hospital, she spoke only with her priest. She was convinced that the only way to regain God's grace once again was to repent—and to that end, she had to disappear, and leave her babies behind. After all, they were the work of the devil.

Jennifer Hartman took to the idea of twins immediately. But it took Richard Hartman much longer to adjust to the doubling of expectations. In most other matters, Richard was far more levelheaded than Jennifer. He'd overcome the Robinson family's snubbing to become the head of his small family, the practical breadwinner.

Yet once Jennifer finally became pregnant after so many years of trying, the sheltered harbor of his orderly existence was exposed to the elements. His life was out of control. It took him a full month to cope with the reality of impending fatherhood, and a month more to begin to enjoy their shared voyage through pregnancy.

But the moment she told him about the twins, he lost control again.

The slightest provocation saw him invoking God's name. He'd mutter "Jesus Christ!" as he walked through their small townhouse, repeatedly smacking himself in the forehead. "Jesus Christ, we've gotta put this place on the market this week, or we'll *never* get a two-bedroom before you deliver!"

"Will you calm down?" said his wife. "The real estate man called me this morning, and he's on top of everything."

"You don't understand!" Richard persisted. "It's a sellers' market these days. Unless we come up with a big enough down payment, we won't have a prayer to get one of those better homes!"

She gave her head a patient shake, an amused smile on her lips. "What I understand, Richard, is that this pregnancy has turned my practical husband into a raving control freak. Why are you so obsessed with real estate? It's really not all that important."

"But—"

She got up and silenced him with a kiss on the cheek. "Come on, let's get out of here. I'll let you buy me dinner, and I'll tell you about the five pounds I gained this week."

"Five *pounds*?" he said, smacking himself in the head. "Jesus Christ!"

It was euphemistically known as "quality time," or "bonding," but to Brad, the moments spent with his son Michael were much more than that. He didn't need an incentive or have to be forced to seek out Mikey's company. While his son kept his wife's memory alive, Mikey was also becoming Brad's buddy. Although still a child, Michael was very much an individual in his own right, with a personality grounded in curiosity. Now, as they were about to set out for a first sail on Brad's boat, he wondered what new challenges his son would provide him.

Brad had learned to sail in his last year at Yale, and it soon became an addiction. Not that he had much time to indulge his craving; during his long years of training, he rarely had more than an afternoon off to get out on the water and get his sea legs. His fantasy was to one day sail across the ocean, or perhaps even around the world. But at this stage of his professional career, a full-time physician's schedule wouldn't allow it.

Although he was by no means wealthy, he spent his money wisely. After six years of practice, he'd accumulated some surplus cash. Other than his son, he had few people with whom to share it. His wife's parents were both dead, and Brad was the only child of a woman long divorced and living in a retirement community in Florida.

The previous fall, Brad had decided to take the plunge. He made a down payment on a Vector 12.5, a forty-foot sloop. He took delivery six months later, and now, early Saturday morning on Memorial Day weekend, he was ready for the maiden voyage.

"All set, Mike?" he said.

"Are you sure we're going to be home by one o'clock?" his son asked.

"I am indeed. What's happening at one, anyway?"

"There's a show on the Discovery Channel. About aliens."

"We'll be back," said his father. "Wouldn't want you to miss that. One of these days, maybe we'll go out at night and check out the constellations. There's nothing like stars over the water. What do you say?"

"Sure."

Eight-year-old Michael had a fascination for anything cosmological. He read countless books about the heavens and, every Sunday, underlined the week's relevant TV listings, often taping shows that aired after his bedtime. At an early age, Mikey was familiar with comets, NASA undertakings, the space program, and theories about the origins of the universe. Brad didn't know where his son got the obsession, but he tried to encourage it.

The boat was moored in a slip in Stony Brook Harbor. Brad helped his son aboard, then turned on the power and checked the fuel and electronics. Satisfied, he started the engine and showed Mikey how to untie the lines from the cleats. Soon they were leisurely motoring north in the channel, toward Long Island Sound.

It was a magnificent late spring morning, with sunlight glinting richly off the dappled trees on the shoreline, and a steady northwesterly breeze. When they were farther into open water, Brad called his son to the helm and showed him how to hold the wheel. Michael grinned proudly, quickly warming to the task. The wind caught his straight blond hair and sent the fine strands flying.

Watching his son, Brad felt a tug at his heart. He put his arm around the boy. Mikey looked up at him.

"Everything okay, Dad?"

"Yeah," he said softly. "I only wish your mother was still here."

CHAPTER FOUR

AmeriCare's annual report was due out the second week in June, and in-house rumor held that it would be spectacular. It was certainly coming at an opportune time. The preceding twelve months had been a year of chaos. A darling of Wall Street as recently as two years previously, since then AmeriCare had fallen victim to financial crisis.

At first a metropolitan New York–based operation, two years after entering the field, AmeriCare, owing to competitive premiums and slick marketing, had subscribers throughout the Northeast. The company's stock price rocketed from nine to sixty dollars per share in a few months. The stock became a fixture in the health care portfolios of premier mutual funds. But then, after several spectacularly successful years, the boom was lowered, largely because the medical directors had approved unusual or expensive care. AmeriCare found itself overextended and underfunded.

The first casualties were the providers. Doctors began to complain that it was taking months, and sometimes up to a year, to be compensated for their efforts. Previously covered services were suddenly disapproved; paperwork increased, and referrals for specialty care decreased. After a rash of bad publicity, subscribers began to fall off, and with them, the company's revenues. Inevitably, as earnings reports turned bleak, mutual funds unloaded their AmeriCare holdings. The stock's price came tumbling down.

There were a series of stopgap measures, but they couldn't solve the problem. Employees were laid off, and crisis meetings were held. It was becoming very clear that unless subscriber attrition could be checked—and, indeed, reversed—they would continue to lose market share to the point where Chapter Eleven would be inevitable. Something had to be done, and soon.

Then, just when things were looking bleakest, there was a shift in mood at corporate headquarters, a shift that soon became a sea change. At first came the rumors that the company was breaking even, and then even turning a small profit. For the first time in months, employees began to smile. Word had it that upper-echelon appointments had been made and certain of their suggestions were starting to bear fruit. Changes in management style and philosophy were taking effect on every level.

Morgan first noticed it during the winter, when memos regarding expanded services recently offered by AmeriCare began to cross her desk. Apparently, someone had decided that one way to increase subscribers was to court them, rather than reject them. Suddenly it became company policy to underwrite the whole field of women's reproductive health, an area previously avoided. A managerial directive circulated to the effect that not only would routine OB/GYN care be approved, but also that they were entering areas most HMOs had gotten out of: advanced infertility treatments, assisted reproductive technologies, and mid-trimester abortions.

Morgan was pleasantly surprised. For eighteen months, she'd been at loggerheads with management over just such expenditures. She was tired of denying claims for the experimental tubal surgery on the woman who'd been raped and suffered pelvic inflammatory disease, for the patient who needed a decent shot at in vitro fertilization, or for the woman who discovered, at four and a half months of pregnancy, that her baby had severe Down's syndrome. Physicians still had to make the requests, but all of a sudden, Morgan was able to grant them. For the most part, she was happily baffled. She was still under pressure to deny expenditures in other areas, such as Nickie Giancola's case, but overall, pregnant women were the unexpected beneficiaries.

Today, a conference had been called. Standing at the podium was the company's radiant CEO, Daniel Morrison. Tall and distinguished-looking, Morrison had a rich baritone and a commanding presence. A former clergyman, he'd long since abandoned the Church to go into hospital administration. After getting his MBA at Columbia, he'd gone on to health care management. The only thing loftier than Morrison's expectations was his sense of self-importance.

Morgan was late arriving, and Morrison paused momentarily to glare at her. She didn't mind. To her, Morrison was both consummate pontificator and buffoon.

"—Once you've all taken your seats, we can get on with the business at hand," he was saying. "I'll keep my remarks brief. On the table before you is the rough draft of the annual report we'll be releasing to the public August first. We are very, very happy with it, particularly the quarter ending May thirtieth. Please take a moment to review it."

The report was rough indeed, eight-and-a-half by

eleven pages stapled together. Morgan knew that when the official document was published in several weeks, it would have a glossy cover and be filled with professional color photos. It appeared that management was eager to get out word of their success. Morgan leafed through the pages. The summary of revenues, net income, and earnings per share came near the end.

Her eyes widened as she read. After many months of decline, all the figures were suddenly in the black. It appeared that not only was income up, but expenditures were down. This was quite a turnaround.

"Now," Morrison continued, "I'd like to take a moment to introduce the man most responsible for this minor miracle. Many of you have already met him, but for those of you who have not, would you stand up please, Hugh?"

To a smattering of applause, a man in his mid-thirties arose near the head of the table. Morgan recognized him immediately. Hugh Britten, Ph.D., was a world-renowned economist. Something of a Bill Gates looka-like, Britten was an award-winning theoretician thought to be a future lock for the Nobel Prize. Morgan had heard he was on the Board, but assumed that he was just nerdy academic window dressing.

"Probably no one has had more of an impact on this company's well-being than Dr. Hugh Britten. Most of you know Hugh as Daley Professor of Economics at the University, but not everyone realizes he's been advising us for almost a year. His suggestions have been crucial to our recent success. I have to admit that I resisted those suggestions at first, but I'm more than happy to eat crow. Dr. Britten, would you like to say a few words?"

Britten acknowledged his greetings with a self-effacing smile. His wavy brown hair was nearly as rumpled as his beige suit. He looked slowly around the table, but his eyes seemed to linger on Morgan. "I really doubt I had that much impact," he said modestly. "But I thank Dan for his compliments. And I'm also grateful to a willing Board of Directors that found itself able to compromise. Basically, my suggestions were economic, simply a matter of supply and demand. Certain areas demanded services that AmeriCare found itself able to supply. And you, in your various divisions, helped implement those suggestions. My thanks to all." With that, he took his seat.

So *you* were behind the changes, Morgan thought. Maybe I misjudged this nerd.

Lectures for medical students at the State University of New York at Stony Brook were often given in classrooms within a nineteen-story circular glass-and-concrete tower known as the Health Sciences Center. Now late morning, one such class was coming to an end. Brad looked at his watch as he switched off the slide projector. "We're nearing the end of the hour, and that's about it," he said to his student. "The take-home message is that we've made little real progress in the diagnosis and management of pre-term labor. The morbidity and mortality that go along with pre-term birth, not to mention the cost, remain very high. There are some fairly promising developments on the horizon, such as fetal fibronectin and salivary estriol levels, but the challenge still remains."

His beeper went off. He paused to check the number: 4050 was the extension for the delivery room. He looked up at his audience. The hundred or so third-year medical students seated in rising tiers in the classroom's amphitheater were still attentive. "I'm afraid I can just take one question." He pointed to the first hand raised.

"I know this isn't on prematurity," said the student,

"but I just wonder what your take is on the NICU deaths. We asked Dr. Harrington, but he didn't say too much."

"Dr. Harrington was the right person to ask," Brad said, surprised by the question. "But he doesn't have any answers yet, and neither do I. Now, if you'll excuse me . . ."

University Hospital served as the primary referral institution for various satellite health clinics, including the clinic at Riverhead. Most patients from that area were indigent Medicaid recipients. Riverhead served a large migrant farm community, and many patients in the area were Hispanic.

Milagros Hernandez was among them. At twenty-four, the Honduran immigrant was expecting her third child. Although nearly full term, she continued to work as a cleaning woman while her young children were cared for by her extended family. The doctors at the clinic told her not to dawdle when her contractions began, because she was already several centimeters dilated. But Milagros was a woman of integrity, determined to finish whatever task she was assigned. Thus when her pains started, she waited until the end of her shift before going to the hospital. Besides, she reasoned, the clinic doctors were men, and she had already been through several false alarms. She decided to trust her own judgment.

Brad quickly left the classroom, took the elevator to the ninth floor, and crossed the bridge to the hospital tower. When he finally reached the DR, the first nurse who saw him pointed excitedly toward one of the labor rooms. "In three, Dr. Hawkins."

Hawkins fought his way through the small crowd spilling into the hall. A laboring woman lay across the mattress, spread-eagle, half on, half off the labor bed.

Her thin floral print gown was hiked up beneath her breasts, baring her abdomen. The woman was grunting heavily, bearing down with uncontrollable expulsive efforts. Eyes closed, teeth clenched, she was perspiring profusely. Around her, the OB team was feverishly at work.

A nurse was trying to adjust a blood pressure cuff on the patient's right arm. To the patient's left, a junior resident fumbled with a tourniquet, obviously hoping to find a vein in which to start an IV. Around the patient's abdomen were two white straps for the fetal monitor. The nearby monitoring strips were unintelligible, either due to strap misplacement, the patient's involuntary pushing, or both. Standing between the patient's legs was an apprehensive female resident.

"What've you got, Dr. Chang?" Brad asked.

"Dr. Hawkins, thank God you're here! She ruptured membranes right before we paged you, and I think she's a breech!"

As if to punctuate that statement, the patient grunted, bearing down heavily. A stream of clear fluid gushed from her vagina, followed almost immediately by a small fetal foot. One of the nurses gasped.

"Damn," muttered Chang.

Brad gazed at the resident, whose face had grown pale. "Done many breeches, Mei Mei?"

"A few," she said hesitantly. "But never in bed. Shouldn't we get her into the DR?"

"Sure, when there's time. What's her history?"

"*Ay, Dios mio*," the woman groaned.

"Mrs. Hernandez is a clinic patient," Chang said. "A twenty-four-year-old gravida four, para two, around thirty-nine weeks, uneventful prenatal course. We didn't know she was coming. Her contractions started about an hour ago, and she was already nine centimeters when she got here. She ruptured membranes as soon as we got her into bed."

"You called anesthesia and peds?"

"On their way."

Two of the nurses quickly unlocked the bed's wheels, but before they began transport, another contraction hit. The patient screwed up her face, bearing down once again. Almost immediately, the first foot was joined by its mate; and as the contraction continued, both fetal shins were expelled up to their knees.

"You can forget about the DR," Brad said calmly, selecting a packet of sterile gloves. "She'll deliver in the next minute or two. And don't worry about that IV," he said to the junior resident. "She'll survive without it. Now let's get her down to the bottom of the bed and pretend we're doing a normal birthing room delivery."

It took four people to get Mrs. Hernandez into position, but soon her buttocks were on the very edge of the mattress, and her bare heels dug into the bed's corners. She let out another forceful grunt, and both fetal legs were propelled outward, to mid-thigh.

"Okay, Mei Mei," said Brad. "You're on."

"I . . . What do I do next?"

Brad realized that Chang was understandably nervous, but not panic-stricken. "The main thing," he said, "is to try not to do *anything* just now. If you're too hasty, you can do more harm than good. Let the kid deliver spontaneously, up to the hips, all right? It won't be long."

The delivery pack was open and ready. Brad unfolded a sterile blue towel and put it in a basin of water. When the pediatric resident barged into the room, asking rapid-fire questions, Brad calmly raised his hand, indicating quiet. One of the nurses paused to wipe the patient's damp brow. Seconds later, another contraction began.

Taking Chang's arm, Brad positioned her directly between the patient's knees.

They didn't have to wait long. The legs-first baby was coming out with its face down and its back up. As Mrs. Hernandez pushed, the lower creases of the baby's buttocks came into view, the child's genitalia between them. It was a girl. With the baby's abdomen being compressed in the birth canal, a sticky plug of greenish meconium was being squeezed out of the fetal anus.

"Show time, Dr. Chang," Brad said, handing her a disposable sterile towel. "Grab the hips just below the thighs and pull downward. Gently."

The resident complied, applying steady floor-ward traction. The fetal body advanced, sliding slowly but easily out of the mother's vagina. Brad checked the fetal abdomen. When the umbilical cord came into view, he manually advanced it, pulling a foot-long loop free. Chang's pulling continued, and soon the fetal scapulae appeared.

"Good, good," said Brad, "this is what we came for. As soon as you see the armpits, rotate the thorax ninety degrees to deliver the shoulder."

"Which way?"

"Doesn't matter. Take your pick."

She soon turned the baby's torso to the left, rotating the left shoulder under the maternal pubic bone. With another cautious tug, the baby's shoulder joint came into view. Brad encircled the fetal abdomen with the moistened cloth towel and lifted, helping support the baby in a makeshift cradle.

"I've got 'er," he said. "Hook the humerus and bring it out."

Dr. Chang swept two of her fingers under the pubis, searching for the fetal arm. Finding it, she swept it down and out for the delivery.

"Perfect," Brad said. "Now take the hips again and slowly swing the kid around a hundred and eighty degrees for the other shoulder."

In steady, stepwise fashion, Brad guided the resident through the remainder of the delivery. Soon the baby's head was out, and Dr. Chang placed the small child on its mother's abdomen. She stepped back to enable others to suction out the baby's pharynx and clamp the cord. Chang looked over at her attending, her face radiant.

"Thanks, Dr. Hawkins. It got kind of easy there toward the end, but I really don't think I could have done it on my own."

"Just mentally replay what we did, because next year, you'll have to." He removed his gloves, clapped her encouragingly on the back, and left the room.

A still-beaming Dr. Chang watched him depart. Like most of the residents, she found something immensely reassuring about the presence of Dr. Brad Hawkins. He was the kind of obstetrician they all aspired to be.

"Forget it," Dr. Schubert said into the phone. "There's absolutely no way I'm going to agree to that!"

"Look, Arnold," said his attorney, "it's either that or go to arbitration, and I don't think you'll prevail. My advice is to bite the bullet and go for it."

"But for God's sake, where is it going to end? What's to stop her from asking for more next month?"

"That's not the way it works. If you take this, I can guarantee you at least three hassle-free years."

Schubert sighed, running his fingers through his already-graying hair. "All right, if that's what you think. But get everything in writing, okay?" He hung up the phone in disgust.

He felt the woman was milking him dry. This was more a mind-set than the truth, for he still had ample assets. He thought that after seventeen years of marriage, he would have understood her better. Obviously, he was wrong. The woman was evil, malicious. A mere six months into their mutual separation, she and the kids were into him for ten grand a month in support, and now the bitch wanted more! What the hell was he paying his attorney for?

His nurse poked her head into the consultation room, waving a sheet of paper. "Just got the fax results on Cutrone."

Schubert took the proffered page and scanned the report. A week ago, he had done an amniocentesis on Alyssa Cutrone, a twenty-five-year-old mother of two. She'd been referred to him because of an elevated AFP level. Alpha fetoprotein was a serum marker for, among other things, Down's syndrome; and even after the results were adjusted for weight, gestational age, and multiple pregnancy, Cutrone's were still high. The only real way to determine if the condition was present was genetic amniocentesis.

Performing an amnio for karyotype—chromosome studies—on twins was no mean feat. It would only be useful if the twins were in separate sacs, as they were in most cases, because each amniotic sac would contain the fluid from that twin alone. And once the fluid had been obtained from one sac, it was imperative not to confuse it with amniotic fluid from the other.

Thus, when he performed the Cutrone amnio, Schubert employed all the usual precautions. He'd used careful sonography to anatomically evaluate both fetuses and map their respective positions, and after he tapped the first sac, he injected a blue marking dye, to ensure that when he entered sac number two, no dye would be present. According to his sonography, baby "A," a girl, and the lowermost fetus, was in the vertex, or head first, position; baby "B" appeared to be a boy, and it was a breech. But the report Schubert was holding was confusing.

According to the lab, one fetus indeed had three twenty-first chromosomes and was a Down's baby, but *both* fetuses were reportedly girls. Apparently, his sonography had been wrong where it came to the genitalia. This presented something of a problem, but not an insurmountable one. The report indicated that the trisomic fetus was the lowermost child, or baby "A." It was "A" that he'd tapped first, and the sac might retain some residual dye. Moreover, if the fetuses were still in the same position, that would be very helpful. Still seething from his phone conversation, Schubert took the report and got up from his desk.

The patient was in exam room one. After speaking with his lawyer, Schubert had no trouble wearing a long face, and he came straight to the point. He held up the sheet of paper. "I'm afraid I don't have good news, Alyssa."

The terrified woman's fingers went to her throat. "What do you mean?"

"I won't beat around the bush. It looks like one of the babies has Down's syndrome."

"Oh my God." Her tremulous voice became a frightened whisper. "Which one?"

"The bottom one, the one that's head first."

Tears came to her eyes. "Oh no, not the little girl!" She had two boys at home.

"Actually, according to the lab, they're both girls."

She wiped her eyes, confused. "But didn't you say—"

"Yes, we thought 'B' was a boy, but sometimes our sonography's off. What looks like a scrotum can actually be a little girl's swollen labia." He tapped the paper he was holding. "The lab's accuracy is almost a hundred percent."

"Is there any chance at *all* that it's wrong?"

"Well, I suppose there's always a chance. But I've never known it to make an error. If the lab says there's a trisomy, that's pretty definite." He paused, studying the look on her face. "Do you want me to call your husband?"

Alyssa shook her head defeatedly. "No, I . . . we've already talked about the possibility. What do we do now?"

"There are a couple of alternatives. I don't know if you're aware of it, but one of the reasons other doctors refer patients such as yourself to me is because I'm a specialist in fetal reduction. Are you familiar with the term?"

"I might've heard of it, but . . ."

"Basically," Schubert explained, "fetal reduction is a technique where women with multiple pregnancies can choose to terminate one or more of them. You've heard of in vitro, right? The procedure was originally intended for in vitro complications, where some women were implanted with four, five, six, or more embryos, and instead of only some of them making it, they all survived. Pregnancies of that magnitude can cause real problems for the mother. Women like that one who recently gave birth to the healthy septuplets are the exception rather than the rule. Most of the time, there are complications, especially extreme prematurity, that can threaten all the babies."

Alyssa said nothing, simply staring at him dejectedly.

"The technique also works on twins," he said. "Do you want me to go over it?"

She shook her head. "Just do what you have to do."

"Would you like me to set it up, then?"

Her chin was quivering again, and she nodded in silence. After a moment, she lifted her head, looking him squarely in the eye. "Do you think I'm making the right decision?"

He nodded. "If it were me, Alyssa, I'd do exactly the same thing."

Ordinarily, he knew, he should talk to her about the risks and benefits of the procedure, the potential complications, and alternative treatments. But Arnold Schubert was a man on a mission. He was desperately in need of money, and he was being paid to help women arrive at precisely the same decision Alyssa had.

Unlike his sister-in-law Morgan, Richard Hartman had no eye for what was normal in pregnancy, and what wasn't. This didn't stop him from offering his observations.

"You sure look big for seven months," he said, staring up at his wife from his perch on the couch.

"Thanks a heap."

He'd always liked watching her put on her panty hose. But now the ankles of Jennifer's shapely legs looked swollen, and her face appeared puffy, especially around the eyes. Even more impressive, however, was the rotundity of her abdomen, which seemed term size. She looked about ready to burst. "You sure there's not a third one in there?"

"That's hilarious, Richard." She took a swig of Evian. "God, I'm always so thirsty. I'll have to ask the doctor about that."

"When's your next appointment?"

"Tomorrow. I wonder if he'll give me a hard time about my weight."

"How much have you gained?"

"Oh, about seven pounds in two days."

"Seven *pounds*?" He sat up smartly and smacked himself in the forehead. "Jesus Christ, do we ever need that bigger house!"

A small group of med students crowded around the chief of neonatology. Word of the conjoined twins had spread through the hospital like wildfire. No one had ever seen anything like it. Although the NICU was a restricted area, all sorts of hospital employees now traipsed through the unit, hoping for a chance to ogle the Siamese monsters.

Dr. Albert Harrington stepped back to give the respiratory technician room to work. He thought her quite good for someone foreign-trained. The tech was a native Haitian, with a lilting, singsong accent. She'd worked at the hospital for six months. She adjusted the ventilator settings in preparation for extubation.

No matter at what age, having a plastic tube in one's lungs was unsettling. Consequently the Nieves children, until then, had been mildly sedated to keep them from fighting the tubes. As they grew more alert, they began moving around and opening their eyes. With their delicate features and dark, flashing eyes, it was obvious they were going to become handsome children. Heads close together, tilted toward one another at a slight angle, what each was now beginning to see was a mirror image of himself. An indistinct blur of larger, white-coated forms loomed around them.

"How is their family coping?" asked one of the students.

"Good question," Harrington said. "The mother is a single mom. She had good insurance and adequate prenatal care. She had a C-section at one of the South Shore hospitals, and her kids were transferred here. But for some reason, after she was discharged from the hospital, she disappeared. The nurses at the other hospital said she seemed pretty freaked out by the whole thing. No one's been able to locate her ever since."

"What happens if you can't find her?"

"Unfortunately," Harrington said, "we occasionally run into that situation. A guardian gets appointed, and eventually the kids become wards of the state."

"Why're are they called Siamese twins?" another student asked.

"Actually, the original set was three-quarters Chinese and one-quarter Siamese," said Harrington. "It's an American term coined by P. T. Barnum for Eng and Chang Bunker, who were a big circus draw for thirty years. They were what's called *thoracopagus* twins, joined at the chest. The Nieves twins share a hip, and they're called *ischiopagus*. But they probably share a few other things through that bridge of abdominal tissue. Once they're successfully extubated, which is what the tech is doing now, we'll do a CAT scan to determine the extent of organs they have in common."

"Can they be separated?"

"Probably," Harrington said. "If it's only gut and liver tissue, which is what we suspect, the surgery will be pretty straightforward, with a good chance for success. But we have a ways to go before we get to that point. They've got to be completely stable and gain a little weight. The legal and domestic issues have to be squared away. If things go well, I suspect the pediatric surgeons will be ready to cut in a couple of months— say, the end of the summer."

Soon, the respiratory technician removed both breathing tubes. With the help and encouragement of the nurses, both twins were soon breathing well, without assistance. Harrington and his entourage watched for a few more minutes before moving on to the next isolette. His teaching rounds lasted another forty-five minutes, after which the group left the NICU and headed en masse for the nearby elevator.

Before the elevator arrived, a distraught nurse rushed into the hall, shouting Harrington's name. At the same time, the overhead PA system started announcing a cardiac arrest in the unit right behind them.

"It's the Nieves twins!" she screamed. "They coded!"

Harrington immediately dashed back into the NICU, white coattails flying. But his efforts were for naught. Fifty minutes later, the frantic team effort at CPR was abandoned. Both conjoined twins were pronounced dead.

For six months, Dr. Schubert's abortion clinic had been doing a land-office business. In addition to the business generated from within the practice, Schubert had numerous referrals from other doctors, as well as certain insurance companies. Three years previously, he'd taken a two-week preceptorship at New York's Mount Sinai Hospital. Eighteen months later, Schubert published his own paper on the subject, and his reputation grew.

Schubert's practice was aided in no small part by the 1998 report of the New York State Task Force on Life and the Law. Among other things, the report's panel suggested that infertility specialists try to avoid techniques that produced high-order multiple births, and, failing that, the doctors should communicate with their patients about the advisability of aborting one or more of what were called "high-order fetuses," or large multiples.

Schubert didn't limit his practice to fetal reduction, however, and his clinic aborted patients between six and twenty-four weeks, the legal limit. His area of expertise was mid-trimester terminations, those between thirteen and twenty-four weeks' gestation. These were avoided by most physicians because they were both complicated and distasteful. To Schubert, they were all well within his competence, not to mention financially rewarding.

That morning, Alyssa Cutrone and her husband arrived at the clinic at ten A.M. She was precisely nineteen-and-a-half weeks pregnant. She had hoped, in this hour of medical commitment, to have the doctor's undivided attention. But there were several other patients nervously waiting. A receptionist handed her forms to fill out, and she gave blood and urine specimens. Then, after a brief counseling session, she had to wait.

Finally, a little after eleven, she was shown to a dressing cubicle, where she changed into a gown. When she was ready, Alyssa was escorted to a treatment room. To her untrained eye, it resembled a small operating theater, with powerful overhead lighting, a central examining table with stirrups, a portable ultrasound machine, and stainless steel supply cabinets. Soon, Dr. Schubert entered, accompanied by a nurse, his broad smile oddly inappropriate.

He asked Alyssa to lie on her back on the table. Despite white draping paper, the Naugahyde was cold against her skin, and she shivered. The nurse wheeled over the ultrasound and covered Alyssa's abdomen with sterile towels.

"As they may have explained in counseling," Schubert said, "we're going to do an ultrasound first, then move on to the injection."

"She didn't really explain much of anything."

"Then I'll go over it," he continued. "You remember the fetus we're targeting is the one on the bottom, Twin 'A.' That's the one with Down's."

Alyssa nodded and silently closed her eyes. She noted how careful he was to say *fetus* instead of *baby*. But she didn't want to discuss it. Right now, she just wanted him to get it over with.

"So we'll confirm it with ultrasound, then get on with the injection. The injection we'll use is potassium chloride, all right?"

Did he really expect her to dispute it? "Okay." She felt the coolness of ultrasound gel being applied to her bare skin.

"I'm using a sterile probe cover to keep everything antiseptic," he said. "I'll start the scan now. Hang on."

Schubert watched the image on the monitor as he moved the probe. It was easy for someone of his expertise to identify separate twins despite the multitude of fetal parts. But as he scanned the abdomen's quadrants, a frown came over his face. The twins were no longer in the same position they'd been in before.

When he performed the amnio, the twins were vertex/breech, with "A" being the vertex. Now, however, the "B" twin had turned, doing a lazy somersault out of the breech position, coming to lie side-by-side with its unborn sister. Both were now head first. Still, the baby on the left-hand side of the monitor was slightly lower, as it had been last week. This Schubert took to be "A." He looked into his nurse's eyes. He'd previously briefed her on what he expected to find, and now her brows were raised in unspoken inquiry.

"Not to worry," he said, pointing at the monitor with his free hand. "This one's the Down's."

Alyssa heard the change in his tone. "Is everything all right?"

"Absolutely. We're just confirming position. Try not to move during the injection, okay?"

Schubert readied the syringe of concentrated potassium chloride, then set to work. Using the probe's needle guide, he numbed up an area of skin with lidocaine, then carefully inserted a four-inch, eighteen-gauge needle into the amniotic sac. His target was the rapidly flickering fetal heart. When his needle touched the fetal thorax, he deftly pierced the chest wall and pericardium and withdrew the needle's stylet. Several ccs of fetal blood shot out the needle's hub. Schubert quickly attached the liquid-filled syringe and injected. The job complete, he withdrew the needle.

He and the nurse watched the monitor, which was shielded from Alyssa's view. On the screen, the fetal heart continued its rapid beating for several more seconds. Then it suddenly quivered in spasm, seeming to flutter momentarily before stopping entirely. Satisfied, Schubert removed the abdominal drapes.

"That's all she wrote, Alyssa."

Her chin was quivering. "Is . . . is the baby—"

"Don't worry about that now," he interrupted. "It's over. Just concentrate on the one that's healthy."

She abruptly sat up, suddenly desperate to get out of there, but unable to hold back the tears. "That's it?" she managed. "Just like that, one of my babies is—"

"Alyssa, *please*," he said. "I wouldn't have done this unless you agreed to it. It's for the best, believe me."

She dried her eyes. "So what happens now?"

"Now, you go home and take it easy for the rest of the day. Then you enjoy the rest of your pregnancy. The fetus we just treated will stop growing, and it may even be absorbed."

"But the other baby's going to be okay, right?"

"Usually. I mean, there's an outside chance you might rupture membranes, or even go into labor. But it's pretty remote. Now, the nurse'll take you back to get dressed."

He watched her somewhat shakily get off the table,

emotionally drained, but physically none the worse for wear. They always took it pretty hard, not that he could blame them. But he couldn't worry about that now. This is what he did, and what he did well.

CHAPTER FIVE

Half-asleep, Morgan distantly heard the ringing of her bedside phone, as if through a tunnel. She automatically lifted the phone to her ear and mumbled "Hello" before realizing her mistake. Squinting at the luminous dial of her bedside clock, she saw that it was eleven-thirty P.M.

Still not completely awake, she waited for the return salutation. When it didn't come, she instantly grew alert, propping herself up on an elbow. *Idiot*, she scolded. This was precisely why she'd bought the answering machine. Her unlisted phone number notwithstanding, Morgan had fallen victim to a problem shared by many single women who lived alone: random prank callers. She'd installed the answering machine as an extra layer of protection. But now, her heart began beating faster. Gazing wide-eyed into the dark, she struggled to remain calm.

"Hello?" she repeated.

"Dr. Robinson?" came the reply.

It was an unfamiliar male voice. "Who is this?"

"This is Hugh Britten. Sorry to disturb you. I still haven't accepted the fact that everyone isn't a night owl like me."

"Hugh Britten," she slowly repeated. "*Doctor* Britten, from AmeriCare?"

"The same. I rarely use the *Doctor* thing, you know. Makes people confuse me with an M.D., when I'm an economist. And call me Hugh."

She pictured his face—the outdated, horn-rimmed glasses, the slightly unkempt hair. "No problem, Hugh. But it *is* a little late. Is there a problem at work?"

"Actually," he went on, "this is a social call. I couldn't help but remember you from the meeting in the Board Room. You were wearing a gray suit, pink blouse, right?"

Rumor had it that despite his eccentricity, Britten was well-off, brilliant, and available. Not that it mattered to Morgan; the guy was definitely not her type. But she could ill afford rudeness toward someone with so much corporate clout. "You've got a good memory," she said.

"Yes . . . I've asked around about you, Morgana. May I call you Morgana? Not meaning to pry, of course, but you're an attractive woman, and I learned that you were unattached. I suppose I was wondering if you'd like to get together. For a cup of coffee, say, or a drink."

She couldn't believe he was actually coming on to her. "Now? You're asking if I want to get out of bed at the witching hour to have a drink?"

"Is that a problem for you?"

"Hugh, I . . . Not right now, I don't think. I'm flattered, really. Maybe I'll be a little more receptive when I'm not so sleepy. So next time you call, give me a ring at work, okay?" She said goodbye and rang off, not sure if her abruptness was kindness, or a terrible mistake.

The next morning, Morgan stared out her office window, rapping her pen impatiently on her desk. She was off men for a while. After her late night experience with Dr.

Britten, the last thing she wanted was the prospect of verbally going head-to-head with Dr. Hawkins.

"Morgan, this isn't like you," said Jennifer. "You told me you'd come with me, and you're usually good for your word."

"I know, Jen. It's just that I'm up to my damn neck in paperwork. Do you suppose you could go without me, and I'll touch base with you later?"

"*Please*," her sister implored. "I'm really not feeling so hot today."

Morgan detected a note of urgency. That didn't sound like Jennifer. "What's going on?"

"I'm fat as a cow, that's what. Do you have any idea how much weight I've gained so far?"

"You're bigger than a bread box?"

"Sixty-four pounds! I feel like a freakin' blimp! At this rate, I'll be over a *hundred* by the time I deliver. My clothes don't fit, my shoes are too tight, and I look like a chipmunk! I don't mean to complain, but something just isn't right."

No, Morgan thought, it wasn't. She knew that mothers of twins often had problems with edema, but generally not of this magnitude. "When's your appointment?"

"In twenty minutes."

"Okay. Pick you up in ten."

On the highway fifteen minutes later, Morgan watched her sister out of the corner of her eye. She hadn't seen Jen in nearly two weeks. Her sister had been rather heavy then, but now she seemed frightfully puffy. "How's your blood pressure?"

"Last week he said it was borderline."

"Did he mention anything about toxemia?"

Jen's eyes darted her way. "You think that's what I've got? Terrific. Will it hurt the babies?"

"I'm not the obstetrician. You'll have to ask him."

Half an hour later, Morgan was seated in Brad's waiting room, alternately reading a magazine or staring vacantly at the fish tank. She'd decided not to go in with her sister this time. Jen was old enough to fend for herself. When the inner door opened, she turned. Brad came out and beckoned to her.

"Could I talk to you a minute, Dr. Robinson?"

"Of course." She followed him to the consultation room. "Is there a problem with Jen?"

"Your sister's got pre-eclampsia," Brad said. "Her pressure's one-forty over ninety, she's got some noticeable edema, and there's one-plus protein in her urine."

Morgan slowly shook her head. "Just how bad is that?"

"Right now, not too bad. Pre-eclampsia is divided into mild and severe. With the severe variety, we have to deliver. With mild, you usually temporize. By temporize, I mean rest," Brad continued, "and lots of it. Some people might hospitalize her, but I think we can manage at home. I tried to reach her husband, but he's tied up. That's where you come in."

"You're asking me to help her rest?"

"*Please*, Dr. Robinson. I know you're in managed care, but you can't be that naïve."

Morgan bristled. She felt her face grow hot, and she knew it was turning the color of her hair. She glared at him icily. "*Naïve*?"

"I shouldn't have to explain it to you. Maybe working in a corporate ivory tower made you forget the basics. Christ, any halfway competent physician should understand the importance of bed rest in this condition."

"God, you have *chutzpah*!" she said, ready to explode. "Now I'm *incompetent*?"

Caught in her penetrating glare, Brad shifted uncomfortably in his seat. "I'm sorry. You're absolutely right. It's just that I've got this foot-in-mouth thing where it comes to managed care, and sometimes I say things I shouldn't." He tried his most apologetic smile.

Morgan sighed. "Okay, okay. Forget it. How can I help?"

"All right, this is what I'm getting at. When I recommend rest, what I mean is, lie in bed and don't get up except to pee, okay? But somehow, that message doesn't get across. No matter how I phrase it, the average patient thinks it's still okay to make dinner for her husband, or go to the store for just a few items, as long as she stays off her feet the rest of the day. She doesn't understand that just a little upright activity can undo the benefit of whatever extra time she spends in bed. So, I have to rely on the families. They're the enforcers."

Morgan could see real concern and sincerity in his eyes. Her umbrage lessened, and she found herself nodding. "I suppose I can do that. Are you looking at some time frame?"

"I'll give her, say, ninety-six hours at home. Then I'll check her again and see what's what. If she hasn't shown any improvement, I'll admit her."

Morgan nodded her understanding. "You've gone over all this with her, haven't you?"

"Yes, I have. But I'm counting on you and her husband."

"We can manage her," said Morgan, rising to leave.

"Dr. Robinson? There is one other thing. I don't know if you've heard, but we just had another NICU death."

She stopped short, startled. "No, I hadn't. That's too bad."

"And it'll get worse once it hits the papers. The hospital has tried to avoid publicity, but some hotshot reporter got hold of the story. It'll make the headlines tomorrow."

"Was it like the others?"

"Identical." He paused. "You know, I was wondering if maybe you and I should put our heads together on this. Maybe we can come up with something."

Morgan checked her watch. "That's an interesting offer, but I have to get back to work. Maybe I can free up some time—"

"I'm not talking about during the workday," he interrupted. "I meant later, after work. You get off at five, right?"

After the late-night call from Britten, her antennae were up. "I'm not following you."

"I'm saying I can pick you up, and we'll go someplace quiet to talk."

She gave a little sniff. "I don't think so, Dr. Hawkins."

He looked genuinely perplexed. "Why not? I thought you were interested?"

"Interested, yes. Foolish, no." She nodded toward his hand. "There's that gold ring on your fourth finger, and there are some family pictures on your office wall."

Brad looked down at his wedding ring. His face broadened into a smile, and he laughed heartily. "Maybe I'm old-fashioned . . . My wife died six years ago."

Her face reddened again. "Well, don't I feel like an idiot? Five o'clock is fine, thanks. And don't forget to call me Morgan."

At first, Alyssa Cutrone thought she'd urinated. Her underpants felt wet, and then something warm trickled down her thighs. But when she went to the bathroom, she was startled to find that she was dripping blood.

She was frightened. There were a lot of things she

didn't know about pregnancy, and many of her symptoms she had been reassured were normal. But vaginal bleeding was clearly not one of them. Frightened, she called her husband, but he'd already left work for the drive home. Then she called Dr. Schubert. He told her to head for the hospital immediately.

Still, she waited for her husband. By then, she was starting to get cramps, which intensified during the drive to University. In the short walk from the ER parking lot, and then during the elevator ride to the eighth floor, her husband had to physically support her to keep her from doubling over.

Schubert had called ahead, and the nurses on maternity escorted her to the triage area. After checking her vital signs, they called in one of the residents. A speculum exam confirmed that the bleeding was coming from the cervix, and a gentle pelvic revealed that the cervix was already several centimeters dilated.

Alyssa was in labor.

The resident said nothing. Schubert could deliver the news. Alyssa was overcome with both pain and anxiety. The nurses started an IV and gave her some Demerol, which helped a little. Then they transported her to one of the labor beds.

Schubert arrived, donning a disposable yellow gown over his street clothes. He was all smiles. "Looks like things are moving along a little faster than we thought," he said. He put on a glove and did a gentle vaginal exam. "That's actually a good sign. You'll pass the treated fetus and not have to worry about it any more."

"Is she in labor?" her husband asked.

"Well, yes and no," Schubert replied. "Actually, her body's aborting twin 'A,' and then the cervix will probably clamp down."

"*Probably? What if it doesn't?*" said Alyssa. "Could I lose them both?"

"Pretty unlikely. Now get some rest and don't worry about it." Still smiling, he strolled out of the room.

Alyssa was angry and upset. In spite of his reputation, Schubert was the most patronizing man she'd ever met. She'd almost expected him to say, "Don't worry your pretty little head about it."

Outside, Schubert told the resident that, although the fetus was small, he thought Alyssa had another four or five hours of labor remaining. Make her comfortable, he said. Give her as much Demerol as necessary to keep her sedated.

But her body had other ideas. Despite the hefty dose of Demerol, within ninety minutes, Alyssa's cervix was fully dilated, and the membranes were bulging. The staff hurriedly put in a call to Schubert's office, but he was tied up with patients. He relayed word that he'd get there as soon as he could. Meanwhile, just keep her zonked, and if necessary, catch the baby. No sooner had he hung up than Alyssa's bag of waters ruptured. The resident did a hurried pelvic and discovered that the small fetal head was already coming down. He stared at the amniotic fluid that dribbled around his fingers.

That's odd, he thought. Hadn't Schubert said it'd probably be stained blue?

The nurses lifted Alyssa onto a stretcher for the run to the DR. They paged one of the neonatology residents, because it was departmental policy to have a pediatrician present at all deliveries, regardless of viability or gestational age. In minutes, a somewhat obtunded Alyssa was in stirrups, draped for delivery. Her husband—gowned, masked, and capped—fidgeted nervously beside the anesthesiologist, who administered nasal oxygen. Everyone paced, awaiting Schubert's arrival.

Alyssa started to bear down. Even though she was semi-conscious, pushing was an uncontrollable reflex. The resident pulled the instrument table closer, awaiting the inevitable. Soon the patient's labia bulged, and a nickel-size patch of fetal scalp began to emerge. It came out haltingly, a two-steps-forward, one-step-back process. Then came another push, and soon the whole head was out, quickly followed by the slightly macerated fetal body.

The resident carefully cut and severed the thin umbilical cord. He carried the limp and lifeless form to the neonatology resident, who placed the fetus supine on a pediatric treatment mattress. Placing his stethoscope on the small chest was a formality, and he quickly confirmed the absence of a heartbeat. Then he carefully examined the child.

The OB resident, meanwhile, awaited delivery of the placenta. His mind was racing. He hoped that the placenta was separate, because if it were fused, or if there were only one placenta for the two sacs, that would prove catastrophic for twin "B." Moreover, he knew it would be wise to administer labor-arresting drugs intravenously, because with the cervix wide open, the remaining baby was certainly in danger. But these were decisions to be made by the attending, not him.

A minute later, while he awaited the placenta, the neonatal resident called him over. They both looked at the stillborn fetus, the neonatologist whispering something in hushed and urgent tones. He pointed out certain features on the fetal palms, and about the face and neck. As they both peered closely at the body, Schubert arrived.

He entered the room with inappropriate enthusiasm. "Everything okay in here?" he said. Alyssa looked at him numbly, and her husband said nothing. Before he could say anything else, the OB resident called him over.

"How'd it go?" Schubert asked.

The OB resident spoke cautiously. "We might have a little problem here, Dr. Schubert."

"What're you talking about?"

"According to him," he said, nodding toward the neonatology resident, "this baby doesn't have Down's. It looks like you might've aborted the wrong fetus."

In Suffolk County, every effort was made to find the next of kin of an unclaimed deceased, especially when it was an infant. A diligent search for Mrs. Nieves, however, turned up little. Therefore, the County Administrator took over. If no family could be found after the mandatory thirty-day wait, he would order the body shipped to Washington Pines for cremation. Until then, the Nieves twins would lie in a refrigerated locker in the University morgue.

Shortly before dark on the day Alyssa went into labor, the morgue lights went on, and the locker was opened. The visitor had already filled out the requisite paperwork, dated twenty-six days hence, indicating that the body had been transported. The locker's retractable stainless steel table was pulled out, and the body bag with the twins was removed. The man stuffed the bag into an oversize Nike carry-on and slung it over his shoulder. Then he switched off the lights, locked the door, and left.

In the hospital's cool underground corridors, the man was met by an occasional passerby, but no one paid attention to what he was carrying. He exited via the service ramp and passed through the covered parking garage en route to the surface lot. His vehicle was a late model Dodge van. Setting his cargo in back, he got in and was soon heading east on the Expressway.

The man's home was out on Long Island between Manorville and Mattituck. Several years previously, he'd purchased the run-down, two-acre parcel, located well off the beaten track in a largely wooded area. The property's buildings included a ramshackle farmhouse and an equally decrepit barn, whose weathered planks hadn't been painted or repaired in decades.

After forty minutes on the highway, he wound through the rutted back roads to his secluded property. Removing his bag from the van, he went directly to the barn and unlocked the main door. The building was deceptive: although outwardly it looked as if the slightest gust of wind could blow it away, the interior was actually reinforced by steel beams. The inner walls were rough and unfinished but sturdy, lending the two-room structure a rugged, frontier appearance.

The man opened the heavy lock, closed the door behind him, and turned on the light. The room was windowless. The overhead fluorescents were pale and bleak, and their bluish tint lent the room an otherworldly appearance. A large black iron cauldron sat in one corner. The near wall was lined with shelves and included space for the beetle box. Most striking of all, however, was what hung on the other three walls.

One wall was covered with animal skeletons, mounted in all phases of activity, from repose to flight to attack. There were seals and hippos, wild dogs and cats, raptors and reptiles. Each was arranged in a strikingly natural pose.

The skeletons on the other two walls were more recognizable: they were humans, artfully hung in an interactive choreography. Two face-to-face specimens appeared to be carrying on a conversation. One of them was pointing to a third, who gave the impression of running toward a fourth, and so on. The skeletons were an ossified frieze, of all sizes and ages, from early infancy to spine-stooped old age.

The man placed his carry-on on the stainless steel table and removed the body bag. Unzipping it, he took out the cold cadavers of the Nieves twins, whose purple thoracic bruises bore silent witness to their unsuccessful CPR. Then he filled the cauldron with hot water and set its thermostat to just below the boiling point. While he was waiting for the water to heat, he gutted both twins with casual indifference, removing their innards and chest contents. When the water reached a brisk simmer, he threw in the eviscerated carcasses.

It would take nearly twelve hours for the skin, flesh, and muscle to separate from bone into a kind of tenderized human stew. After the rendering was complete, what remained of the Nieves twins would be unrecognizable.

It would be twelve hours before the beetles would feed again.

CHAPTER SIX

For her meeting with Brad, Morgan was thankful she'd worn what she did that day. She'd chaired an AmeriCare staff meeting earlier that morning and had chosen to go with the strong power look: the dark gray, double-breasted linen suit. While it wasn't cocktail wear, she reminded herself that they were meeting to discuss work-related matters.

She had mixed feelings about meeting him at all. He had already proven that he could be either charming, or narrow-mindedly infuriating. But deep down inside, she acknowledged that both of them were single, and she wouldn't have minded his asking for a date. Not that she was sure how she would have responded if he *had* asked her out socially. Some women would doubtless consider him youthfully attractive, but her own tastes ran to more sophisticated men. And while he was undeniably professional in his work, his antics with the fish tank struck her as juvenile, and she didn't know *what* to make of the nudist publication.

Moreover, he seemed to have preconceived notions about what kind of people worked in managed care. His attitude toward her job was prejudiced and hostile. The more she thought about it, the more Morgan realized that she and Brad would be in for rough sledding if they were to have a relationship.

She was late. The Radisson wasn't far, but with rush-hour traffic, she didn't arrive until half past five. Parking her Nissan in the lot, she breezed into the lobby and took the escalator to the second-floor piano bar.

Brad was waiting. Still casually dressed, he wore a blazer over an open-collar shirt. He had a square jaw and a bronzed complexion that suggested long hours spent outdoors. When he got up to meet her, Morgan saw that he was a bit taller than she.

"Glad you could make it. Can I buy you something to drink?"

"What're you having?" she asked.

"Just iced tea."

"That sounds good to me."

He signaled to the waitress, pointed to his nearly empty glass, and held up two fingers. They both took their seats. The pianist played an old Sinatra tune.

"Your office is nearby, isn't it?" Brad said.

"Just down the road. Ten minutes, barring traffic. Before we go any farther, Dr. Hawkins—"

"Brad."

"Brad." She smiled. "I'd like to apologize for what I said in your office. I guess I'm naturally suspicious where it comes to married men."

"Sounds like you're speaking from experience."

"You might say that. I've gotten burned more times than I'd like to remember. I don't know what it is about marriage that makes single women attractive to some men."

"Never married yourself?"

"Oh, I came close once," she said. "I lived in the city

then. I suppose it was one of the reasons I came out here."

When the waitress brought their drinks, Brad took a long sip of his tea. "What was the other reason?"

"I'm not really sure. You see, I was in a private practice there—"

"Really?" he interrupted. "Why would anyone give that up? Why would someone as smart as you waste your time with an HMO?"

Morgan found herself glaring at him over the rim of her glass. That was precisely the kind of prejudiced, narrow-minded remark she found so infuriating. Still, she was determined to be patient. "To start with, I was low man on the totem pole in the group, working sixteen hours a day, seven days a week."

"What group?"

"One on the East Side, working out of Cornell," she said. "I'd just finished my residency at Beth Israel, and I was so eager to get into practice, I signed on right away. It was a high-power, six-person group, very prestigious, and I suppose I was flattered they asked me. But most of them were a lot older than I was. I wound up spending a lot of time in the trenches."

"Sounds demanding."

"To be honest with you, it wasn't just the hours," she said. "For one reason or another, the practice had a lot of real sick kids, and more than their share of oncology patients. A couple of them died—always when I was on call. It did a number on me. I suppose I got a little gun-shy. Then, there was this man I got involved with, and . . . Well, I took a hard look at everything going on in my life, and I decided I needed some distance." She stared at him. "Why are you smiling?"

"It's nice to know I'm a good judge of character," he said. "I *knew* you had what it takes to be a real doctor."

Morgan folded her arms defensively across her chest. "I *am* a real doctor. What *is* your problem with managed care, anyway?"

"It's not my problem," he said, calmly sipping his drink, "it's theirs. The folks who run HMOs think they can reduce everything to an economic science. What costs to cut, what claims to deny, how much paperwork they can shove down patients' throats before they just give up and walk away. This isn't managed care. It's *un*-care."

"I'm sorry you've had problems, but what does that have to do with me?"

"Nothing, probably. But you're management, and I don't see anyone on the management side suffering. And it's not doctors like me who suffer the most. For instance, take your sister. There are a couple of very sophisticated blood assays I'd like to run on a patient like her, and guess who won't pay for them? AmeriCare. They say they're not of proven usefulness, so they denied them. Now, what kind of provider is that? Suppose one of those tests could save her life? Would it be worth it then? Like I said, in the end, it's always the patients who suffer the most."

She applauded lightly. "Very noble sentiments, Doctor. But you make it sound like I'm the one behind some giant conspiracy."

"If I did," he said with a shrug, "I apologize. It's just that my experience with managed care hasn't been very positive. Look, Morgan. AmeriCare doesn't deserve you. Have you ever thought about going back to clinical medicine?"

She had a wistful look. "I miss the work, sometimes. The kids were a pleasure to work with. But I don't miss the tension, and certainly not the tragedy. Who knows? Maybe I'll go back someday. What about you?"

"I love what I'm doing," he said. "I'm not sure I did at first, when we first came out here. But I had a lot of distractions. First, Mikey was just a baby then—"

"The boy in the pictures in your office?"

He nodded. "He's eight now, and he's a handful."

"And the woman?"

A dark and brooding look replaced the easy smile on his face. "That was my wife, Danielle. She got killed in an idiotic riding accident."

"I'm so sorry."

"Thanks." He looked away, sighing, wondering if he was overly maudlin. "Funny how it all seems so recent, but it was a long time ago. Michael was barely two then."

"It was pretty hard for you, wasn't it?"

"More than you know. After she died, I got a live-in housekeeper for my son and threw myself into my work. Twenty-hour days were just the therapy the doctor ordered. In the beginning, I took call even when I didn't have to, anything to keep from being alone with my thoughts."

"All work and no play?"

"Not quite," he said. "In my time off, what there is of it, I spend every moment with my son. I've been doing a lot more of that recently . . ." His voice trailed off. "But the reason I suggested this meeting, what I'm after, is your take on the hospital's NICU deaths."

"Why would you think I'd know anything about that?"

He paused. "I'm plugged into what's happening in the OB department and in the nursery. I've looked at the charts of the kids who died, and there's something peculiar going on."

Her lids narrowed. "Peculiar in what way?"

"When four newborns who are supposedly on the

mend suddenly crap out and die, that goes way beyond coincidence. So far, the only common thread I found is that all those babies were yours."

She frowned. "Mine?"

"They were all insured by AmeriCare."

She wasn't sure she'd heard him right. "What in the world are you implying?"

"I'm just making an observation. What do you suppose are the odds of that happening?"

Morgan looked away angrily. She'd known about the insurance coverage for the first three, but had presumed it was a coincidence. She hadn't been aware of the coverage for the fourth. Still, it was *preposterous* for him to connect an insurance company with a string of unusual hospital deaths. Trying to remain calm, she said, "I'm not sure I like what you're suggesting."

"I'm not suggesting anything. I'm saying they were the insurer of record, times four."

"Honestly, Brad. I know you hate managed care, but do you actually think an HMO would . . . stoop to anything so . . . What you're talking about is criminal."

He gave a noncommittal shrug. "I don't think anything. I'm just looking for answers."

"But what would the company have to gain, other than financially?"

"You said it," he observed, pointing a finger at her.

"A *financial* motive?" He was sounding more and more ludicrous, and she looked at him dubiously. "That's positively ridiculous!"

"Think so? Remember that Nigerian woman who gave birth to octuplets in Houston a while back? The total cost was over a million dollars. You think managed care companies don't care about expenses like that?"

"That's different."

"Not really. Let's run the numbers, okay?" he said.

"Take these Siamese twins, for example. Clinically, they were doing pretty well. In another month or two, maybe, if they remained stable, they'd be up for surgical separation. But off the top of your head, what do you think the hospital bills for a month of NICU are? Round numbers."

"Oh, about a hundred grand, but—"

"Okay," he continued. "Now multiply that by the total months they'd be spending in the NICU, then throw in a few weeks of care on a regular newborn floor. Now, add up all the consultations, the various surgeons' fees, and the dozens of sophisticated lab tests. When you do the math, you're talking maybe half a million dollars." He let the numbers sink in.

"That's just about the most asinine thing I've ever heard!"

"A company man, huh? The figures don't add up to your HMO liking?"

"My math is fine, thank you. What doesn't add up is the logic. You know, I'm starting to take this personally, and I have half a mind to get up and leave! What you're implying—"

"Like I said before, I'm not implying anything."

"Fine," she said vehemently. "But what you're talking about doesn't happen in a vacuum, or by coincidence. It requires human participation, and it's also a capital crime!" He just stared at her smugly, saying nothing. "You *can't* be serious!"

Finally, under her persistent stare, "Maybe it is a little far-fetched," he admitted. "I just wanted to hear what your trained HMO mind thought about it."

"My *what*?"

"Please, spare me the righteous indignation, okay? Save it for some gullible senior resident who's been force-fed into thinking managed care is medicine's salvation. You may not admit it, but you know damn well that what I'm saying has merit."

"God," she said with disgust, "you are one arrogant, suspicious piece of work."

"Fine," he said condescendingly. "If this little irate act of yours is over, you can do us both a favor. I realize this is asking a lot, and I know we're talking about the people you work for, but can you keep your eyes and ears open at AmeriCare? For Christ's sake, babies are dying! If you find out something, maybe you can let me know, okay?"

Morgan's fists tightened around the edges of her chair. She glared at him. "You want me to spy on the people I work for?"

He sighed theatrically. "Jesus, asking you to keep an open mind is asking the impossible."

Morgan jumped out of her seat, her fury barely restrained. "You know what you can do with your insane theory," she said, storming out of the crowded bar.

What Jennifer found so unexpected about pregnancy was her increased sensuality. She loved the changes in her body—the curves, the heaviness, the *zoftig* roundness. Her sexuality increased in tandem with her body-awareness. Despite weight gain, swollen ankles, and shortness of breath, she frequently felt aroused, often at the strangest times. The degree of her moistness sometimes embarrassed her.

Richard was the usually enthusiastic beneficiary of this increased desire. His wife wanted to have sex more frequently than at any time in their marriage, including on their honeymoon. And she wanted to make love in the oddest places, including the living room floor and the bathtub. It wasn't unusual for them to have sex two and three times a day. For the first time in her life, Jennifer Hartman became multiorgasmic. Were it not for certain emerging fears, Richard might've thought he'd died and gone to heaven.

Enjoy the libidinous excess though he did, deep down, Richard was frightened of hurting his wife or the babies. He became somewhat timid in his sexual expression. He had no trouble getting an erection or climaxing, but his sexual assertiveness vanished entirely. During intercourse, he was content to lie there and let his wife do all the work. This didn't seem a particular burden to Jennifer, who was experiencing a newfound sexual freedom. She was more than content to play the aggressor. Thus, although the missionary position had become impossible, she took to mounting him from above, from the side, or with him behind. All he had to do was stay hard.

It had been the romantic culmination to a long day. Spent, they lay side-by-side, nestled like spoons. His arms around her, Richard slowly drifted off. Moments later, Jennifer nudged him softly in the ribs.

"Richard? Richard, you awake?" Before he could reply, she abruptly sat up in bed. She threw off the covers and looked down at the mattress. "I think something's coming out."

He opened his eyes sleepily. "What'd you say?"

"There's water or something. I'm leaking."

"Huh? Where?"

"I think my water broke."

Now wide-eyed, he leapt out of bed. "Jesus Christ!"

He quickly dialed Dr. Hawkins' number and reached the service. According to them, Brad was off that night. Richard was patched through to the covering doctor, who instructed them to go to University's delivery room. Five minutes later, they were in the car, en route to the hospital. Jennifer brought several bath towels and had to change them frequently, as they quickly became saturated beneath her.

When they finally reached the hospital, they parked, entered through the ER entrance, and took the elevator to the eighth floor. The doctor who'd spoken to them was already there, attending two other patients in labor. He had the nurses take Jen to the triage room, where she was undressed and gowned, checked for vital signs, and had a fetal monitor attached. Soon, the doctor came in and introduced himself.

He had her prenatal record on file, and he knew she was carrying twins. Both fetal heart rate tracings were good, and fortunately, the uterus wasn't contracting. Labor, at least at that moment, didn't appear imminent. Then he performed a quick sonogram. The first baby, the girl, was head first, and the boy was a breech. On the monitor, they both had good movement and tone. Finally, he performed a sterile speculum exam, visually assessing Jen's cervix and taking cultures.

"The fluid's nice and clear," he said, "and the cervix looks closed. That's a good sign. We really don't want you going into labor at this point, if we can avoid it. What we're going to do is start an IV and put you on antibiotics to protect against infection. Then we'll give you something to help you get some rest."

"What then?" Richard asked.

"Then," the doctor said, "we wait."

Brad was back on call and making rounds by seven A.M. Standing at the foot of Jen's bed, he tweaked her big toe through the sheet, nudging her awake.

"Get any sleep?" Brad said. Richard snored soundly in a bedside recliner.

"Oh, hello," she said, blinking. "Some. It's kind of hard to get comfortable with all these monitor straps. And I keep leaking. How much fluid is there, anyway?"

"More than most people think. It'll slow down some, but there's always more being produced. Now, this is what we've got in store for you," he said, sitting on her bed.

"Are the babies okay?" she asked.

"So far, so good. You probably know that the biggest risk comes from prematurity. We'd love for you not to go into labor now, but sometimes the uterus has a different idea. So just in case, we've given you some steroids to help with the babies' lungs if they decide to come early."

"What if I do go into labor? Isn't there a drug that'll stop it?"

"Well, yes and no. Yes, there are drugs, but there might be reasons we won't want to use them. There are a lot of last-minute factors involved, judgment calls. Hopefully, we won't get to that point for quite a while. If it were up to me, I'd like you not to go into labor until at least thirty-two weeks."

"Thirty-two weeks? That's another month!" She looked to him for a response, but Brad simply nodded. "Am I going to stay here until then?"

"We're going to keep you in the labor area twenty-four hours or so, and if everything goes well, we'll transfer you up to the antepartum unit. You can move around more freely there. But with twins, ruptured membranes, and your blood pressure a little iffy, we're going to keep a close eye on you."

Jennifer struggled to take it all in. She silently looked away, sighing deeply.

Brad got up. "I'll be back later. Is there anything I can do for you in the meantime?"

"Yeah," she said. "My phone's not hooked up yet. Can you call my sister? Explain what's going on, doctor to doctor?"

*   *   *

"Extraordinary," said Britten. "Just exquisite. Way beyond anything I ever imagined."

The man smiled. "It is lovely, yes?"

"*Lovely*'s not the word. More like *unique*. Are there any others you know of?"

"I know there's one in Hamburg," the man said. "Not exactly the same, but still Siamese. And I've heard there might be one in Hong Kong."

"There's one of everything in Hong Kong. But Hamburg, huh? Probably some Nazi memorabilia, from their camps. That would diminish its value considerably."

"A specimen like this is very rare," the man said. "Priceless." He had long, artistic fingers, and strong hands, with prominent ligaments and trimmed nails. He took a moment to adjust the specimen's position.

The Nieves twins' skeletons were skillfully mounted, facing one another obliquely, a posture reminiscent of Romulus and Remus. They were joined by a thin bridge of bone at the hip, a slender, two-centimeter band connecting their iliac crests. One of the twins raised a bony hand to point at something distant, while the other's skull was turned in that direction, its mandible slightly lowered, as if its mouth were open. They seemed still alive, frozen in movement.

"Priceless?" said Britten. "Nonsense. Everything has a price. And I have a feeling that's exactly what you asked me here to talk about."

They were in the barn on the man's Eastern Suffolk property. Britten was a collector, and for several years, he'd known this man as a supplier. Indeed, Britten had purchased a magnificent juvenile female skeleton from him not six months before. They generally met in a neutral location, but today the man had told him to come here, claiming to have something unusual.

"It might be too early to talk price," the man continued. "The specimen should cure at least another month."

"Fine, fine. I'll let it cure all it wants. How much?"

"For something of this quality, I couldn't take a penny less than a hundred thousand."

"I came here to negotiate, not get raped," Britten said. Then, after a beat, "I'll give you twenty-five."

The man shook his head with annoyance. "You won't find another like it in this hemisphere."

Another offer was made, and then a counteroffer, until finally, after several minutes, they agreed on a figure. At length, the two men shook hands, satisfied.

Each had what he wanted.

CHAPTER SEVEN

EAST AFRICA 1980

No one knew the mites were in the marijuana until it was too late.

As the young men were growing up, *cannabis sativa* played an increasing role in their rituals. It hadn't always been that way. Traditionally, the plains tribesmen of East Africa used drugs sparingly in their ceremonies; but their offspring were children of their generation, and as such were quite familiar with kif, cannabis, and coca. It was easy to grow the hemp plant around Nairobi, especially in the more temperate hillside regions. Worldly young Kenyans were increasingly involved in the drug culture.

One member of their circle, a tall, strapping nineteen-year-old named Makkede, was the first to stumble on the cache. It was halfway up the mountain, hidden in an acacia thicket and covered with a weathered tarpaulin. When Makkede lifted the tarp, he was met by a familiar, musty odor. There, under the cover, were several dried bales of what was unquestionably Kenyan marijuana—valuable treasure that, he suspected, had been either lost or abandoned. But that wasn't all he discovered. Under the tarp was also a nearly decomposed human cadaver, covered with tattered clothes and strips of drying flesh.

Later, Makkede's friends surmised that the dead body was that of a murder or suicide victim involved in the drug trade. Makkede himself didn't get that far in speculation. He was so pleasantly surprised by his good fortune that he immediately decided to celebrate. Nearby cadaver or not, he rolled himself a large blunt and lit up. Ten minutes later, when his friends caught up with him, Makkede was pleasantly stoned.

Ten minutes after that, however, he grew short of breath. He developed air hunger, and his lips became horribly pale. Wide-eyed and panicky, Makkede began gasping for air—deep, croupy inhalations as he frantically turned to his friends for help. But there was nothing they could do. As they stood around helplessly, Makkede's eyes rolled backward in their sockets, and he collapsed to the ground. The raspy gurgle that came from his throat sounded as if he were drowning. Soon a pink froth rose to his lips, and his hands twitched wildly. Moments after, he was dead.

At first it was rumored that Makkede had succumbed to witchcraft, or that he'd fallen victim to a *thalu*, or curse. After Makkede's body and the decomposing cadaver were removed and examined, the police took numerous samples, and investigators swarmed over the scene. It took nearly a month to discover what really happened, and it would have remained a mystery forever had it not been for the fortuitous presence of Dr. Richard Fielding.

On sabbatical from Cambridge, Fielding was one of the world's foremost entomologists. His specialty was the *arachnidacea*, the class comprising spiders. He spent his year off traveling and studying the arachnids of sub-Saharan Africa. As luck would have it, Fielding was visiting a biologist friend at the University of Nairobi when a specimen of the suspect marijuana came in. The police had sent plastic-wrapped samples of the cache to experts in the sciences, hoping to discover the presumed toxic substance that killed Makkede. It was an unlikely stroke of good fortune when the biologist asked Fielding to help examine the product.

But what Fielding found would remain a mystery for nearly twenty years.

At Jennifer's request, Brad spoke with Morgan and filled her in on what was happening. She seemed genuinely grateful that he'd called, and there was no mention of their unpleasant parting. She thanked him and then rang off after saying she'd stop by the hospital on her way to work.

Afterward, Brad went to a hastily called meeting in the conference room outside the nursery. He was the representative for obstetrics. Others came from pediatrics, the nursing staff, administration, and infectious diseases.

When everyone had arrived, Dr. Harrington held up a copy of that morning's *Newsday*. "Unexplained Deaths Plague Intensive Care Nursery," read the headline. The front-page article went on to chronicle the four cases at University. It was written in generalities, because so little was known about the deaths. But there were the customary journalistic histrionics, including interviews with families of the dead babies. At the heart of the article was the question about the safety of the University Hospital NICU.

"As you can imagine," said Harrington, "the switchboard is being inundated with calls from the press and worried parents. We've gotten a preliminary inquiry from the State Health Department, and rumor has it that the JCAH," he said, referring to the Joint Commission for Accreditation of Hospitals, "may be paying a visit.

Some of the people in your department"—he looked at Brad—"said patients are pressuring them to go elsewhere. Is that true?"

"It's a little early yet," Brad said. "The full-time staff isn't hearing much, but I imagine the private guys are under the gun."

"The Dean has asked me to help come up with an official response to the article. I'd like to get everyone's thoughts on this. Meg?"

"Well, we're pretty much stuck with the catch-all diagnosis of SIDS," Meg Erhardt said. "But given what we now know about SIDS, none of these kids had the cardiac or EKG component."

"No prolonged Q-T interval or arrhythmia?" Harrington asked.

"Not in these four cases. All these babies were monitored, and we've gone over the tracings. It just isn't there."

"What about coffee drinking?" Brad asked. "There've been a couple of reports showing an association between heavy prenatal caffeine intake and SIDS."

"We questioned the mothers," Meg said, "and we haven't found a pattern."

"What about drug use, or an infectious component?" Harrington asked the representative from infectious diseases.

"All the urine tox screens and cultures were negative, bacterial and viral. Sputum, blood, urine, you name it, aerobic and anerobic. Nothing unusual has grown out. We can't find an indication of overwhelming sepsis, and anyway, the clinical pictures just didn't fit."

"No, they didn't," Harrington agreed. "If anything, it looks like some kind of primary pulmonary process—the sudden, profound hypoxia, then collapse."

"Did any of these newborns have a post?" Brad asked.

"Just one, the second. The autopsy didn't show anything unusual." Harrington eyed the rest of the staff. "Look, people. I don't have to tell you how urgent this is. Some of our babies have died, and we damn well better come up with an answer."

They questioned, argued, and hypothesized for the better part of an hour. Yet in the end, they knew little more than when they'd begun. What they agreed on was issuing a noncommittal statement reassuring the public and indicating that their research was ongoing. But for Brad Hawkins, the idea of babies dying without explanation was intolerable. There had to be *some* culprit— some reason.

And he was determined to find it.

When Morgan visited her sister at University, it was the first time in two years she'd set foot in a hospital. As soon as she entered the spacious fifth-floor lobby, she was beset by mixed feelings. On one hand, she was entering an emotionally charged atmosphere. Her pediatric patients had died in places not unlike University. On the other hand, being in a hospital gave many physicians a not-unpleasant feeling of power. It was here that they alone could joust with fate in the serious contest for human lives. On balance, Morgan's positive feelings won out. It felt good to be in a hospital again.

After seeing that all was well with Jennifer, Morgan still had a little time before she had to be at work. As she stood in front of the elevators, she glanced to her left and saw the entrance for the newborn intensive care unit. She wondered how she would react to being in a nursery again. On a whim, she decided to go inside.

Passing through a pair of automatic doors, she found

herself facing a spacious family waiting area. It was
empty. Proceeding around the circular corridor to her
left, she soon came to the NICU entrance. Its doors were
clearly marked, "Staff Only." Morgan assertively pushed
her way through.

To her left was a staff lounge. Morgan stopped in its
doorway and spoke to the two nurses standing at the
coffee-maker.

"Excuse me, I'm Dr. Robinson. I'm a pediatrician.
I'm not on staff here, but I was visiting my sister on
labor and delivery. Would you mind if I looked
around?"

"Sure, no problem," said one of the nurses. "Anything in particular you want to see?"

"No, just curious."

They waved her ahead. Morgan walked around
slowly, taking in the familiar sights and sounds: the occasional hiss of a respirator, the muted beeping of a
monitor, the pungent smells of ammonia and alcohol.

Passing the first few isolettes, she gazed at the tiny
infants lying there. They seemed so small, so helpless.
But when she came to the third isolette, she stopped in
her tracks. A child was lying on its back, clad only in a
diaper. Its entire left leg was swollen and misshapen.
The disfigured mass was grape-like, purplish and shiny.
Above the diaper, the child's abdomen was distended.
Morgan's heart started racing, and her knees felt weak.
She turned to a passing nurse.

"Is that congenital osteosarcoma?" she asked, pointing to the isolette.

The nurse nodded. "They don't have a biopsy yet,
but that's the working diagnosis."

"It's already metastasized, hasn't it?"

"That's what they think. God, what a pity."

As Morgan turned away, the horrible memories

rushed in, and for a moment she thought she would faint. A wave of despair swept over her like an oppressive blanket. She felt as if she were suffocating. It was all she could do to put one foot in front of the other and shuffle out of the nursery. She stumbled through the automatic doors and rested heavily against the corridor wall, breathing deeply. Staring vacantly ahead, fighting the frightening images in her brain, she barely felt the hand on her shoulder.

"Morgan?" said a familiar voice. "Morgan, are you all right?"

She turned and saw Brad. After a few seconds, she nodded shakily.

"God almighty, you're white as a proverbial sheet. What's going on?"

She nodded unsteadily toward the automatic doors. "The nursery . . ."

Morgan's face had the ashen look of freshman nursing students at their first encounter with the dying. He kneaded her shoulder reassuringly. "Hey, it's okay. We all have days like this. Want to tell me about it?"

For some reason, she did. "There's a baby in there with osteosarcoma. It's horrible, it already has abdominal mets, and . . ."

"And that reminds you of one of your patients?"

Her head bobbed weakly up and down. "One of the last patients I had. It was awful. I really worked hard on the kid, days at a time, and I guess I became a little too attached to him. I didn't want to admit it, but the handwriting was on the wall. There was no saving this baby. He lasted about a month, and then . . ."

For the next few minutes, as she slowly caught her breath, Morgan told him about the case. It had been an exercise in medical frustration and futility, and emotionally, it had taken its toll on her. It was one of the deaths

that had eventually caused her to walk away from medicine, at least temporarily. Brad asked an occasional
question, but for the most part, he listened. Finally, as
her strength and color returned, Morgan looked at her
watch.

"I've really got to get to the office. Thanks for listening. I'm sorry if I sounded like a melodramatic idiot."

"No need to apologize. You know, we doctors are
our own worst critics. Sometimes we're much too hard
on ourselves. We try to deny it, but we're flesh and
blood, with real feelings, and real vulnerabilities. It takes
a certain amount of maturity to admit it."

She looked up into the eyes that had so recently
seemed so hostile. Now, they were brimming with compassion. Morgan was suddenly conscious of the warmth
of his hand on her shoulder. She gave him a faint smile
as she pulled away and headed for the elevator.

On the drive to work, she replayed the conversation
in her mind. Morgan was annoyed that she'd shown such
weakness, and equally annoyed that Brad had seen her
like that. His opinion of anyone who worked in managed
care was already low enough. On the other hand, he'd
shown an empathic, sensitive side that she hadn't noticed in a man in quite some time. His narrow-minded
prejudice notwithstanding, perhaps she was wrong about
him.

Morgan's secretary greeted her with a timid smile,
then nodded toward the interior office and shrugged.
Morgan took this to mean she had unwelcome company.
She found Dr. Martin Hunt and CEO Daniel Morrison
waiting for her. Morrison looked at his watch.

"You're ten minutes late, Dr. Robinson."

"I wasn't aware we'd started using time clocks."

"This company demands the most from its employees," Morrison went on. "Especially those in positions of authority, like you."

"Sorry. I was visiting my sister in the hospital. Next time I'll be more prompt."

"Actually, it's not your punctuality that concerns me," said Morrison. "It's actions like this." He lofted a piece of paper toward her desk, where it floated onto her blotter.

Morgan picked it up. It was a copy of the appeal she'd written to the Board, before Nickie died, outlining her concerns in the event the Giancola transplant was denied. In it, she asked the Board to reconsider its policy. "Is there a problem with this?"

Morrison looked at Hunt, then back at Morgan. "The biggest problem, Doctor, is that you don't see that it's a problem. For God's sake, administrators don't write appeals, patients do! It's your job to play mister nice guy, to field the appeals from the patients and their doctors. But in the end, we expect you to make the appropriate denial." He paused. "Do I make myself clear?"

She wasn't sure she understood, and she was starting to feel angry. "You're saying you want me to string them along?"

"Morgan . . ." said Hunt, rolling his eyes.

"What I want is for you to enforce the rules! AmeriCare has administrative policies, Dr. Robinson," Morrison continued. "They're made by the Board, with input from company physicians like you. We listen to their advice, but we make the decisions. And those decisions are final. What we do *not* need is someone to rock the boat and to question our collective wisdom. Am I making myself clear?"

The man was glowering at her defiantly. Morgan wanted to stand her ground, to argue the rightness of her cause and the injustice of their policy. But she knew her argument would fall on deaf ears. Their minds were made up. And it was suddenly clear to her that managed care was nothing more than a bottom-line business, with the attitude "Patients be damned." It was also clear that she would soon be moving in the direction of a career-changing decision. "Perfectly," she said, through tight lips.

"Fine," Morrison concluded, rising to leave. "So long as we both understand each other."

As Morgan watched both men stroll toward the exit, she suddenly thought of Brad's comments about AmeriCare's financial motives. They'd sounded like ridiculous speculation before, but in light of the CEO's adamancy, the idea seemed more plausible now. "Mr. Morrison?" she called.

"What is it?" he snapped, turning around.

"By any chance have you been following those new-born deaths at University's NICU?"

"Just what I read in the papers. Why?"

Hunt shot her a cautionary look. "This isn't the time or place, Morgan."

She refused to be deterred. "Did you know that we insured all four of them?"

Morgan thought she detected the slightest hesitation before he replied. But Morrison's voice was steady, and his eyes were cold. "No, I didn't. Now, if you'll excuse me . . ."

Something about that man, Morgan thought. His tone rang of insincerity. Morgan closed her door and sat at her desk, chin in her hands, deep in thought. Clearly, her beliefs and those of her employer were incompatible. But beyond that, she was starting to feel that there was something peculiar going on here. And she was beginning to think that she might have an ally in—of all people—Brad Hawkins.

*   *   *

That afternoon, after office hours, Brad briefly returned to the hospital. He found Morgan in Jennifer's room. Brad nodded a greeting and leafed through the bedside chart.

"So far, so good," he said to the patient. "How're you holding up?"

"Not bad, but it's hard to get any rest. It's so busy around here."

"That it is. We'll see if we can get you through the night without too much commotion, and then tomorrow morning, we'll order up some peace and quiet."

"How're my tests?" she said.

"The lab work is normal. And the official ultrasound shows good interval growth since your last sonogram. Right now, the only thing you have to worry about is staying in bed. Where'd your husband go?"

"He wimped out on me," Jennifer said. "He's not too keen on hospitals. I told him to go to work."

"Probably just as well. All right," he said, putting down the chart. "I'll stay in touch with the nurses tonight, then I'll be in to see you bright and early. If you have any questions, just holler."

As he left the room, Morgan got up and followed him out. "Excuse me, Dr. Hawkins?"

"What happened to 'Brad'?"

She took his arm and continued walking. " 'Dr. Hawkins' was for my sister's benefit. She overreacts when I'm on a first-name basis with any man I haven't known for twenty years. How is she, really? Is there anything you didn't want to say in front of her?"

"Nothing gets by you, does it?"

"I was just wondering about her blood pressure."

"You're right, it's still a little up. Nothing worrisome yet, and bed rest is the right treatment. Fair enough?"

"Yes, thanks. Look, Brad. About this morning—"

"No more apologies, Morgan. I meant what I said outside the nursery."

"That's what I'm talking about," she said. "I want to thank you for that. I always thought of myself as a tough cookie, but that poor kid, well . . . it just got to me."

"I was glad to be there. It's good to see you're human."

"You mean, for an HMO employee?"

He laughed. "I guess I am a little inflexible about that."

"That's a mild way of putting it. By the way, is there anything else you want to tell me? Like what went on at a certain staff meeting that I understand you went to this morning?"

He stopped, looking at her poker-faced. "What meeting?"

"Come on, Brad. Why don't we put our heads together on this NICU problem?"

"Tell you what," he said. "I think we both could use some fresh air. I'll pick you up tomorrow morning and take you someplace where we can talk about it."

"All set on the bow cleat, Mikey?"

"Ready, Dad."

Brad untied the stern and tossed the line onto the slip's mooring. "Okay, release it." When they were free, he worked the throttle and wheel, steering them out into the channel.

Morgan sat beside him in the aft cockpit. She was grateful for the invitation. It was time for a little fence-mending. They were both headstrong and opinionated. But it was clear that they both regretted the sharpness of their words. A morning sail was a good way to clear the air.

Moreover, as he'd implied, they could both use a break. She certainly didn't consider sailing together as much a "date" as an opportunity—a chance to find out more about the NICU deaths, to discuss her sister, as well as to relax. Besides, it couldn't be a date if he'd brought his son along.

To Morgan's untrained eye, the Vector was an impressive craft. It was sleek and low-profile, with teak decks that contrasted nicely with a jet-black, fiberglass hull. She hoped she and Brad could sail along as smoothly as the boat.

Eight-year-old Michael was a handsome, outgoing child, a towheaded tyke with mischievous blue eyes. Morgan could detect a strong resemblance to the picture of his mother in Brad's office. Morgan had immediately hit it off with the boy. He had a laughing, inquisitive manner and an innocent impetuousness.

"He really seems to know his way around the boat," she said.

"Think so?" Brad asked with a note of pride. "This is only our third time out, but he's a natural."

Morgan hesitated for a moment. "Speaking of natural," she said, "there's something I've been meaning to ask you. I know this is none of my business, but the first day we met in your office, I noticed you'd been reading a nudist magazine. You're not going to start taking your clothes off out here, are you?"

Brad looked at her oddly, then burst out laughing. "That wasn't my magazine! One of my more seductive patients sent it to me. God, can you picture that? A nudist gynecologist? Talk about a busman's holiday!"

Morgan was relieved, but she kept her feelings to herself. She glanced overhead. A front had come through during the night, and the sky was now clear, with an

occasional fair-weather cloud. "When does the actual
sailing start?"

"Once we're well out into the Sound. It's too
crowded in the channel."

"How long have you had this boat?"

"A little more than a month," he said. "It was a gift
to myself. She's got the works, all right. Swim platform,
GPS, autopilot, electric windlass, water maker, you
name it. We won't need everything on a day sail, but it
comes in handy on a long trip, or overnight."

"People can sleep on board?"

"Oh, definitely. Room for six." From the helm, he
stole a look at her. Morgana Robinson was certainly attractive. She had a very fair complexion, and her wind-
swept red hair was barely restrained by a headband. She
wore warm-up pants with a V-neck and a short-sleeve
white top, with a windbreaker loosely tied around her
shoulders. He handed her a tube of sunscreen. "Want to
try some of this? You can get a pretty bad burn on a
day like today."

Carried by an eighty-two-horsepower diesel, they mo-
tored steadily up the channel, rounding the point, then
taking an easterly course. A carefree Michael pranced
around the deck in his lifejacket. Thirty minutes after
embarking, Brad handed Morgan the wheel, with instructions on how to keep a bearing of two-seventy-five.
He and his son went forward to raise the sails. Soon,
with the wind behind them, they were making a steady
ten knots. Finally he rejoined her at the helm.

They were heading into a light chop, and the bow
gently rose and fell. The sun was now strong in her face,
and Morgan had to put on her polarized Bolle's. She
glanced at Brad, who appeared confident and at ease.

"You really like this, don't you?"

"A lot," he said, nodding. "There's something about

an open sea. The way the sun and wind work together. I'm not sure why, but out here, I get this spiritual feeling. When I sail, I feel like I'm really part of the universe. A sort of cosmic connectedness, if that makes any sense."

"I don't mean to change the subject, but by any chance did you happen to see my sister this morning?"

"Yes, just before I signed out. Her pressure's okay, she seems comfortable, and there's no sign of labor. I sent her up to the antepartum unit."

"What're the chances she'll make it another month?" Morgan asked.

"Fair, at best. She's gotten through the first twenty-four hours, but about seventy-five percent of patients like her still deliver within a week."

"That high?"

"I'm afraid so," he said. "But assuming she doesn't get an infection, the good news is that there's also a seventy-five percent chance of infant survival. The odds improve each day."

They continued sailing east, past Port Jefferson and Wading River. While Michael cavorted above and below decks, Brad taught Morgan the rudiments of sailing. She was an enthusiastic student, quickly grasping his instructions. When they drew abreast of Shoreham, they reversed course and tacked into the wind. The three of them made an efficient crew.

"What do you think?" Brad asked. "Ready to give up the HMO life?"

"Don't tempt me. If every day were like this, who'd want to go back?"

"For real sailors, every day *is* like this. Depends on your attitude."

"Speaking of attitude," she said, "are you willing to

tell me what went on in that staff meeting yesterday morning?"

"Why not?" he said. "Much ado about nothing, if you ask me. The Dean wanted different departments to get together and come up with a reply to the newspaper article. Which we did, for what it's worth."

"What did you decide on?"

"Oh, some double-talk that diplomatically avoids saying how little we know. A 'no threat to the public, we're covering all angles' kind of thing. Which is pretty much true."

She saw the suggestion of a frown on his face. "You're not satisfied, are you?"

"I just hate being in the dark. Babies are dying, Morgan. And you know what really bothers me? Only one of those kids had an autopsy. I realize that in SIDS-like cases you rarely find anything, but it was still worth taking a look, right?"

"Couldn't hurt," she agreed. "And somehow I have the feeling that's precisely what you intend doing."

"The way I see it—"

He was interrupted by the chirping of his beeper. On its panel, he saw that the number indicated was the hospital delivery room. Even though he'd signed out for the weekend, he'd instructed the nursing staff to notify him in case of certain emergencies. Brad took the mobile phone out of his jacket, dialed the number, and spoke with a nurse. A look of concern crossed his face.

"It's your sister," he said, putting the phone away. "She might be going into labor."

Once they docked, Brad dropped off his son and quickly drove to the hospital with Morgan.

"How often are her contractions?" Morgan asked.

"According to the nurse, every four minutes. I told

them not to examine her unless she felt like pushing."

"If she is in labor, can you stop it?"

"No. Some places administer prophyllactic tocolytics, drugs to stop labor," he said. "But no study so far has shown that giving them to patients like your sister improves neonatal outcome. Antibiotics, yes. Antenatal steroids, yes—and she's gotten them both. But at this point, if her contractions lead to real labor, tocolysis won't help."

They parked in the doctors' lot and took the elevator up to maternity. Forty minutes had elapsed since Brad had first been paged. The nurses had also notified Richard Hartman, who abandoned his weekend bowling league to dash to his wife's bedside. Looking pale, Richard stood forlornly in a corner of the labor room when Brad arrived.

Jennifer was in the midst of a contraction. She moaned softly, panting her way through the discomfort. From the nearby monitor, Brad could tell that the contractions were coming every three to four minutes. When it was over, he took Jennifer's hand.

"Good, Jen. You managing okay?"

"No, I'm not. This really sucks, you know?"

"So I've been told," he said. He let go of her hand and put on an examining glove. "Let's see what's happening, okay?"

Her lower body was still covered by a bedsheet. After helping her draw her legs up, Brad reached under the linen to perform an exam. Slowly, gently, he probed inside her vagina, assessing the cervix. At length, he withdrew his hand and discarded the glove.

"Am I dilating?" she asked.

"Yes, about four centimeters. Here we've gone and done all this fancy footwork, and it seems your body has decided the issue for us."

"Oh, no. Does that mean I'm in labor?"

"Seems that way," he said. "Look, Jen. I want you to understand what I'm saying. We can't stop what's going on—"

"But—"

"Listen, just listen," he said soothingly, patting the back of her hand. "I know you didn't sign on for this, and I realize you didn't even start your Lamaze classes yet. But sometimes, despite our best intentions, nature won't wait. This means you're going to deliver today."

Jennifer was speechless. Brad glanced at Richard, who was slowly shaking his head.

"I didn't bring the camera," he muttered.

"Don't worry," said Brad. "Everything's going to turn out okay. The babies are eleven weeks early, but they have strong heartbeats. The steroids will help their lungs, and the antibiotics should prevent infection." He watched the fetal monitor. "Another contraction?"

She squeezed his hand, grimacing, as beads of sweat broke out on her forehead. Forty-five seconds later, the pain was over, and she fell back heavily against the pillow.

"The first baby's still head first," Brad continued, "and judging from baby B's heartbeat, it's still breech. Now here's what I recommend. I'm not sure there's anything to be gained by putting you through a few hours of labor, and it could be risky for the little guy on top. It might be better all around if we did a section." He paused to look at both of them. "Is that okay with you?"

Jennifer looked nervously at her husband. Richard sheepishly shrugged his shoulders. "Your call, Jen."

She looked back at Brad. "When're you going to do it?"

"Soon as you say the word."

"I have just one question," she said.

"Shoot."

"Can you give me a bikini cut?"

Forty minutes later, with the consents signed, Jennifer's abdomen prepped, and the epidural anesthetic administered, they were ready to operate. Jennifer lay on her back, tilted slightly to her left, her abdomen covered with sterile drapes. Richard was shielded from the operative site, and he sat at the head of the OR table. Gloves steepled in front of him, Brad stood on the patient's left.

"Everyone ready?" he asked of the anesthesiologist, the scrub nurse, and the two pediatric residents.

"How about a skin test?" the anesthesiologist said.

Brad nodded and, using a forceps, tested the abdominal skin to determine the effectiveness of the anesthetic. The epidural was perfect. "Good level," he said.

Getting a thumbs-up from the anesthesiologist, Brad took the scalpel. He was assisted by a second-year resident and a med student. Though he often let the resident do most of the surgery, he decided to begin this case himself. He first made an ample bikini incision, which he carried through the fascia and peritoneum. Soon the glistening, swollen uterus came into view.

Working cautiously, Brad made a low, transverse incision through the thickened uterine muscle. As the incision widened, the scalp of baby A became apparent, its dark hair sleek and moist. The resident inserted a swab to obtain a culture of the residual secretions. Then Brad reached into the uterus, cupped the baby's head in his left hand, and lifted it out of the incision. The small body immediately followed. After suctioning the baby out and clamping its cord, he handed the infant to the pediatrician and went after baby B.

"Intact membranes on number two," he said.

Unlike the first baby, the amniotic sac of the second

hadn't broken. Using an Allis clamp, Brad ruptured the second sac. The fluid that gushed out was disturbingly turbid, a sickly yellow color. After first finding the breech's small legs, he then located its tiny heels. Working cautiously, he gently extracted the baby's hips, thorax, and head. He was concerned that the little boy seemed less vigorous than his sister. But after suctioning thick secretions from the baby's throat, he finished with the cord and gave child number two to the second pediatrician.

The remainder of the procedure was straightforward. Once the babies were delivered, Brad helped the resident with removal of the placenta and surgical closure. In the background, the pediatricians and nurses were busy with their charges. Jennifer, sedated but awake, began asking questions about her children. The pediatricians offered lukewarm assurances, telling her to hold on. Turning toward them, Brad saw that "B" was being intubated. He didn't like that one bit.

Soon, both pediatric isolettes were wheeled out of the OR and rushed to the NICU. Brad finished fifteen minutes later, closing the skin with a row of stainless steel staples. Removing his mask and gloves, he shook hands with Richard and Jennifer, promising to keep them posted on the babies. No sooner had he stepped into the hall than he got a call from the NICU.

"Dr. Hawkins," the resident said, "we've got a little problem with baby 'B.' This kid looks septic as hell."

CHAPTER EIGHT

While Richard accompanied his wife to recovery, Morgan followed Brad to the NICU. Inside the entrance, she paused. She could see a flurry of activity around her new nephew. Nurses, technicians, and residents were intent on their work with the infant, attaching wires, tubes, and monitors. Their presence made him seem even tinier than he was. Periodically Brad spoke with one of the residents. Ten minutes later, he motioned to Morgan, and they went out into the hall.

"It looks like he has early-onset group-B strep," he said.

"A strep infection? I thought Jen was getting antibiotics."

"She was. But as you know, antibiotics *reduce* the incidence of infection, not prevent it entirely. The preliminary strep test is positive. If the cultures are too, then that settles it."

"Wonderful," Morgan said. "I don't know how to tell her."

"Let me handle it."

In the recovery room, Jennifer was resting comfortably. A small dose of narcotic had been added to her epidural, taking the edge off her anxiety. Richard sat by the stretcher, holding her hand. Both Hartmans nervously eyed Brad when he entered.

"This is what we have so far," Brad began. "Your daughter's doing great. She's breathing on her own without a respirator, just getting a little oxygen. It's a little early, but I have a feeling she's going to be fine. Your son's having a little tougher time."

Jen squeezed Richard's hand but said nothing.

"As of now," Brad continued, "it looks like he's got an infection. The working diagnosis is something called early-onset group-B strep."

"I don't understand," said Richard, frowning. "Isn't that what you tried to prevent with the penicillin?"

"That's right. But we're not always successful."

"Is it bad, this strep?" Jen said.

"Group B strep is a pretty common germ," Brad said. "Ten to thirty percent of pregnant women have it. Only a fraction of their babies get infected, but when they do, it can be a problem. We don't usually divide bacteria into good germs and bad germs, but if we did, group B strep would be a bad guy."

"What can it do?" Richard asked. "This isn't what happened to those babies that died, is it?"

"No, it's not. What happens depends on a lot of things. Most of the time, with proper treatment, the kids do fine. But if things turn sour, this kind of strep can sometimes cause sepsis, pneumonia, and meningitis. In a worst-case scenario, it can even cause death."

"Oh my God," Jennifer sobbed.

"Just remember that usually doesn't happen. This NICU is excellent, and they're doing their best for him. One of their nurses will be down to talk with you soon. So just keep your chin up and hang in there, okay?"

Brad left recovery and went to the nurses' station to

complete his chart. Moments later, Morgan appeared, looking angry.

"Don't you think you were a little hard on them?" she asked. "My sister just had major surgery, and I'm not sure they really wanted to hear all the depressing facts."

"I don't enjoy telling people about possible complications, Doctor, but I can't do it any other way. The plain truth is that at this gestational age, a lot of these kids are going to get real sick, and maybe fifteen percent of them will die. You're a pediatrician, and you know that. If you have a better way to explain that fact, I'll be the first one to listen."

Brad Hawkins was the kind of workaholic who mixed business with pleasure. Although he was off call that Sunday, he made rounds on his own patients, taking his son with him. Michael already knew his way around the hospital.

"Hello, Dr. Hawkins," a deep voice called, as they were walking down one of the building's less accessible corridors.

Brad turned and saw a tall black man approach, smiling broadly. "Hello, Nbele," he said, taking the man's extended hand. "What's new and exciting?"

"Same old, same old, Doctor. Is this the young man I met at football last year?"

"That's him. Michael, say hello to Nbele."

"Hi," his son offered. "Are you a football player?"

Nbele laughed richly. "*I* call it football," he said in an accented voice. "Your father calls it *soccer*. Yes, I play. What about you?"

"Sometimes. I'm not real good at it."

"They've got you working on Sunday?" Brad asked.

"Oh no, I have a few errands to run." To Michael,

"Maybe we can play together some day, yes?"

"Sure."

Still smiling, Nbele waved and walked away. Brad led his son down the corridor.

"Is he a doctor here?" Michael wanted to know.

"No, he works in the pathology department."

"He sure does have a funny name," Michael said.

"He does, doesn't he? He comes from somewhere in Africa, and he can tell some wonderful stories. Someday, we'll have to invite him out on the boat."

Twenty-four hours after he had aborted the wrong twin, Arnold Schubert received a phone call from the Chairman of the department of obstetrics and gynecology. The Chairman upbraided Schubert for what he called "the worst negligence I've seen in a decade." He assured Schubert that the whole incident would be reviewed at the next departmental quality assurance meeting. Any further lapses in judgment, he said, would result in Schubert's immediate suspension.

Schubert hung up, unnerved. He hadn't received such an old-fashioned ass-kicking since he was a teenager. He hoped the incident wouldn't make the papers. Worse still, he would probably get sued over it.

For Arnold Schubert, the pressure was mounting.

Morgan lived in a fashionable townhouse complex in Fort Salonga. It was a little after nine A.M., and she was just about to leave for the hospital when the doorbell rang. She wasn't expecting anyone, but on a beautiful Sunday morning, it might be anyone, from environmentalist to evangelist. She cracked the front door open and peered outside.

"Good morning, Dr. Robinson. Am I getting you at a bad time?"

Morgan was astonished. It was Hugh Britten. What in the world was he doing there? Had she overlooked a message saying that he was coming by? "Dr. Britten, I . . ." She stood there open-mouthed.

"I was just in the neighborhood," he continued, "and I was wondering if you'd like to get that cup of coffee. Or brunch, if you'd prefer."

"Do you live around here?"

"No, I don't."

He was gazing at her fixedly, just as he'd done in the Board Room, a curious puppy dog look. Yet she felt unnerved by its intensity. He was wearing an impossibly geeky outfit, a strange mixture of vintage seventies and eighties: a wide-collar polyester shirt, a grandfatherly cardigan, and hound's-tooth slacks. If clothes indicated one's intentions, she had no idea what he had in mind.

"My sister just had twins, Dr. Britten, and—"

"Hugh."

She forced a polite smile. "Hugh. I was just leaving for the hospital."

"Which one?"

"University."

"Want me to drive you over there?" He gestured toward his car. "We could grab a bite on the way back."

Looking beyond him, Morgan saw an immaculate Infiniti sports utility vehicle at the curb, a Yuppie indulgence. "Actually, I'm a little pressed for time." She punched the door-side buttons of her alarm system, armed it, and stepped outside, closing the door behind her. Then she took him by the arm, gently turning him around as she made for her own car. "And I have a few personal things to take care of. So I'm going to have to say no."

He seemed to stiffen, and he pulled out of her grasp.

"If I didn't know better, Morgana, I'd think you were avoiding me."

"Look, Hugh. It *is* kind of short notice. You don't just call someone in the middle of the night, or show up at their front door, and expect them to drop everything."

He glared at her. "So I'm socially inept, is that it?"

Morgan willed herself to remain patient. Britten was, after all, the brightest rising star for AmeriCare. "Right now, all I'm saying is that I've gotta run." She waited a few seconds for him to take the hint, but Britten stood rooted. Morgan shrugged. "Suit yourself." She turned and headed for her car.

"I'd be very careful if I were you, Morgana," he called to her. "I'm in a position to help you a great deal in your career. But if you keep treating me this way, I can also do just the opposite."

She halted. Good Lord, he was threatening her! Could he possibly think that intimidation was the way to a woman's heart? Morgan felt her hands ball into fists. Nostrils flaring, she was about to whirl around and confront him when she caught herself. Telling him off could well prove a hollow victory, indeed. There was absolutely no question that he could make things rough for her at work. And after her recent encounter with Morrison and Dr. Hunt, she could find herself out of a job in the blink of an eye. When she chose to leave she wanted it on her terms. It might be better to be tactful, at least for the moment. Morgan calmed herself, took a deep breath, and turned back to him. "Tell you what. Come back at noon and we'll go out for that coffee, okay?"

From Morgan's townhouse, Britten drove to his office at AmeriCare. He had information to ferret out. Although his position was part-time, he'd insisted that the quarters provided him were spacious and fully equipped. Entering the posh office, he turned on the computer and logged onto the system. After accessing Morgana Robinson's personnel file, he discovered that she'd listed her sister, Jennifer Hartman, as next of kin.

Britten's fingers were lightning-quick at the keyboard. He wound his way through the networks until his keystrokes delivered him to UHIS, the University Hospital Information System. Within minutes, he was smiling. Jennifer Hartman was indeed a patient there, having recently delivered twins, both of whom were in the NICU. Fifteen minutes later, he'd found out everything there was to know about the three patients. One of them, the little boy, was quite ill.

They lunched at the Old Dock Inn. Although the restaurant was crowded, they managed to get a small table by the window, with an impressive view of the water. Britten chose the soft-shell crab platter while Morgan contented herself with a salad and coffee.

"Your sister's well, I trust?" Britten asked.

"As well as can be expected. She's having a rough time. She went into labor eleven weeks early and had a C-section. Now one of her babies is critical."

"I'm sorry to hear that. What's the problem?"

"A group-B strep infection," Morgan said. "Do you know what that is?"

His smile was condescending. "My dear Dr. Robinson," he said, "even though I'm not a physician, not much happens at University Hospital that I'm unfamiliar with. My degree may be in economics, but my area of expertise is health care."

"I didn't mean to offend you by—"

"It takes a lot to offend me," he went on. "Not that the academic powers-that-be haven't tried. Do you know that last year I was nominated for provost of the entire state university system?"

"No," Morgan said, "I hadn't heard."

"Neither had anyone else," Britten said, "which was my main problem. Apparently, the nomination was just a formality. The trustees had already made their choice, and they didn't expect any of the other nominees to take the position seriously. But I did."

From the vehemence with which he said it, and the fire in his eyes, Morgan didn't have to be a psychiatrist to see how intensely wounded he'd been by the snub. She had the feeling Dr. Britten didn't take wounding lightly. "That must have been hard on you," she said.

"Actually, it worked to my benefit. It made me get my priorities straight. I decided my greatest usefulness was in the private sector, and I think my performance at AmeriCare this year has borne that decision out."

"I take it you have no love lost for the higher-ups in the university system."

He smiled. "Alas, no."

"So now that we've established what makes Hugh Britten run, maybe you can tell me why you wanted to get together with me."

He waited until the waitress put down their orders and left. "Isn't it obvious?" he said.

She looked at him oddly. "I'm sorry?"

"Look at me, Morgana," he said. "I'm thirty-seven years old, and I have no illusions about my physical appearance. I've never been one whose looks swept women off their feet. But I have a fair amount of money, and most people would concede that my future's very bright. I've gotten where I am by my intelligence, by being goal-directed, and by going after exactly what I want. By almost any definition, I'm a good catch." He paused. "Why don't you think about it?"

"Why don't I think about what?"

"Please, Morgana, don't be obtuse. I no longer want to live alone. I've had my eye on you for quite some time. With your looks and personality, and with my brains, we'd make an unbeatable combination, don't you think?"

The sinking feeling that began in her stomach spread through her entire body in nauseating waves. He wanted her. Staring at the peculiarly contented expression on Britten's face, Morgan concluded that he was either the ultimate socially inept creep, or else a very dangerous and driven man.

CHAPTER NINE

A year ago, Arnold Schubert's residence had been a palatial home in Head of the Harbor. Since his marital separation, his quarters had shrunk to a modest two-bedroom apartment in St. James. Although his present digs were a far cry less lavish than those to which he was accustomed, he still had his music, and more important, his freedom. If only, he thought, he had the money to go along with it.

Emotionally, he was strung out. The quickly averted eyes in the hospital corridors convinced him that everyone was talking about the way he had botched the twin abortion. Yet much as he feared getting sued over it, a lawsuit had seemed much too premature; it generally took a minimum of a year for a plaintiff's attorney to go through all the medical records and obtain a preliminary expert opinion . . .

Until yesterday, when he received a certified letter from Alyssa's attorney. "This is not a subpoena," it explained. But because of Schubert's "gross negligence and incompetence" in the matter, the Cutrones intended to seek damages of ten million dollars. The letter ended with a suggestion that he consult his malpractice carrier immediately.

Late the next afternoon, still shaken, he was in the living room listening to Verdi when the phone rang. The doctor sighed. Ever since the start of his marital problems, he'd resumed taking more call, needing the income it generated. But being on call came at a price, not the least of which was its impact on his dwindling serenity. He reluctantly picked up the receiver.

"Enjoying your Sunday?" the caller asked.

Schubert recognized the voice immediately. "Yes, thank you. It's been quiet so far."

"Ah, solitude. Would that we had more of it. You certainly deserve every minute you get. Which brings me to the purpose of my call."

Here it comes, Schubert thought. "Which is . . . ?"

"Which is that you're doing an excellent job. Abortion numbers are up across the board, both early and mid-trimester. It's already having an impact for us—and for you. But if we're going to keep it that way, we have to avoid mistakes, don't we?"

Schubert stiffened. "What're you talking about?"

"Incompetence, as if you didn't know! Easily avoided mistakes, like aborting the wrong twin! And if that wasn't enough, then you had to abort the one you should've taken care of in the first place. Good God, man, a first-year med student wouldn't make a blunder like that!"

"I—"

"You, nothing! Use your head, for heaven's sake. We've got a good thing going here, and if you start to screw it up, we're all going to be in hot water. Get my drift?"

Schubert understood. The caller had a reputation for intensity, the kind of single-mindedness that brooked no errors or second chances.

*   *   *

After rounds the next morning, Brad went to see head pathologist Bernard Kornheiser. Brad had been bothered by the lack of autopsies in the neonatal deaths. In all cases where the cause of death was obscure, it was helpful to have pathological confirmation to pin down the etiology. But apparently, a post-mortem exam had been done in just one case, the second. Even if Kornheiser hadn't personally performed the autopsy, at least he might be able to go over the slides with Brad.

"That was the Strickland kid, right?" the pathologist asked.

Brad nodded. "Little girl with Listeria sepsis."

Kornheiser retrieved the slides. "I did that post myself. Scrawny little kid. A preemie, right?"

"Thirty-two weeks."

Inside the slide folder was the final anatomical diagnosis. Kornheiser unfolded the paper. "Seventeen hundred eighty grams. She was pretty emaciated by the time she died. There wasn't really anything unusual about her case. In fact, her sepsis and pneumonia had resolved by the time of death."

"So what killed her?"

Kornheiser shrugged. "What kills all these SIDS-like cases? We don't know. They die for no apparent reason. Her organs showed typical stigmata of infection, but nothing out of the ordinary. Did you want to see any slides in particular?"

"The lungs, I guess."

Kornheiser ran his index finger down the slides, which were in a slender, book-like cardboard folder. "Let's see . . . here we go." He plucked out a slide with his thumbnail and placed it on the microscope's stage. His microscope was a pricey Zeiss, a top-of-the-line twin-headed teaching model. He adjusted the focus knob. "Take a look."

Brad bent over, swiveling the head his way. He put his eyes to the oculars and worked the fine focus, trying to identify what he was seeing. "Where exactly is this?"

"Proximal alveolar bed. The main thing you notice is the resolving inflammation. Still a fair number of polys, but they're being replaced by lymphocytes. There are a few eosinophils here and there."

"The pink stuff in the alveolar lumen is edema fluid?"

"Right."

"Isn't there a lot of it?" Brad said. "The alveoli are filled with it."

"It's a little more than usual, maybe," Kornheiser conceded. "But you sometimes get that from the trauma of CPR."

"With all this edema and those eosinophils, could this be some kind of allergic reaction?"

"You've been reading too much, Brad," said the pathologist. "From what I understand, none of the four cases had an allergic manifestation."

"Right, but . . . what about some sort of toxin, or poisoning?"

"None that I could see," Kornheiser said. "If there was, I'd have found characteristic lesions in other organs, like the liver."

Brad straightened up. His brow was furrowed. "Mind if I borrow these slides?"

"Help yourself." Kornheiser slid over the folder. "Exactly what is it you're looking for?"

"Anything I can find."

Forty-year-old Simon Crandall was one of the curators in the entomology division of Manhattan's Museum of Natural History. He was also a forensic biologist, with specialties in anthropology and entomology. The latter was an area in which he was a recognized expert, and with a background in both entomology and forensics, he was a frequent visitor to crime scenes. On top of that, his anthropology credentials made him into a sub-specialist in bone identification. Crandall conducted most of his business from an office in the museum.

"A police officer is here to see you, Dr. Crandall."

"Show him in."

The clean-cut man who entered Crandall's office wore an inexpensive gray suit and carried a briefcase. After displaying his NYPD shield, he introduced himself as Kevin Riley.

"What can I do for you, Detective?"

"Could you identify this for me, Doctor?" Riley removed a large bone from his briefcase.

"Let's take a look." Crandall examined the bone, turning it over in his hands, using a magnifying glass to scrutinize its articular surfaces. "Where'd you get this?"

"A shop in the West Village called Skulls N Things."

"Must be a new one," Crandall said. "I know most of the bone collectors around here, and I never heard of them."

"They opened a few weeks ago, and they were running a special. According to them, this is supposed to be a gorilla femur, price slashed from a grand to seven hundred fifty."

"It's a femur, all right. Human female. Usually goes for around seventy-five bucks."

"You're shittin' me."

"You're new to this racket, aren't you, Detective?" asked Crandall.

"Is it that obvious, Doc?"

Crandall smiled. "For your initiation, I'll give you a brief overview to Commercial Osteology 101." He returned the bone and leaned back in his swivel chair, hands folded behind his head.

Skeleton collecting, he explained, had been a pastime since antiquity. Although considered morbid and outré by the general public, there was always a small group of the anatomically curious who were fascinated by ossified remains. There were few laws against bone collecting—sale or possession of the remains of endangered species, like the gorilla, being one—and the regulations that existed were loosely interpreted. Almost anyone could get into the business.

In fact, Dr. Crandall continued, there were about fifty "natural history" stores across the U.S. selling a wide variety of items, such as human funny bones, sharks' teeth, animal skulls, lizard spines, and human teeth. About ten of them were "bones only" shops. What was once an obscure hobby practiced by Southwestern ranchers had evolved, over the years, into a worldwide business in which items were sold by mail-order, over the Internet, and in upscale urban boutiques.

"Are we talkin' about normal people, or some kind of pervert?" Riley asked.

"Ordinary as you and me. At one time the customers were mainly museums and medical students, but now the collectors come from everywhere. And it's a booming business. The market is growing really fast. Prices skyrocketed after India, which was one of the world's largest suppliers of human bones, banned their export in 1986. Animal skulls, particularly the exotic types, sell for around one hundred dollars, while the best human specimens go for nearly ten times that. Something truly rare and unusual can command five to six figures. Because of the money involved and lack of regulation, the industry is unfortunately susceptible to large-scale fraud and criminal activity."

Crandall leaned forward, raised his eyebrows, and asked the detective if he had any questions.

"Yeah, just how do they make these skeletons, anyway? Legitimately, like for medical schools?"

Crandall smiled to himself. He always enjoyed watching the expressions on people's faces when he explained the process of stewing fresh human cadavers and allowing them to be picked clean by hundreds of carnivorous beetles.

Predictably, Riley paled, and his Adam's apple bobbed in his throat. "Are you shittin' me, Doc?"

"Not at all, Detective. It's one of medicine's macabre little secrets."

Suddenly the officer seemed anxious to leave. "I appreciate your patience, Dr. Crandall," he said nervously. "This bone stuff must make you a busy man."

Crandall nodded. "You know what worries me, Detective? Like any niche business, there are some die-hard collectors. They'll stop at nothing—and I mean *nothing*—to get the specimen they want."

Brad Hawkins had been up since four A.M. administering oxytocin to one of his patients in labor. The process, known as "pitting out," required his presence until the patient delivered. The exhausting task often took hours. At ten o'clock, with the patient still undelivered, he put on a cover gown and went down to the cafeteria for a break. No sooner did he sit down than he was joined by Meg Erhardt.

Among the nurses, Brad, an attractive, intelligent man with a promising future, was considered something of a catch. The only problem was his standoffishness. Some saw it as snobbishness, but Meg recognized it as the pain of a man who had once been deeply in love. She'd known Brad for several years; and at times, when she talked about her own family, she could see the pain overwhelming him.

Meg considered this vulnerability very appealing, and it was one of the many reasons she pursued him. Meg was an assertive go-getter, and very attractive, but although they'd dated several times, she had yet to break through his self-imposed emotional barriers. That didn't stop her from trying.

"Did you hear about that baby at North Shore?" she asked.

"What baby?"

"They had a newborn death that sounded just like ours."

"When was this?"

"Yesterday evening," she said. "A preemie, four weeks old. It was finally starting to get better when it had unexplained cardio-respiratory failure. A friend of mine who works over there called me."

"I hope this isn't some sort of weird infectious thing," Brad said. "You know, I took a look a the Strickland kid's autopsy slides, and for a moment, I thought there was something either toxic or allergic going on."

"Why'd you think that?"

"Something on one of the slides." He paused. "You know what we have to find, Meg, is a common denominator."

"You mean a piece of equipment, like IV tubing?"

"Right," he nodded. "Something you might not expect, something ordinary that was used in every case. Something . . ." He stopped in mid-sentence, mouth agape, staring at her.

The dark look that swept over his face frightened her. "What's wrong?" she asked.

"Health coverage," he slowly said. "Who was that baby's insurer?"

*   *   *

The following morning, the brief article about the latest death appeared on *Newsday*'s page five. As Jennifer lay reading the paper in her postpartum bed, she felt a chill run through her body. The article, which summarized the four other deaths and the noncommittal statements made by hospital authorities, went on to speculate about causation and whether there would be more. This was precisely what terrified her.

"How's it goin', Jen?"

She looked up to see Sarah Berkow smile at her from the doorway. They'd both delivered on the same day, and Sarah had been her roommate until yesterday, when she was discharged. But Sarah's child was also in the ICU suffering from respiratory distress.

Jennifer gestured toward the paper. "Did you see this article in *Newsday*?"

Sarah nodded. "Scary, isn't it?"

"*Scary*'s not the word. If I'd known there was a problem . . ."

"I know, but you know how the press exaggerates, so maybe . . ." Her voice trailed off. "Still, this place always had such a good reputation. Anyway, I was just down to see Ellen, and she seems all right. Thought I'd stop in to see how you were doing."

"Thanks, Sarah. Physically, I'm doing all right. Emotionally, it's another story. The fact is I'm terrified about Benjamin."

"I suppose there's some comfort in knowing we're not alone in this," said Sarah.

When Sarah left, Jennifer quickly got out of bed, put on a robe, and went to the NICU, feeling angry and helpless. Why had no one told her about what the paper called "the NICU problem"? Had she known, she might well have chosen another doctor and a different hospital. Maybe it wouldn't have made any difference, but at least it would have given her *some* semblance of control.

Her daughter Courtney, now four days old, continued to improve. She was breathing very well for a newborn her size, she was taking small feedings, and she was only mildly jaundiced. The pediatrician said her prognosis was excellent.

Her son Benjamin was a different story entirely. Ben lay in isolette 104, in the center of the NICU. Lying diapered on his mattress, he looked pathetically frail. A white blindfold shielded his sensitive eyes, and a blue glow radiated from the bili-blanket beneath him. An Air Shields warmer/light was overhead, and a SensorMedics oscillating ventilator fed humidified air to his endotracheal tube. He barely moved at all. He had two IVs, a urinary collection bag, and all sorts of monitors. Sensor wires led everywhere. Tethered to his life supports, Benjamin looked like some sort of lab experiment, more electronic than human.

No one had told Jennifer her son's odds of survival, and she didn't ask. Not that she really wanted to know. The sobering facts were that a child more than ten weeks premature, of very low birth weight and with massive bacterial sepsis, had at best a fifty percent chance of meaningful survival. Although Ben was on the receiving end of all the appropriate therapies, the deck was stacked against him. There was little his mother could do except wait and pray.

And pray she did. She had never been a particularly religious woman, but she felt desperate, and right now she would do anything that might help her child. At the side of the isolette, she put her finger in Ben's tiny, motionless palm, thinking that, if she couldn't hold him, perhaps some sort of physical contact might help impart strength, if not to him, then at least to her.

She prayed to God, and to Jesus. To Buddha, and to

the Great Spirit. She prayed for the will to continue, for divine intervention, and for the caregivers' skills. But most of all, Jennifer Hartman prayed for a sign. Deep down, she was losing hope, and without some sort of encouragement, she didn't know how long she could continue.

CHAPTER TEN

Several days after he'd first met with Dr. Crandall, Detective Riley called with a request from the assistant medical examiner that he come to a crime scene to examine a dead body. An official consultant to both the ME's Office and the NYPD because of his credentials as both an entomologist and bone expert, Crandall was often called when an expert was needed for a forensic investigation.

Crandall kept the tools of his trade in a suitcase in his office. In addition to latex gloves and a magnifying glass, he had protective clothing, surgical instruments, a small artist's brush, various insect aspirators, and assorted folding nets. Everything was ready to go by the time Riley arrived. As they walked to the unmarked police car, Crandall asked where they were headed.

"Staten Island, Doc," said the detective. "Near Great Kills. They think it's Sal De Paolo's daughter, and they need to pin down the time of death."

"The Mafia guy?"

"The same. Nineteen-year-old kid, disappeared ten days ago. You read about it?"

Crandall shook his head. "I don't really keep up with crime."

"Word on the street is that De Paolo's boys might be muscling in on that bone business we talked about. It's unregulated, and there's a lot of money to be made. That's why I got assigned to this case. If this body turns out to be De Paolo's kid, some people think it might be a revenge killing." He paused. "Tell me somethin', Doc. How'd you get involved with forensic entomology, anyway?"

"Professional curiosity, I guess. How much do you know about what I do?"

"Not much," Riley said. "I've only been on this job a month."

"Then you'll have to put up with the standard ten-minute rookie lecture. As far as dead bodies go, there are several methods for establishing the time of death. First there's histological, which is from tissue slides. Then there's chemical and bacteriological. For the garden-variety corpse, any good ME can pin down the time from those three techniques. But sometimes, especially when the body's outdoors in the summer, you might use botanical or zoological methods. The last is where I come in."

"Zoological?"

"I study the cadaver's fauna, mostly insects. If you can identify the species that are present in their various stages, you can give a pretty good estimate of the time of death."

As they drove, Crandall explained precisely what happened to a cadaver in the field. "After putrefaction, four different categories of insects might feed on the carrion at various times. First there are the necrophagous insects, such as blowflies and their larvae. Next, the predators and parasites of the necrophagous insects, particularly *coleoptera*, or beetles. Carrion beetles usually avoid competition with blowflies by visiting the carcasses at a later, dried stage of decomposition. Next come the omnivores, such as wasps and ants, and finally there are the adventive insects, like spiders

"First," Crandall continued, "I make a general inspection of the body to get a rough idea of the stage of decomposition, the same as the ME would do. The rate of a body's decay depends on ambient temperature, season and microclimate, humidity, type of exposure, and other environmental factors, all of which I take into consideration. If I carefully collect all the data on site, and couple it with a detailed entomological identification, I can usually arrive at a fairly precise time of death."

They crossed the Verrazano-Narrows Bridge and arrived on site fifteen minutes later. The cadaver was found barely thirty feet from Raritan Bay. The two men parked and headed for the yellow crime-scene tape. The murder victim was lying on a marshy plain thick with reeds and tall grass. A gust of wind swept toward them off the water, filled with the stench of death. The odor of decay overpowered Riley, who promptly regurgitated his breakfast onto the roadside. Crandall handed him some paper napkins.

"Should've warned you about that," he said. "You want a mask?"

Still pale and shaken, Riley said, "Will it help?"

"Not really."

"Then what's the point?"

"My feelings precisely," Crandall said. "You get used to it after a while. The stench alone pins it down a little, say from around three to eighteen days. But that smell's so powerful, I'll bet the date's in the latter half of that range. You up to this?"

Riley's voice was weak. "I'll try."

They ducked under the tape and walked in the direction indicated by a police officer. The bulrushes had been pushed aside, trampled into a makeshift path. Several yards into the overgrowth, they came upon what was left of the body. The naked young woman lay on her side, arms raised over her head. Patches of long blond hair clung to her scalp. Crandall hunched down and opened his suitcase as he eyed the cadaver.

Other than being obviously human, little of the corpse was recognizable. The eyes and lips were gone. Although the victim was Caucasian, what remained of the exposed flesh was nearly black. The tissues were beginning to shrivel, and as internal gases escaped, the body had started to collapse inward on itself. Here and there, especially around the face, bones were beginning to protrude.

Unaffected by the stench, Crandall took out a hand lens and closely inspected the head. The nasal passages were thick with slimy grubs, and yellowish maggots slithered in and out of the eye sockets. Given the temperature and the humidity, they were fewer than Crandall would expect for what might be a ten-day-old cadaver. He took out his forceps and several liquid-filled bottles. Over the next ten minutes, he carefully selected different species of insects, killed them in carbon tetrachloride, and then transferred them to ethyl alcohol for preservation.

When he was finished, Crandall put everything away, closed the suitcase, and went to find Detective Riley, who had retreated to a far corner of the crime scene. Minutes later, they were on the highway.

Back in his office, Crandall examined his species both macroscopically and microscopically, making careful notes. It took him two hours to finish. The predominant insect forms were *creophilus* and some *creophilus* larvae, *gamasids*, parasitic wasps, and *ptomaphila*, with less abundant amounts of blowfly larvae and *trichoptera*.

Given the insect prevalence and various stages of development, Simon Crandall concluded that the cadaver was thirteen days old.

If the De Paolo woman had been seen ten days ago, she clearly couldn't be the murder victim. If the police wanted to find the mobster's daughter, they'd have to look someplace else.

"I'm really getting worried about her," said Morgan. "All she does is hang around the NICU staring at Ben's isolette."

"She's a worried mother," Brad said. "That's how they act. I see it all the time."

"Come on, Brad. She's almost never home, and she hardly sleeps. I haven't seen her eat a thing. That can't be very healthy, can it?"

Brad smiled to himself. Only a mother, he'd come to realize, could show that degree of selfless intensity and devotion. It was an all-consuming behavior that to others seemed to border on the psychotic. "All right, I'll talk with her. But I honestly don't expect her to change much until Ben's off the respirator."

"Just how likely is that?"

He shrugged his shoulders. "We'll just have to wait and see."

They both sipped their coffee. Getting together in the hospital cafeteria had become a daily ritual. The prickliness of their early relationship had vanished. Now they both seemed to look forward to sharing a coffee, although at present, their relationship remained strictly professional.

It had been days since Jennifer was discharged, after a flawless recovery. She wanted to remain in the hospital to be close to her children, but even her sister's considerable clout with AmeriCare couldn't keep Jen there unnecessarily. And since she could rarely reach her sister at home, Morgan took to stopping off before work or during lunchtime to keep tabs on her family.

"Heard from good old Hugh recently?" Brad asked.

"Not in a few days." Morgan had told him about Britten's late-night phone call and his odd early-morning appearance at her door. "I'm sure a lot of women would be flattered, but . . . Did you know that he'd been up for provost last year?"

"Yep. It was a big story on campus for a couple weeks." He peered intently at her over the rim of his coffee cup. "You up for a little unsolicited advice? Steer clear of that guy, Morgan. Word is that once he latches onto something, he's as tenacious as a piranha. I don't think it's over yet between him and the university. The man can be ruthless."

Morgan looked away, trying to hide her rising concern. She hadn't mentioned the e-mail from Britten, or the phone calls at home that she let go unanswered. It was one thing to have her own suspicions, but another thing entirely to have them confirmed by someone else.

EAST AFRICA 1981

He gutted the brown goat first.

Animals were the key to understanding God's will. The god Ngai expressed herself through their grazing patterns, or—if one was in a hurry—through their entrails. And now, he was in a hurry.

As son of a *mindumugu*, or witch doctor, he had a responsibility both to himself and to his people. By the age of twenty, he had become an apprentice game warden and university student in biology. Scandal was to be avoided, and it was a sin to shame the tribe. Makkede's tragedy had brought the police to their door, and now his continued use of the hemp plant was getting him in trouble with the authorities. It was rumored that the police would arrest him soon. Steps had to be taken, but first, it was essential to verify the threat. This was why he'd gathered the goats.

He was a handsome man, tall and thin-nosed. He paused from his long climb, savoring the faint evening breeze that rolled up the hillside. This was truly God's country, and this was his home. Looking into the distance, his gaze fell upon the ridge of granite-hewn mountains, *Ildonyo Ogol*, cloaked in thorn and acacia. Beneath him, facing the rift, the breathtaking sweep of the Serengeti unfolded as far as the eye could see, thick with wildebeest and kongoni, impala and zebra. He breathed deeply and moved on, pulling the goats behind him.

Reaching the clearing, he tethered the goats to a stake and lit a fire. For the next hour, he dug a wide pit in the ground and carefully lined it with overlapping banana fronds. Then he waited for the darkness, until the sky was inky black and the stars glittered overhead. At length, he stood up and chanted a benediction. Moistening the fronds with water from a gourd, he sprinkled them with a sacred powder from an ivory flask.

It was time.

With a glance at the heavens, he unsheathed his knife and approached the white goat. He smoothly split its nose and rubbed powdered lime into the wound. Undoing the tether, he walked the bleeding goat clockwise around the pit, leaving a blood trail. Then he repeated the process with the brown goat, circling in the other direction.

The night air was fragrant with mimosa. Putting his

knife away, he began to choke the brown goat until its knees buckled and it was nearly dead. When its opalescent eyes turned cloudy, he used the *panga* to open the goat up and let out its guts. After ripping apart its belly, he clawed the intestines free until they lay glistening on the dry earth. The animal was barely alive when he finally cut its throat. After dispatching the white goat in similar fashion, he freed the goats' intestines from their attachments and dragged the steaming guts into the pit. Uncoiling their slick loops onto the fronds, he hunkered down to read the entrails.

His eyes narrowed in concentration. Properly slaughtered, a sacrificial goat's innards told a story. A skilled *mindumugu* could read them as if they were a book. In the firelight, he carefully studied the cooling mass, using a stick to poke through the coils, searching for meaning. At length, he came to understand that the authorities were indeed after him, and it was only a question of time before he was in custody. Satisfied, he finally straightened up. The time had come to leave his native land.

With the coming of daybreak, the vultures would arrive and circle overhead. Drawn by blood and stinking viscera, marabou storks would come prowling among the corpses, corpses that, under other circumstances, might have made fine skeletons. But by then, he would be gone. Having discovered what he set out to, he retreated down the hill, abandoning the clearing to the raucous night symphony of *fisi*, the hyena.

CHAPTER ELEVEN

AmeriCare's atrium was a magnificent entryway with floor-to-ceiling glass windows and Italian marble walls. It conveyed an impression of power, and every time Morgan entered the building, she was imbued with a feeling of strength. But that feeling came at a price. There was a remoteness to the place, a certain coldness that left its mark on the employees.

And it didn't come from the building's architecture alone. Not long after she was hired, Morgan came to realize that the atmosphere of almost any managed care organization, with its incessant claim denials and efforts at cost containment, was one of stingy short-temperedness. Early in her tenure, she was accustomed to breezing through the atrium with a smile and cheerful hello for everyone. But the most she ever elicited from the security guard was a testy grunt, and other employees seemed equally defensive. After a while, she stopped trying.

One of the rare exceptions to company moodiness was her secretary, Janice. A bouncy, outgoing blond, Janice always had a ready smile and encouraging word for her boss. Janice was Jennifer's age—several years

Morgan's junior—and Morgan treated her more like a sister than an underling.

"How's your sister, Morgan? And your nephew?" Janice asked.

"They're both hanging on by a thread," she said. "It's touch-and-go with Ben, and Jen's her own worst enemy. Anything come up while I was out?"

"I got that file you wanted. It's on your desk. And Dr. Hunt's been nosing around looking for you."

"What does he want?"

"He wouldn't say, but honest to God, he's starting to give me the creeps."

Morgan knew what Janice meant. The Martin Hunt she'd first met when interviewing for the AmeriCare position seemed cast from a different mold than other senior administrators. In contrast to the quarrelsome stodginess of people like Daniel Morrison, Dr. Hunt had a lively affability that was decidedly out of place in the halls of AmeriCare. In fact, it was largely his outgoing personality that had convinced her to take the job.

This stemmed partly from his formal medical training. Ever since the early eighties, medical school curricula adapted to the changing demands of an increasingly consumerist society. Whereas med schools previously stressed the disease-oriented, case-management approach, suddenly they began to pay attention to ethical consideration, preventive care, and doctor–patient communication, where an even personality and an ability to listen were paramount. It was important that young doctors were viewed less as "M. Dieties" and more as trusted advisers. Hunt had gone to school early in that era, and Morgan thought he had learned his lessons well.

However, unlike her, Martin Hunt was never a practicing physician. Ten years older than Morgan, married and with nearly grown children, Hunt had given in to financial pressures. The growing managed health care industry made attractive offers, and he went right into administrative medicine after one short year of postgraduate training. Despite the organizational stuffiness, he fit right in.

For Morgan, Dr. Hunt came to act as a buffer between her and administrators like Morrison. Yet the one thing that set him apart from her was his relative lack of experience in direct patient care, and the emotions and anguish it brought. Likeable though he was, Martin Hunt was a man without compassion. Initially Morgan thought she could tolerate that lack, but it was now becoming a sore point between them.

Morgan's glance flitted from her computer to the folder on her desk. In it was a copy of the pediatric chart on the child who'd died at a North Shore University Hospital. By now, the clinical scenario was depressingly familiar: a seriously ill newborn who, despite initial setbacks, slowly appeared to be getting better. Then, inexplicably, came the profound adverse pulmonary event and cardiovascular collapse. In this case, a three-day-old little girl had suffered seventy percent third-degree burns in a house fire. In the ensuing month, she had undergone multiple surgeries and skin grafts, during which her kidneys had failed. But with dedicated care, she was finally starting to show improvement. Her prognosis was guarded but stable, and it was starting to look like she'd live to spend the next few months in the NICU. And then, like the others, she died.

Morgan shuddered. She was in a profession accustomed to finding answers, and in this case, there were none. Even worse, this child was also an AmeriCare insured. Brad's observations about statistical likelihood reverberated hollowly in her ears: what, exactly, were the odds against AmeriCare being the HMO in every one of the recent NICU deaths? Skeptic though she was, she had to concede that the odds were very, very high.

She was working on financial projections on her computer. Much as she didn't want to think about a possible financial motive behind the deaths, she was understandably curious about the monetary impact they were having on her company. Using a printout from the University Hospital business office, Morgan collated the charges for the first three children who had died in their NICU. She hit a few keys and did the math. On average, the babies cost the company one hundred seventeen thousand dollars per month. If the same average costs applied to newborns four and five, and if each child had been expected to remain in the nursery another three months before discharge, then AmeriCare stood to save a million and a half dollars from their deaths.

Morgan pursed her lips. That was hardly a phenomenal amount of money in the health care business, but it wasn't inconsequential, either. Little savings here and there, repeated dozens of times, could make a tremendous difference indeed. It was certainly in keeping with the company's attempts at cost containment. What other changes had AmeriCare made to get in the black, changes Hugh Britten took credit for?

Her intercom buzzed, and Janice announced that Dr. Hunt was back again. Morgan exited her computer program and got up just as her boss walked in.

"What's up, Morgan?" he asked. "What're you working on?"

"Same old stuff, Marty. Claims and authorizations. Did you want something, or are you just keeping an eye on me?"

"As a matter of fact, I am. You know I'm your friend, Morgan. I'll go to bat for you when others won't. I just want to make sure you're staying out of trouble."

"You bet," she said with a smile. "A team player all the way."

"Good. I'm counting on you, Morgan. Don't let me down."

When he was gone, Morgan returned to her computer. She punched up the case mix for the entire field of reproductive endocrinology for the past three months. According to internal company statistics, the number of infertility patients was way up, thanks to aggressive marketing. But infertility expenditures had not risen. Questionable and expensive treatments were being discouraged and office procedures encouraged. Moreover, the big-ticket expenses for assisted reproductive technologies like IVF had been contracted to a single provider group, at a remarkably low price. As for obstetrics, the total number of deliveries was up, but interestingly, so was the number of abortions. The increase in terminations actually offset the rising birth rate.

Morgan concentrated on the figures. Abortions were up across the board, not just in the mid-trimester, which is what she would have expected. The largest abortion provider was Dr. Arnold Schubert, who for some reason contracted for a very low reimbursement rate. Morgan temporarily stored that fact away and then did a side-by-side tabulation of total abortions versus total deliveries. The results were eye-opening. The cost to the company of a normal delivery, including physician and lab fees, anesthesia, and the hospital proper, was upwards of five thousand dollars. An abortion ran them at most five hundred. Over the course of a year, AmeriCare stood to save a great deal of money.

Morgan made a hard copy of everything she'd discovered and put it in her desk drawer. She felt sobered, and a little sickened, too. The figures didn't lie; and like Brad, she was coming to believe in the improbability of coincidences, particularly where money was concerned.

Much as she wanted to deny it, Morgan was fast reaching the conclusion that her employer's financial health was firmly rooted in someone else's misery.

The dramatic increase in Arnold Schubert's abortion practice had come as the result of slick marketing techniques. His was the only full-page color ad in the Yellow Pages, under three listings—Abortions, Clinics, and Physicians and Surgeons. Never mind that it added thousands of dollars a month to his phone bill. The expense was more than offset by his increased revenues.

He also advertised in newspapers, magazines, and local penny savers. He bought air time on radio stations that catered to females in the eighteen-to-thirty-four age range. But perhaps his greatest marketing coup was his direct appeal to physicians. He mailed attractive promotional brochures to every practice on the Island, highlighting the caring, quality nature of his facility. Finally, he sent mailings to every woman covered by AmeriCare.

The greatest flaw in Schubert's professional character was that he was a perfectionist. He wanted every operation to go without a hitch. Even the expected rate of medical complications caused him undue emotional distress. In early abortions, a complication rate of one percent was considered acceptable. Given the volume of Schubert's practice, that meant he perforated one uterus per week, overlooked an occasional ectopic pregnancy, or was troubled with excessive bleeding from an incomplete abortion. While other doctors might have taken this in stride, considering it the price of doing business, Schubert lost sleep over it. He was a man at odds with himself, a man who desperately needed the patients and their money, but who hated his own desperation.

The pressure was becoming too much for him. After

a lengthy internal debate, he finally phoned his benefactor at AmeriCare.

"I think I want out," Schubert said, explaining about the failures that were haunting him. "I realize how you've helped me out, but I'd rather let someone else carry the load."

"I see," the man said slowly. "Now that the money's rolling in, you no longer need the income."

"It's not that," said Schubert. "And I certainly appreciate what you've done for me. It's just that I . . . I'm not sure I can take this pressure much longer."

"Now you listen to me, Doctor," the man hissed. "A deal's a deal, and I fully expect you to live up to your end of the bargain! I've worked too hard to have you suddenly develop cold feet. You damn well better remember what you have to do, or the whole world will find out what you did!"

The man wasn't initially sure why he decided to take the mites out of Africa, other than having a hunch that the insects might someday prove very useful. Technically, it was a minor challenge. As heir to a wealthy *mindumugu*, he was much more than a simple tribesman. He had both the funds and generations of tribal tradition to apply to the task, he was much more than a simple tribesman. By the age of twenty, he was an apprentice game warden and university student in biology. Alas, repeated run-ins with the law forced him to leave his native land.

Long-term preservation of the insects was relatively simple. Several species of mites had been reported to survive over a century on a comparatively small supply of hemp. All one needed was the proper combination of humidity, warmth, and darkness. It had been far harder to get the briefcase-size cache of marijuana into the U.S., but he did, traversing a little-used logging road that crossed the Canadian border. Ultimately, after he bought his property, he kept the marijuana in a sealed basement storage bin. All he needed to do was add more cannabis substrate every year and occasionally mist the product.

It was not a task to be taken lightly. He'd seen what the mites had done to Makkede, and he had no intention of sharing that fate. Whenever he worked with the insects, he took all the necessary precautions, adding some that might be superfluous: using complete biohazard gear, industrial respirators, and an air-controlled room with negative flow that vented outdoors. Though not environmentally safe, it was a set-up worthy of a university toxicologist.

Before he left Africa, he'd read a copy of Makkede's autopsy report. After emigrating, he regularly kept up with the entomological literature, and as far as he could determine, no one had replicated Dr. Fielding's apparently forgotten discovery. But he realized that all his work would be for naught if he couldn't periodically evaluate product efficacy. He knew it was possible that, favorable growth conditions notwithstanding, the mites could lose their virulence over the years. Thus it was necessary to test his supply.

Since his other abiding interest was collecting animal skeletons, doing the research was easy. For a man of his connections and background, there was no shortage of animals at his disposal. For what he had in mind, he needed live specimens. His first sacrificial subject was a macaque.

In his hermetically sealed room, the man suited up and placed the animal in a cage. As if it knew its intended fate, the monkey began to screech piercingly. The man covered the cage with a sheet of transparent plastic, through which he snaked one of the hoses of a hookah.

Lighting a small quantity of tainted marijuana, he brought it to the point of smoldering and directed airflow into the delivery hose. He realized that although some mites would be killed by the heat, others would be dislodged to float in the smoke.

As he watched through his goggles, wisps of white smoke entered the cage. Predictably, the monkey became frantic. Eyes watering, he began a frenzied hopping between bars of the cage. After several minutes of intense excitement, he gradually became tranquil from the hemp's narcotic effect. Lids growing heavy, the macaque slumped to the cage floor and began playing with his genitalia.

For a few more minutes, he masturbated contentedly. And then the mites attacked his lung tissue. The monkey started to cough, his face contorting into a grimace. He began leaping about once more, filling the air with high-pitched shrieks, furious to escape. His nose grew thick with mucus, and a pink froth bubbled about his mouth. His lips turned a grayish-blue, and his chest started heaving desperately. Mercifully, the struggle only lasted a short while. Soon the animal fell onto its side, and its eyes rolled backward into their sockets.

In further experiments, other animals fared no different than the monkey. The pulmonary reaction to the mites affected all air-breathing vertebrates, both young and old, though it was most pronounced in primates. Over the years, at twelve-month intervals, the man repeated what he came to think of as potency testing. The mites remained just as virulent as when he'd first seen them at work on an African mountainside.

When the opportunity arose, administering the mites to newborn lungs proved somewhat more challenging, since he had to remain undetected. What he needed was a foolproof delivery system. He studied the problem for months and finally decided that the equipment was right in front of him. Since his job in the hospital gave him ready access to respirators, a little tinkering with the apparatus was all that was required.

Respirators and ventilators had a wealth of tubing for gas delivery. The heart of each unit was an electrically operated piston or bellows pump, computerized for optimum efficiency. When the pump was working, it delivered humidified air, with or without supplemental oxygen. Conduits of various sizes ultimately led to the patient-recipient. He concentrated his efforts on the tubing.

He removed dried leaves from tea bags and substituted the tainted cannabis. Then he rolled each bag into a slender cigarette and carefully sealed the ends. These would be thin enough to fit the respirator tubing below the downstream filter. When a rush of pump-driven air swept through the bundle, mites would be released in large numbers and carried toward the potential victim.

Once he felt the technique was perfected, he tested it on a tracheotomized goat. In the room, he tethered the animal to a pole, hooked the respirator to a tracheotomy adapter, and turned on the machine. Then he retreated a safe distance. It didn't take long before the goat was dead, fifteen minutes after its first breath of marijuana-tainted air. He was ready. He had no doubt the method would work equally well on humans.

His tests complete, it was time to celebrate. He disposed of the goat and cleaned up the room. He'd been a hemp-head for over twenty years, and nothing else could soothe his nerves, or be quite as rewarding, as a lungful of tetrahydrocannabinol. He rolled a thick joint, lit up, and inhaled deeply. Within seconds, molecules of THC began attaching to receptors in his hypothalamus, working their magic on dopamine and serotonin release.

His senses metamorphosed, and, grinning beatifically, the man leaned back and mentally merged with the euphoria.

It never occurred to him that his decades-long, twice-daily marijuana consumption was a problem. Not only was he unable to admit his dependency, but he also reasoned that he deserved some heady escapism from the pressures of his work. The fact remained that his addiction was a dangerous blind spot in an otherwise cunning character. It had gotten him into considerable trouble before.

CHAPTER TWELVE

Brad Hawkins' Nissequogue home was a fixer-upper when he bought it, and over the subsequent five years, he had fixed it up considerably. The twenty-five-year-old ranch was of modest size and equally modest construction, in frequent need of repair. As he rarely socialized, summer weekends found Brad at home when he wasn't aboard his boat. But this would be the first time in years that he'd invited guests over.

He found a Weber charcoal kettle grill on sale in a local discount store, along with an electric charcoal igniter. Brad loved to cook, and he decided that grilled pizza and fresh fish should cover everyone's tastes. He had the fish market cut the tuna and bonito into thick steaks, which he divided into ingot-like rectangles. He coated the fish with a dried seaweed and sesame seed crust, then seared the steaks over a high flame. He cut thin slices and served them with a ginger–miso sauce over a bed of greens. His guests were impressed.

"Where'd you learn your oriental cooking?" Morgan asked.

"Just picked it up," he said. "It's fast, and Michael loves it."

"It is superb, Dr. Hawkins," said Nbele. "A very delicate flesh. It reminds me of the flamingo fish of Lake Turkana, back home."

"Where's *home*, Nbele?" Morgan asked.

"Equatorial East Africa. Kenya."

"Do you have family here?" Morgan asked.

"I have a cousin here, and a sister in Montreal. Everyone else is back home."

"Anywhere near the Rift Valley?" Michael said.

"Very near," said Nbele. "Not many Americans know about it."

"Did you hear aliens landed there last year?"

"No, I didn't," said Nbele. "Where did you learn about that?"

"The UFO news on Yahoo. It's got really neat stuff."

Nbele smiled. "When I was a boy, we used to see aliens all the time."

"Really?"

"Oh, yes. They came to the mountains, at night. Some people thought they were huge birds, like vultures. But others believed they came from another world."

"Nbele," Brad cautioned, "Mikey believes you."

"But it's true, Doctor. My people claim these are gods, and they have been visiting us for centuries." He wiped his lips with his napkin. "Come, Mikey. Let's play soccer. I will tell you all about it."

Brad watched his son eagerly jump up and lead their guest toward the backyard. "It's like the Pied Piper. Mention the word *aliens* and he'll follow you anywhere. Sometimes I wonder about that kid."

"Don't squelch his imagination, Brad. It's perfectly healthy. Children his age are naturally curious."

"Spoken like a true pediatrician. Speaking of medicine, you have any more thoughts on the newborn deaths and your employer?"

Somewhat reluctantly, Morgan told him about what her computerized financial projections revealed: that although AmeriCare did stand to save a comparatively small amount of money from the NICU tragedies, the amount paled in comparison to what it would save from the increase in abortions. "Do you know Dr. Schubert?" she asked Brad.

"Sure I know Arnie," he said. "Kind of a loner, but a hard worker."

"Does he seem like the type to, well, pump up the abortion numbers? Say, at the expense of term pregnancies?"

His eyebrows raised slowly. "That never occurred to me. Schubert's a funny guy. Nobody really knows him. Word also is he's getting raked over the coals in a messy divorce."

"So, he could use the money?"

"Couldn't we all?" Finished with the meal, he pushed his plate away. "Did you learn anything else?"

"I did a computer search for similar cases," she said. "The State Bureau of Vital Statistics keeps tabs on all recorded deaths by cause. I was able to log onto their database and sift through their records. So far as I could see, the only similar deaths in the state are the ones we already know about."

"Come inside a second, Morgan. I want to show you something." He led her away from the patio and into the house, toward a small study just off the bedroom. A microscope sat on the desk. Taking a slide out of its cardboard folder, he put it under ten-power magnification, centered the image, and waved her over. "Take a look."

She put her eyes to the oculars and adjusted the focus. "What am I supposed to be looking at? Pathology wasn't my best subject."

"Mine either. This is a slide from the Strickland kid, the only NICU infant that was autopsied."

She studied the slide, moving it slowly across the stage. "Lung tissue?"

"I'm impressed. See anything unusual?"

"Well, this looks a little like an asthmatic. I did a lot of pulmonary in the city. Loads of edema here, and a ton of mucus production."

"Kornheiser thought you might see that from the CPR," he said.

"He's the expert, I suppose. I remember a few cases like this in kids who had anaphylaxis," she said, referring to an exaggerated allergic reaction to a foreign protein as a result of previous exposure to it.

"These babies were a little young for that, don't you think?" Brad asked. "What about a first-time allergen? You see all those eosinophils?"

She flipped to high power. "Yeah, I do. An interesting thought. What kind of allergen did you have in mind?"

"There you've got me. See anything else?"

She slowly scanned the slide. "No, I . . . what's this, an artifact?"

He bent over and looked through the eyepiece. On the very edge of the slide was what appeared to be a tiny insect, greatly magnified, not visible to the naked eye. It resembled a louse. "I don't know. Not the kind of thing you'd expect to find in an airway, is it? Jesus, you suppose Dr. Kornheiser has the crabs?"

That brought a chuckle from her. She was still smiling when he put the microscope away and led her back outside. She realized that Dr. Hawkins had a comic side, and she very much liked the feel of his hand on her arm.

The most remarkable aspect of Hugh Britten's skeleton collection was its diversity. Although he collected animals of all sorts, humans were the focal point. He was particularly proud of his assortment of monsters, especially the Nieves twins, his most recent acquisition. Yet he considered his collection incomplete. There was always one more specimen to add, the more unusual the better. Right now, his sights were set on a virtually headless baby.

Anencephalic monsters were fetuses that lacked most of the brain, and consequently, developed no cranium. For whatever reason, the cerebrum failed to develop, leaving only a primitive brainstem. Lacking an upper skull, the anencephalic had only a maldeveloped jaw and maxilla. Its fist-sized head had two grotesquely bulging eyes that most closely resembled those of a flounder. Without a cerebral cortex, it was incapable of living more than a few days.

The problem for Britten lay in locating a live specimen. Anencephalics were few and far between, a scarcity complicated by advancements in prenatal diagnosis. Widespread use of the alpha-fetoprotein maternal serum screen and early ultrasound usually identified problems like anencephaly, allowing affected fetuses to be aborted. It was a rare woman who chose to proceed with such a pregnancy. In anencephalics identified late in pregnancy or at birth, almost all were born to women who had refused antenatal testing. If he wanted to add one to his collection, Britten would have to locate such a patient.

Ultimately, this proved rather easy. AmeriCare was a leader in the computerization of outpatient medicine. After he was appointed, one of Britten's first suggestions was that the company use a computerized database for all of its reproductive infertility patients. Obstetrical practices, in particular, were asked to enter all patient data into the company's mainframe. In theory, by prompt identification of potentially overlooked problems, AmeriCare managers could intercede to cut costs. All Britten now had to do was enter the keyword *anencephaly*. The computer would do the rest.

His patience was rewarded. Virginia Ryan, of Yonkers, New York, was in her thirty-fifth week of pregnancy when her fetus was diagnosed anencephalic. Her obstetrician's staff duly logged the finding into the system, where it was flagged by Britten's computer. He was delighted with the discovery. He quickly had his secretary phone the obstetrician's office to learn the Ryan woman's intentions.

The office manager was happy to unburden herself. The patient was proving a tremendous problem for them, not to mention the fact that the doctor was terrified of getting sued. It seemed that Mrs. Ryan came from an Irish Catholic background that encouraged large families and discouraged abortion. Birth defects, to their way of thinking, were an expression of God's will. One of the patient's sisters already had a child with Down's syndrome. Thus, thirty-six-year-old Mrs. Ryan, mother to five healthy children, had refused any and all prenatal testing. Her problem went undiagnosed until her physician, concerned over his persistent failure to feel the fetal head, had insisted on a sonogram. The sonographic result was clear and unmistakable.

Initially, Mrs. Ryan seemed very blasé. She claimed that it was just one of those things, and she could always have another child. At present, she planned to deliver the baby when it was time, and then get on with her life.

As Britten saw it, the preferred option was for her to abort. But according to New York law, she was already eleven weeks beyond the legal limit. Britten checked her computerized demographics. With an annual family income of thirty thousand dollars, the Ryans were people of very limited means. In an era when money talked, Hugh Britten decided to speak very loudly indeed.

Posing as one of AmeriCare's medical directors, he called both Mr. and Mrs. Ryan to express the company's concerns. AmeriCare, he said, was there to do anything it could for Mrs. Ryan; her welfare was paramount. Then he lied, claiming that he'd already discussed the situation with her obstetrician. The course of action they were recommending was immediate delivery. No, he continued, this wasn't an abortion. Her pregnancy was too advanced for that. Rather, inducing labor was the best solution for Mrs. Ryan and everyone involved. And, to help with their grief, the company was going to give them five thousand dollars toward expenses, if they acted promptly. He promised to call back later that day.

The Ryans' reaction was predictable. As long as it wasn't an abortion, they were both willing to go along with the medical recommendations. They knew God worked in mysterious ways. What did they have to do, where did they have to go, and when would they get the money? Britten promised to get back to them.

What Britten now needed was the right person to do the job. The doctor handling it would have to act professionally, competently, and with the utmost discretion. And it would have to be someone Britten could rely on to keep his mouth shut, someone beholden to him.

It was time to get in touch with Dr. Schubert.

Schubert was no longer eager to receive calls from his AmeriCare contact—from the person who had fed him case after case, the person who helped ease his financial predicament. And not unexpectedly, after their recent exchange, the doctor's mood bordered on the choleric. "I may have spoken rashly the other day, Dr. Schubert," Britten began. "I want to take this opportunity to apologize. We've all been under a great deal of stress lately. I've been re-thinking what you said."

Schubert immediately grew suspicious. That didn't sound like the AmeriCare *wunderkind* he'd been dealing with. "You're starting to see things my way?"

"To a certain extent, If what you were saying is that you want to cut back, I can more than understand that. Now that you've gotten the program up and running, so to speak, it shouldn't be hard to spread both the work and the wealth around. It won't be the same as dealing solely with you, of course. And I'll still depend on you for supervision and management. But as for the actual work, I think we can start distributing it to other providers."

"I see," said Schubert, who didn't really see at all. Britten was ruthless, and he didn't trust him not to exact retribution. "And the finances . . . ?"

"I still expect your best efforts, Doctor. As a token of my good faith, I propose to continue our present arrangement."

"That's very generous." He paused. "What about my old hospital records?"

"Once everything's wrapped up, you'll get the originals. I have no further use for them. There is one other thing, however. Something of a favor."

Here it comes, Schubert thought. "And that is . . . ?"

Britten outlined his proposal for Mrs. Ryan. He spoke quickly, anticipating Schubert's reservations. Just when he sensed that the doctor was about to say no, he added the sweetener. "Call it a bonus," he said. "A token of appreciation." Schubert's assistance in this matter was worth ten thousand dollars in cash.

"That's a lot of money," Schubert said slowly. "But I don't understand why you're getting involved in this business."

"It's an internal AmeriCare matter," he smoothly

equivocated. "Let's just say it's important to statistics that make up the company's bottom line."

Such a patent falsehood made Schubert immediately suspicious. But he bit his tongue and kept silent. What the man was asking him to do was outrageous. Technically, he supposed, it might be considered a medically indicated pre-term delivery. But many things—the secrecy, the use of his clinic rather than the hospital, the proposed falsification of documents—were illegal, or quasi-legal at best. What's more, he didn't trust Britten. Yet the man had him over a barrel in more ways than one. And besides, the money was not inconsequential.

Against his better judgment, Arnold Schubert agreed.

Now eleven days old, Courtney Hartman, her mother's fears notwithstanding, was a robust and vigorous child. She was taking formula heartily. Like most newborns, she had initially lost some of her birth weight, but her appetite was so good that she'd had a net gain of three ounces. She required little of the NICU's high-tech equipment.

Her brother Benjamin, however, continued to have problems. He required every type of NICU apparatus available. He never regained his lost weight. Pale and scrawny, his size hovered around the one-thousand-gram mark. Treatment of a severe strep infection was a long, involved process. But, although it was still too early to tell for certain, he seemed to be showing some slight improvement.

For the first time, his X ray showed that his chest might be clearing. Evidence of patchy pneumonia remained, but it was less dense. His ventilator settings were changed for the better. Weakened though his lungs were, it seemed as if they might need less oxygen. This was encouraging news, and the nursing staff did its best to convey their optimism to Jennifer Hartman. But she wasn't easily reassured.

She remained terrified for both Benjamin *and* Courtney, even though her daughter was flourishing. Jennifer envisioned an ominous cloud hanging over the NICU, and until both her babies were discharged, she couldn't relax. And she wasn't the only parent who felt that way. Ever since the Nieves twins had died and the newspaper article broke, worried mothers and fathers hovered protectively around the NICU. Parents with children in the nursery could visit around the clock, and no matter what the time, the eighth-floor hallways were crowded with small knots of anguished parents seeking strength in numbers.

Jennifer acknowledged most of them with a numb nod. The only one she shared her feelings with was Sarah Berkow. A gutsy woman, the daily grind was wearing even Sarah down. The dark circles under her eyes attested to her lack of sleep.

"I don't know how much more of this I can take, Jen. When are they going to find out what killed those babies?"

It was the same question Jennifer kept asking herself, a question to which she had no answer. "Anything new with Ellen?" she asked.

Sarah shrugged and shook her head forlornly. "I honestly don't know anymore. They *say* she's doing a little better, but I can't tell. Can I trust them to tell me the truth? I think I've lost any objectivity I had. What about you?"

"I try to believe whatever they tell me, and as of today, they say Ben's improving."

But in truth, haunted by what she'd read in the papers, Jennifer had recurrent nightmares about her son's sudden deterioration. She pictured him being carried off in the company of angels, or simply failing to breathe, growing cold and stiff on his insulated mattress. Obsessive fears about his imminent death plagued her, and she was still more than a little worried about Courtney. Twelve days after the twins' birth, Jennifer's bedside hovering had grown even more intense.

An oppressive sense of impending catastrophe clung to her like a shroud. Now, when she walked over to see her son, Jennifer's depressed, shuffling gait resembled that of a Parkinson's patient. She wasn't wearing any makeup, and she hadn't combed her hair. Her appearance made the staff uneasy, and most of the nurses avoided making eye contact, instead watching Jennifer out of the corners of their eyes. She neared the isolette and halted in front of it.

"Hello, little man," she said mechanically.

Jennifer bent forward ever so slowly, like a turtle emerging from its shell, inspecting her son. There was something frighteningly still about him. He lay there in a white diaper and white eye protectors, an endotracheal tube in his throat and an IV in each of his tiny, marbled hands. Benjamin didn't appear to be moving at all. Jennifer bent even closer, feeling the pounding of her heart. The respirator rhythmically cycled with a muted *whoosh*, and Ben's fragile chest expanded. But other than that . . .

She lifted a trembling finger and slowly moved it toward her son's flesh. The overhead radiant heat was warm on her icy hand. After a moment's hesitation, she finally touched the skin of his tiny thigh, pushing it slightly in, as if testing the doneness of meat. Ben still didn't move. Jennifer's heart was instantly in her throat. It took all of her strength to advance her finger to his doll-like hand where, surprise of surprises, his tiny fingers slowly closed around hers.

Jennifer choked, stifling a cry of relief. Tears filled

her eyes, and her chin started to quake. Every so often, the baby's fist gave a reflex squeeze. To Jen, it was the most wonderful sensation in the world. How she wanted to scoop her son up in her arms and cradle him to her bosom! She hovered there another ten minutes, nearly overcome with emotion, wishing that the warmth of Ben's small, encircling hand would never end. Finally, it was time to go. Jennifer reluctantly withdrew her finger and lowered her lips to his ear.

"I love you, little guy."

As she walked away, her depression returned. She kept looking back over her shoulder, fearing that she'd find the isolette empty. Everyone who watched her shook his head in sympathy.

Her family, her doctors, and the nursing staff had all done their utmost to help her, putting their arms around her shoulder and repeating the most optimistic information. When that didn't work, they appealed to her common sense. Nothing got through to her. In the hall outside the NICU, Jennifer stood still as a statue, haggard and bleary-eyed, staring back at her son.

"You've been avoiding me, Morgana."

Startled, Morgan whirled. Britten emerged from behind a half-closed door, a smug expression on his face. Arms folded, he took a step forward. "Hugh," she finally acknowledged.

"I don't like having to track you down," he went on. "Business with pleasure, you know? But I've tried over and over to reach you at home, and all I get is that damn machine. Didn't you get my messages?"

"Hugh, we've already been through this."

"Yes, but maybe you didn't realize how persistent I am. A long-term relationship is like a business deal, and

I took your first response to be the beginning of negotiations."

She shook her head. "I meant what I said when we had lunch. I'm very flattered by the offer, but I'm not looking for a commitment, long-term or otherwise."

His patient smile was unwavering. "In time, you'll come to think differently. The way I look at it—"

"Maybe you don't have a lot of experience with the opposite sex, Hugh. But these days, when a woman says *no*, she means it. No mixed messages, coy come-ons, or double entendres. Just *no*. I don't know how to put it more plainly than that."

"I see." His lips pressed into a thin line, and his jaw muscles began twitching beneath his cheeks. "This is your final word? There's no chance you might reconsider?"

"I'm sorry, but that's it."

"Well, then. At least let's have dinner tonight to fête our non-relationship."

She had to laugh in spite of herself. "God, *persistent*'s not the word! What do I need to get the message to you—Western Union?" She started to walk away.

"You enjoy poking fun at me, Morgana? A sly little witticism at my expense? I dislike pulling rank, but I will, if that's what it takes to convince you."

She walked on in silence.

"Your sister, for instance."

Morgan halted, feeling a chill come over her. Torn between fear and fury, she turned around ever so slowly. "Are you threatening me, Hugh?"

"Dear Morgana," he said, smiling unctuously once more and raising his palms in a conciliatory gesture. "I'm only trying to convince you of my seriousness. I intend to keep on seeing you, and I'll use whatever it takes—your job, even your family. If you consider your sister's insurance coverage a bargaining chip, so be it."

The instant she hesitated, Morgan knew she was lost. Britten was childish and vain, but he also wielded considerable power. She'd grown positively sick of the HMO scene, and it was now only a question of when she'd quit, but her family . . . Whether by legal means or not, Britten was in a position to terminate the Hartmans' coverage.

Spending even a few minutes alone with Britten would be a bitter price to pay, but she conceded that it was unavoidable. Morgan squared her jaw, resisting the urge to clench her teeth. Until Jennifer and the babies were safely out of the hospital, she couldn't afford to offend Britten.

She felt the bile rise in her throat but swallowed it down. "Okay, Hugh. You win. Where do you want to eat?"

Minutes later, having planned their rendezvous, Morgan turned and walked away. But she'd only gone a few steps when she bumped into her secretary. Janice had obviously overheard the whole conversation.

"How long've you been standing there?" Morgan asked.

"Long enough," Janice said sarcastically. "Far be it from me to interfere with a budding romance."

Morgan shook her head and sighed. "He's got me in an awkward position, Jan. Christ, I'm sick of this place! I'm damned if I do and damned if I don't."

"For God's sake, Morgan, you don't have to sleep with the guy. Not yet, anyway. Maybe he just wants to go out to eat."

"No, this is *way* beyond a dinner date." She went on to explain the extent of Britten's annoying attention. "You know, the more I think about it, the more I'm inclined to report him for sexual harassment!"

"Definitely not a good idea," Janice clucked. "Not if you want to keep your job. Dr. Hunt's already on your case. And especially not if you want to run interference for your sister. Keep your chin up, boss. You'll think of something."

Thirty-year-old Melissa Alexander was nearing the end of her pregnancy. Assertive and intelligent, she was also very much a feminist, outspokenly so. During her early years under a gynecologist's care, she'd had a great deal of difficulty relating to the male-dominated specialty. To her way of thinking, no man could ever be as empathic to her very personal gynecological problems as a woman. She sought out several female OB/GYNs, but they, too, failed to meet her high expectations. She wound up changing physicians as quickly as some women changed hairstyles.

Yet Melissa desperately wanted a baby. It didn't matter that she wasn't married; marriage had never been a priority. But when she tried to conceive, she wasn't able to. Where it came to fertility, her well-ordered life suddenly went out of control. Determined as she was, Melissa approached the infertility in a logical manner, only to be thwarted by her insurer. AmeriCare had seemed to place every conceivable managed care stumbling block in front of infertility patients. Then suddenly, a year ago, they changed their policies without explanation.

Melissa had had a hard time getting pregnant because she suffered from endometriosis. Some of her health care providers labeled her an "endometriosis personality," a syndrome which linked the physical condition to a high-strung, intense, demanding nature. Typically, these patients were often medically well-read. They asked innumerable questions, demanded precise explanations, and insisted on lengthy office visits, quickly outstaying their welcome. Most doctors considered them a pain in the ass.

Melissa had finally gotten pregnant with the help of a University Hospital infertility specialist, but she didn't take his recommendations about OB care. She did her own doctor search instead. Initially, she found no individual or group with whom she felt comfortable: too many men; too interventionist; or too disinterested. It wasn't until her fifth month of pregnancy that she stumbled upon a situation to her liking.

The practice, located in a working-class suburb, consisted of three physicians and two female nurse-midwives. It was the latter who piqued her curiosity. Melissa was unaware that midwife providers were a good deal for AmeriCare, as they reimbursed considerably less for midwifery services.

Initially, she made an appointment for an interview with some skepticism, wanting to find out if there were anything about a midwife's philosophy that she could live with. But once she met the midwife, she was so impressed that she immediately signed on as a patient.

This particular midwife was in her early sixties. She had a laid-back but patient manner, and she listened more than she talked, which suited Melissa. The woman explained that their approach was very much hands-on and machines off: they were very low-tech and non-interventionist, preferring to let nature take its course. Melissa was thrilled. The only drawback was that the practice relied on "collaborative management," meaning that she'd have to meet at least one of the doctors before reaching term.

Of the three physicians, the most recent addition to the practice was a young woman. Melissa scheduled her next appointment with her. She found the junior physician reasonably pleasant, but lacking the midwives' encouraging bedside manner. She was content to see the midwives exclusively for the remainder of her pregnancy. The midwives did most deliveries, although the physicians would take over in the event of complications or emergencies. Melissa doubted she'd have any problems.

Britten picked Morgan up at nine. They dined on trendy nouvelle cuisine, and Britten was on his best behavior, doing his utmost to play the genial suitor. But Morgan's polite attentiveness was insincere, and she forced the food down without tasting it. She smiled woodenly at his increasingly off-color jokes. Too much depended on indulging him. But, when he suggested his place after dinner, Morgan had had enough and begged off with contrived sweetness.

"Come on, Morgana," Britten wheedled, "I'm not such a bogeyman. Just for a few minutes, then I'll take you home. There's something I really want to show you."

"What might that be?"

He put a finger to his lips and winked. "If I told you, it wouldn't be a secret, would it?"

Throughout her feigned interest during dinner, the heart-rending image of her underweight, scrawny nephew, desperately fighting an infection, lying nearly naked and blindfolded and attached to a maze of tubes, filled Morgan's mind. For little Benjamin's sake, she had to humor Britten.

Morgan sighed, then nodded, telling herself that the nerdy types were usually harmless. "Sure. What's a few minutes more?"

During the ride to his place, Britten's cloying effervescence was almost more than she could bear. How any woman could put up with his peculiarities for any length of time was beyond her. No wonder he had to go to such great lengths to get a date. The evening had long ago become an endurance contest. The real shock began when she stepped through his front door.

She couldn't believe her eyes. Animal skins and rugs covered the floors and walls. Morgan recognized zebra, lion, and bear, but there were other species she couldn't identify. Jaw dropping, she slowly walked forward, a moth drawn to a light. Like the man, the interior of the home was highly eccentric.

"What do you think?" he asked.

She couldn't quite think of what to say. "It's . . . *interesting*, Hugh. Very colorful."

"Thank you. I'm rather proud of it. Come on, I'll show you around."

Beyond and to the right of the foyer was a den. The walls bristled with antlers of every shape and size. Some were fastened directly to wooden plaques, others came with skulls attached, while still others were life-like stuffed heads, neck-and-shoulders mounts of custom taxidermy.

"Very lifelike, aren't they? Huh?"

"You might say that," she said. "Is everything real?"

"Of course they're real. Some are priceless."

Britten's house was enormous, and Morgan followed him uncertainly into a hall where the light suddenly dropped off. The corridor was a narrow and serpentine labyrinth. The sparse overhead lighting came from recessed high-hats, whose limpid beams cast pale spots of light on the curving walls. At first, the walls were bare and unadorned. But as she followed Britten around a winding curve, her gaze fell on a dimly lit circle. What she saw made her gasp, and she thought she might stop breathing.

There, ringed by the faint incandescent glow, were

two shrunken heads. The brown facial skin was deeply lined, like corrugated hide. The eyelids were sewn shut with heavy black thread. The lips were pierced, held together by vertical wooden skewers. Each head was suspended by a chain made of small, linked shells attached to the scalp. Morgan turned in horror to look at Britten. His face was radiant.

"Remarkable, aren't they?"

She was at a loss for words. "I . . . you *collect* these things?"

"I do indeed. They're all unusual, some even one-of-a-kind. These were Maori tribesmen. Come on."

Morgan followed in halting, tentative steps, and Britten's extraordinary collection of human skeletons unfolded before her astonished eyes. She gawked, mouth agape, caught between being appalled and fascinated in the odd way of people looking at a horrifying car crash, unable to turn away.

Britten's collection was more artistic than anatomical. The bony remains were skillfully hung in evocative postures, suggesting the frozen movement of dance. It was almost as if an invisible puppeteer hovered just out of view, manipulating the limbs. As the bizarre display continued, what struck Morgan most was the increasing anatomic oddness of the skeletons.

Each specimen showed greater evidence of maldevelopment or disfiguration. Two dwarfs were paired like bookends. From her classes in embryology, Morgan recognized rickets in a skeleton with bowed legs and protruding shins. In another, syphilis produced a skull that seemed oddly squared. Several specimens also revealed the distended, brittle thin heads of hydrocephalus. The display was something out of P. T. Barnum's freak show. Morgan shook her head incredulously, unable to believe that someone actually relished so bizarre a collection.

"Never seen anything like it, have you?" he asked, all smiles.

"No," she said, too shocked to put her feelings into words. "Is this everything, or is there more?"

"That's all there is at present. Right now, I'm looking into an anencephalic."

"But why, Hugh? What do you get out of it?"

"You don't find all this inspiring, even spiritual?"

"To me," Morgan said, "it's a collection of human suffering."

"Nonsense!" he scoffed. "A collection like this isn't about suffering! Rather, I think of it as the ultimate connection with our humanity. For example, if just one piece of our chromosomes was out of place, or if our mothers had eaten this instead of that," he said, gesturing to the wall, "you and I might be up there ourselves! These specimens are humble reminders of just who we are, Morgana, and what we sometimes become. It's a link with our past, with man's evolutionary history. Deformities like this not only suggest our limitations, but also our tremendous potential, don't you think?"

To Morgan, his argument was as grotesque as his collection. Its convoluted reasoning somehow defined the man, logic mixed with lunacy. But this wasn't the time, she realized, to argue the psychopathology of his hobby. "Why are you showing me all this?"

He walked toward her with a saccharine smile and took her hands in his. "Because, dearest Morgana, I want to share all of this with you. You're the first person to ever see my entire collection. I don't want to have any secrets from you. If we're going to share a future together, I want you to know everything about me. And I want you to be part of this."

A dreamy, adolescent look came over his face. He tried pulling Morgan toward him.

Repelled, she pushed him away. "Stop it! You said just a few minutes, and the time's up. Take me home."

He held fast to her wrist. "You don't know what you're saying. Didn't I make myself clear? I want us to be partners, in this and in everything!"

"You're sick!" She wrenched her hand away and hurried down the winding corridor. "I'll take a cab."

Britten came after her, calling her name, telling her to stop. Morgan began to run. She couldn't stand the thought of him touching her. He was repugnant, slimy and reptilian, and decidedly unbalanced. She had to get away.

As she ran through the winding hall, she knocked into the conjoined twins. They crashed to the floor and came apart in death, fractured at the hip. At the end of the corridor, just as she grabbed the door handle, Britten seized her shoulders.

"Wait, for God's sake!"

But Morgan fled, pulling out of his grasp and barging into the room beyond, frantic to escape the man and his disgusting collection.

"You don't understand!" he shouted after her.

She understood, all right. Genius or not, Britten was a psychopath, hopelessly infatuated with her. He was a man possessed, determined to have her, whether by persuasion or coercion, as if she were another creature to add to his collection.

Desperate to make Morgan stop and listen to reason, he leapt toward her. She twisted away and he stumbled, his head smashing into the metal desk. The air went out of him, and Britten fell to the floor.

The sickening sound of impact made Morgan stop. Forcing herself to turn around, she saw Britten lying motionless. As she watched, the deep gouge in his forehead grew thick with blood that seeped into his eye socket. His eyes were closed, his body was still, but his breathing was deep.

She wanted to get the hell out of there, but the physician in her made her stop. After a moment's hesitation, Morgan knelt and examined Britten's wound. It was a serious laceration, but there was no sign of a fracture. She took a tissue off the desk and pressed on the cut. The flow stopped only momentarily. The gash would probably require stitches. Checking his carotid pulse, she found it strong and full. Morgan stood up, satisfied that all he probably had was a deep gash and a concussion.

She reached for the phone and dialed 911. Britten should be taken to a hospital. As Morgan spoke to the dispatcher, her gaze fell on some papers half hidden on Britten's desk. She suddenly recognized what they were, and her fingers grew cold around the receiver.

She hung up and picked up the pages. They were photocopies of the data she'd downloaded from her computer, the information she'd uncovered about AmeriCare's recent financial savings. Either Britten knew her password and had accessed her files, or else he'd broken into her office. He had been watching her, and he probably knew everything she was doing.

Morgan felt violated. Sickened, she phoned for a cab, quietly stole from the house, and fled into the night.

CHAPTER THIRTEEN

Morgan didn't want to be alone. Visions of Britten's bizarre skeletons danced through her head like disjointed marionettes in a nightmare. Not sure where to go at that hour, she finally gave the cab driver Brad's address.

It was one in the morning when she arrived, and she prayed he wasn't at the hospital. She knew she was taking a risk. Their first meetings had been so barbed that she wouldn't have asked for his help if her life depended on it. But at the moment, she thought of him as a steady, dependable presence. She hoped he wouldn't mind the intrusion.

And he didn't. When Brad saw Morgan's panic-stricken face at his door, she looked so wounded and vulnerable that his instinct was to put his arms around her. Gently, he drew her inside.

"What's wrong?" he asked, thinking something must have happened to her sister, or one of the twins.

She reluctantly pulled out of his grasp and sank onto the nearby couch. Now that she was safe, the real horror of what happened at Britten's house hit her. Morgan's tightly pressed lips turned downward, and the tears she'd been struggling to hold back began to flow freely, running down her cheeks in mascara-stained streaks.

She told Brad everything, from Britten's veiled threats about her job and her sister to her discussion with Janice about sexual harassment. She went on to describe the horrifying skeleton collection and Britten's rantings about a shared life. Brad held her hand and listened without interrupting. When Morgan finished, she wiped her eyes while Brad stroked her hair soothingly.

"I *knew* that guy was bad news," he said angrily, "but I didn't realize how bad."

"Do you think I should call the police?"

"If you're not going to press for sexual harassment, going to the cops would be a leap. Anyway, what're you going to tell them? That he made a grab for you, fell, and bumped his head? That he took files from your computer? Besides, if you bring in the law, there's no telling how he might react."

"What do you think I should do?"

Brad took a deep breath. "Don't do anything. Let him get his head sewed up and figure out what happened. Put him on the defensive. Take off from work for a day or two. Nut case or not, he might realize what an idiot he's been. With any luck, he might even apologize."

Morgan nodded uncertainly, then smiled. "Thanks for listening. I'm not really sure why I came here, but I'm glad I did." She felt cold. "You know, I'm still scared about going home alone. I hate to ask you this, and I don't want to impose, but would you mind if I sacked out on the couch tonight?"

"Hey, no problem. There's a guest bedroom next to Michael's. Come on, I'll get some fresh linen."

The room was small but comfortable. Outwardly, Morgan was exhausted; but inside, she was still wide awake and trembling. She knew it would take a long while before she fell asleep.

She stripped down to her bra and panties and pulled back the bedcover. She would have preferred to sleep naked, but she wanted to have something on in case Michael walked in. Out of curiosity, she opened the nearby closet. The fragrant aroma of cedar filled the air. She stepped inside and turned on the light. The clothing was a woman's, probably Brad's wife's.

Morgan recalled the picture of the attractive woman in Brad's office. For several seconds, she wondered about her, and about her life with Brad. Brad had said almost nothing about his wife, and now, as Morgan stood amidst her clothes, she felt as if she were intruding. She self-consciously rummaged through the clothes until she found a worn flannel nightshirt. Hoping Brad wouldn't mind, she slipped out of her underwear and put the shirt on. Minutes later, she was curled up comfortably in the small bed. Soon, she was asleep.

Brad woke at his usual hour of six, thinking about Morgan. Despite the prickly start to their relationship, he'd discovered that he felt increasingly comfortable with her. Moreover, Morgan was awakening feelings long dormant within him. Of the other women he'd recently known, none fueled the sparks of fantasy the way Morgan did. When he knocked on her door a few minutes after he got up, he was looking forward to having breakfast with her.

There was no answer. He turned the knob and pushed the door open. "Morgan?" he called softly. "Morgan, you up?" Brad opened the door wider and tiptoed into the room. Faint rays of daylight slipped past the drawn curtains. He walked into the near-darkness, closing the door behind him.

He could dimly make out the outline of her head against the pillow, the strands of her fine russet hair splayed loosely across the linen. He parted the curtains slightly, letting in more of the morning light. Morgan continued to sleep undisturbed.

She was sleeping on her back, the quilt at her waist. Something about the way she looked stirred a longing within him. Looking closely, Brad saw that she was wearing one of his wife's old nightshirts. He suppressed a pang and slowly sat on the edge of the bed. He touched Morgan's forehead, instinctively brushing back a few wisps of hair.

Morgan's eyes opened. She saw him indistinctly, as if in a dream. His hair hung loose and unbrushed over his ears, and his robe was open to his waist. Morgan found something terribly appealing about him. Still not fully awake, she found her attraction to him overwhelming. Her arms rose automatically to encircle his neck.

Morgan closed her eyes and pulled his head closer. In the room's pale light, their faces slowly came together. His lips gently touched hers, brushing against them softly, like velvet. Her slightly parted lips were hot and dry. His mouth moved sideways in light and grazing strokes, and he was amazed by the warmth that radiated from her skin. Soon her tongue was touching his mouth, and he felt himself beginning to stir.

His lips slowly trailed down her skin, coming to lie in the hollow of her neck, where he felt her pulse beating rapidly. With a low and contented moan, Morgan pressed against him, straining at his gentleness. She reached under the covers and lifted up the nightshirt.

In the dim light, Brad could just make out a V-shaped cleft of browned, lightly freckled skin. How delightfully Irish, he thought. As they descended across her sternum, the tan blotches grew larger, coalescing into irregular coppery islands. Brad's hand moved slowly down the middle of her chest. Morgan placed her hand atop his.

She slid his fingers to one of her breasts and pressed them tightly around it.

She was breathing more heavily now. Brad looked into her eyes and saw the longing. His hand cupped her breast, and when his thumb brushed across the areola, her stiffening nipple signaled her eagerness. She urgently reached for his head, clasping her fingers behind his neck, pulling his face to her bosom. His lips explored her tautness, and he made slow circles around her areola with his tongue. Then he closed on her firm nipple and, for several seconds, suckled contentedly.

Morgan groaned. She let go of Brad's neck and grasped his robe, slipping it off. Desperate for the touch of his chest against hers, her fingers dug into the muscles beside his spine. When his ribs met hers, she arched her back and pressed fiercely against him.

In deft movements, she centered his lower body between her legs. Feeling the restraining cloth of his boxers, Morgan impatiently hooked her thumbs into the elastic waistband and pulled the briefs free. Then she clasped his hips, sinking her nails into his muscled buttocks.

He was now completely aroused, and Morgan felt him press himself between her legs, but then back off. He pulled his lips from her breast to gaze into her eyes. She saw intensity there, tinged with uncertainty.

"Do you—?" he asked.

"It's okay," she whispered, silencing him with a kiss. "I'm on the pill." She drew his face back to her breast.

He found her eagerness contagious and maddening. With her hips starting to work beneath him, Brad grew incredibly stimulated. He ached for her. His pelvis started thrusting against hers, and he fumbled between her legs. Morgan brushed his hand away.

"No," she said. "Let me."

When she took hold of him, he couldn't restrain a throaty moan. She guided him into her body. She was indescribably wet, soft and smooth, all heat and lubricity. Her legs encircled his waist, and their hips began a slow and intimate dance. They swayed in synchrony, the cadence of their movements increasing along with their desire.

He kissed her neck, her shoulders, her breasts. Soon neither of them could hold back any longer. They both neared the brink and then exploded over it into the sensual beyond. Finally spent, damp with perspiration and with muscles quivering, Brad's cheek fell tenderly against hers.

Moments later, he slipped out of her and rolled onto his side, an arm draped loosely across her chest. He touched her lips with his fingertips, exploring the feel of her. "I didn't mean for that to happen," he said.

"God," she said lightly, "don't tell me you're HIV positive."

"No." He waited a beat. "You?"

"No, sir. You're not saying you're sorry it happened, I hope?"

He smiled. "What do you think?"

"I think," she said, "that your good intentions might do you in some day."

He kissed her lips warmly. "Got to get up, Morgan. Have to make Mikey's breakfast, and then make rounds. I'll be back later."

When he slipped out of bed, Morgan contentedly watched him leave the room.

Later that morning, Hugh Britten entered his office at AmeriCare sporting a black eye and a sutured laceration on his forehead. Martin Hunt saw him in the hallway and inquired about the injury, but Britten didn't reply.

He didn't say a word to anyone, and it was apparent that his mood was even darker than his eye. He went right to his desk and turned on the computer. Once it was powered up, he logged onto UHIS and retrieved the latest data on Benjamin Hartman. To his surprise, the infant seemed to have turned a corner. Against all odds, the child was not only holding his own, but actually showing modest improvement.

That fact brought a smile to Britten's lips. He made a quick financial projection. The Hartman child would be in the NICU at least two more months. At the current reimbursement rate, Benjamin Hartman would cost AmeriCare at least a quarter of a million dollars. Pursing his lips, Britten shook his head. That wouldn't do.

Morgan had decided to follow Brad's advice and take a few sick days. She had no desire for a confrontation with Hugh Britten. Besides, she wanted to linger at Brad's house, savoring the afterglow of their lovemaking. She wanted to unwind, to get a feel for his home, to think about where they were heading. By mid-morning, she finally left and went home to change. Then she went to the hospital.

Outside the NICU, Morgan saw Sarah Berkow, who rushed up to her with a big smile, reporting that her daughter was considerably improved. Although Morgan was pleased for Sarah, she found Jennifer looking worse than ever. Her eyes were sunken into sockets made dark by sleeplessness and fatigue. The yellowed sclerae were laced with a web of tiny red capillaries. Frail and stoop-shouldered, Jennifer looked as if she'd dropped thirty pounds.

Jennifer's fear that something horrible would happen to her son was unshakable. There was no reasoning with her. Now that Benjamin was beginning to show modest improvement, it was Jen's obsession that had become a cause for concern.

"Come on, Jen," said Morgan. "You're not doing your son or daughter any good by becoming a zombie."

Jennifer's hoarse voice was strained. "I'm trying, Morgan. I'm doing everything I can. I know I'm not paying much attention to Courtney, but . . . if I don't watch Ben, who will?"

"Richard will. The nurses will. *I* will. You can't watch over him every waking moment."

"I have to, don't you see?"

"Why?" Morgan pleaded. "Just tell me why!"

"I know it sounds crazy, but if I'm not here all the time, I know something terrible's going to happen to him, just like with the others."

"Oh, Jen, Jen," Morgan said. "You're absolutely right, it *does* sound crazy. You're under a lot of stress, and you're overreacting. Listen to me. There's a doctor on staff here whose job it is to listen. He's a shrink, but he's really a great guy. You'll like him. He has an office downstairs, and he says he'll see you whenever you want. *Please*."

"Nice try," Jen said, with a wan smile. "And I promise I will, just as soon as Ben comes home with me."

Morgan shook her head and walked away, frustrated. Although she was a doctor, she couldn't help her sister at all.

Dr. Schubert made special arrangements for the Ryan delivery. To insure privacy, he scheduled the procedure for early evening, after his clinic normally closed. He estimated that the procedure would take twelve hours. He'd need only one assistant, a reliable woman who'd worked for him for years. The rest of the staff didn't have to know anything.

The Ryans drove to the clinic in tense silence, too filled with emotion to speak. Mrs. Ryan's eyes were welling with tears. She knew she was doing the right thing, but she had invested a lot in this pregnancy, emotionally.

They arrived at seven. Schubert wasn't particularly interested in explaining the details of the procedure, and fortunately, the Ryans weren't terribly keen on knowing. He had Mrs. Ryan sign a consent for obstetrical delivery. Then, after she changed into a patient's gown, he ushered her into a treatment room and put her on the exam table. Once she was in stirrups, Schubert inserted a speculum to expose the cervix. The cervix was purplish-gray, swollen by pregnancy and five prior deliveries. Schubert could tell that it was already at least a centimeter dilated. He daubed its opening with iodinated antiseptic and grasped the anterior lip with a prong-like instrument.

Several plastic-wrapped packages were on a nearby table. Each contained a brown twig-like laminaria, three inches long and an eighth to a quarter-inch wide. Schubert unwrapped one, grasped an end with a long packing forceps, and gently inserted the other end into the cervix. Laminaria were hygroscopic, and they worked by absorbing moisture. Over the next several hours, they would swell to three times their original width, dilating the cervix. Schubert inserted six.

Schubert then filled a hollow plastic applicator with an unusually large dose of prostaglandin gel and placed its tip beneath the cervix. The prostaglandin would bring about uterine contractions. Depressing the plunger, he deposited an ounce of gel into the upper vagina. When he was done, he packed the lower vagina with gauze, carefully removed the speculum, and had Mrs. Ryan sit up.

Since prostaglandins could also cause intense nausea,

diarrhea, and fever, Schubert gave his patient some Tylenol, an antispasmodic, and an antiemetic with a sip of water. Next, he showed her into the clinic's recovery room, where he had her lie on a stretcher. He started an IV and then sedated her with a potent narcotic/tranquilizer combination. Soon Mrs. Ryan was snoring soundly. Finally, Schubert started an intravenous drip of oxytocin, a drug that enhanced uterine contractions. It was time to wait.

The office assistant showed Mr. Ryan into the recovery room to be with his wife. With all the preparations made, Schubert went into his office and closed the door. Catching up on his journals would take several hours. If he got tired, there was a comfortable couch. He turned on a desk lamp and got down to work.

At ten o'clock, Mrs. Ryan was in the full throes of labor. By then, each laminaria had swelled to cigarette-size. Schubert removed the laminaria and discarded them. He was pleased to see that the cervix was already five centimeters dilated, and the membranes were bulging. It would be best, he decided, to let them rupture on their own. Finally, after giving Mrs. Ryan another large dose of sedation, he returned to the office to lie down. His assistant would call when necessary.

He'd barely drifted off when she rapped on the door. Checking his watch, he saw that it was a little past midnight. In the recovery room, Mrs. Ryan was grunting heavily, still out of it, but beginning to bear down. From long experience, Schubert associated the grunts with the end stages of labor. Quickly re-examining her, he found that she was fully dilated, with tense and fragile membranes. The instant he touched them, they ruptured.

The warm, yellowish fluid gushed out over the stretcher, filling the air with a slightly alkaline odor. His fingers still inside her, Schubert felt the doughy mass that was the fetal buttocks. The baby was a breech. Once the buttocks and hips were delivered, the thorax would shortly follow, and then the aftercoming head—actually a misnomer in this case, for the head was nonexistent. Watching the patient push, Schubert glanced at her pasty-faced husband.

"You sure you want to be here for this, Mr. Ryan?"

"I was there for the others, Doc. I think she'd want me to hang around."

"She was awake for those, wasn't she?" Schubert said. "Usually, when the husband stays, it's to share the birth with his wife. But she's out of it. And I'm not really sure you want to see what's going to happen."

Mr. Ryan looked away as he mulled things over. Finally, he nodded. "Okay, you're the doctor. I'll be out in the waiting room. Just let me know when it's done, all right?"

Once the father was gone, Schubert began work in earnest. After putting on a disposable surgical jumpsuit, he pulled Mrs. Ryan to the end of the stretcher, where he placed knee-crutch stirrups in their attachments and positioned her legs in them. By now she was pushing uncontrollably, yielding to an involuntary reflex as the fetal buttocks pressed down on her pelvic floor. While Schubert watched, her perineum began to bulge. Soon her labia began to gape, swollen by the descending breech.

Schubert noticed that the baby was a girl. For the time being, he kept his hands off, letting the baby deliver spontaneously. A gelatinous gob of dark greenish meconium exuded from the fetal anus. Soon the fetal buttocks had been completely expelled, and the breech had delivered up to mid-thigh. Schubert took a towel and grasped the baby by its hips. Not concerned about newborn viability, he pulled harder. Within sixty seconds, the entire baby had been delivered.

Without looking at it, Schubert wrapped the child in a blanket, covering it completely. He then placed the bundle on Mrs. Ryan's considerably smaller abdomen while he cut the umbilical cord. That done, he took the baby into another room and placed it on an exam table, allowing nature to take its course. He still had to deliver the placenta. In no rush, he returned to his patient. Fifteen minutes later, the placenta finally came out. He wrapped it for disposal with the red-bagged medical waste. Then, somewhat reluctantly, he went back to the exam room.

He procrastinated because he knew it often took infuriatingly long for anencephalics to die. But he didn't have the time, and right now, he was in no mood to wait. He unwrapped the receiving blanket to check for the presence of a fetal heartbeat. The moment its shoulders were exposed, Schubert found himself staring at the small, misshapen remnant of a head.

Much to his annoyance, the baby was still alive. Its moist, bulging eyes stared up at him, appearing to look in two different directions at once. Its purplish, bow-shaped lips pursed in and out, a reflex sucking movement. The child made intermittent gasping efforts, like a fish out of water. Repelled, Schubert averted his eyes, put on a stethoscope, and listened for the heartbeat. The pulse was very slow, but definitely present. There was no telling how long it could remain like that.

He was prepared for this eventuality. He'd already readied a ten-cc syringe with concentrated potassium chloride, and he reached for it without hesitation. There was no need to use an antiseptic. He placed the tip of the syringe's eighteen-gauge needle next to the child's sternum, centered it, and plunged the needle into the baby's heart. After quickly injecting the entire ten-cc bolus, he smoothly withdrew the now-empty syringe and once again listened with his stethoscope.

It took no more than ten seconds for the heartbeat to disappear. Once it did, Schubert rewrapped the body and returned to Mrs. Ryan. Still heavily sedated, she snored loudly and uninterruptedly while he checked her uterus. Satisfied that it was well-contracted, and the postpartum bleeding was minimal, it was time to show the deceased to its father.

Schubert's intention was to shock Mr. Ryan into immediately severing any emotional ties he might have had toward the baby. Picking up the dead child, he marched to the waiting room. After motioning the man to remain seated, Schubert unceremoniously handed over the still-warm bundle. Ryan took it, looked down, and gasped.

The color immediately drained from his face. His jaw dropped, and his mouth fell open in shock and horror. For a moment, Schubert thought he might faint. But then Mr. Ryan appeared to steady himself, and he looked up at the doctor.

"Did you show this to my wife?"

"Not yet," Schubert said. "She's still sleeping."

"Does she have to see it? She's a strong woman, but, my God . . . this might be too much for her."

It was the response Schubert had been hoping for. "No, she doesn't. If you want to, I can take care of things. What usually happens is to have the body cremated. Then we'll return the ashes to you for burial."

Ryan slowly nodded. He handed the bundle back to Schubert. "I appreciate that. Do you think you could baptize the baby? It'd mean a lot."

"I'd be happy to."

"How soon before my wife wakes up?"

"Oh, a few hours. There's no point in your waiting.

Why don't you go home for a while? We'll call you once she's ready to go."

Schubert had no intention of performing a baptism. Once Mr. Ryan left, he made his call. The man told him he'd need a few hours. After once more checking on his patient, Schubert lay down on his office couch. Like many obstetricians who'd mastered the art of drifting off in unusual circumstances, he was soon asleep.

At four A.M., the front door buzzer sounded. Schubert got up and answered it himself. He hadn't been told precisely who was coming. On the phone, the man had an unidentifiable foreign accent. But Schubert wasn't prepared for the tall, angular black who now stood before him. The man's face had a slightly gaunt and weathered look, but his frame was all bone and sinew, radiating power. Schubert stared at him without speaking.

"You are Dr. Schubert?" the man finally asked.

"Yes, and you?"

"I have something for you." He handed Schubert a quart-size jar of what appeared to be ashes. "Don't worry, they will pass for human. I believe you have something for me?"

Schubert nodded and took the jar. "Right this way." He showed the man to the exam room, avoiding the recovery area, Mrs. Ryan, and his assistant. Finding what he came for on the treatment table, the man unwrapped the blankets and gazed at the anencephalic's features. A broad smile washed over his face, revealing glistening white teeth.

"Magnificent," he said with undisguised glee. "I have never seen one before."

Schubert grew annoyed. "Just get rid of the damn thing!"

The man carefully rewrapped his parcel, tucked it

under his arm, and left the office without another word. He had a great deal of work ahead of him. In addition to preparation of the specimen, he'd been instructed to ready another batch of mites. He'd be very busy, but then, that was precisely what he was being paid so handsomely for.

Jennifer looked on the verge of collapse. Although the staff was sure she took catnaps, no one had actually seen her sleep in days. She shuffled along with the listless lethargy of a concentration-camp survivor, with haunted, sunken eyes that stared blankly ahead.

Ordinarily, the NICU staff welcomed new parents; caring for the entire family was part of their job. But there were other families on the unit besides the Hartmans, and some had started to complain about the increasingly strange-looking woman who was wandering around. Finally Dr. Harrington drew Jennifer into the hall.

"This is serious, Jennifer," he said. "Frankly, I couldn't care less what other parents are saying. But the fact is, you look like you're about to fall over—"

"I—"

"Let me finish," he continued. "We're all worried about you, but we're just as concerned about the babies here. If you stumbled, or knocked over an isolette, nobody's going to forgive you. And you'll never forgive yourself."

"I'm not going to fall."

"Probably not, but can you afford to take that chance? We can't. Look, I've already spoken with your husband, and he agrees. I'm sorry it has to be this way, but I have to insist you get some rest, okay? The nurses aren't going to let you back here until after the eleven o'clock shift change. And I strongly suggest you go home for the night."

"You just don't understand," she softly persisted.

"Maybe not, but that's the way it's got to be. Now go on. Your son is doing better and better, and the nurses will keep their eyes on him."

With one last forlorn look toward Benjamin's crib, Jennifer exhaustedly shook her head and pressed the elevator's *down* button. Exiting at the hospital lobby, she slowly made her way toward the comfortable seats near admitting. She slumped heavily into one and sighed, glancing at the clock, wondering just how quickly the hours would pass. She didn't dare close her eyes, but given her fatigue, they soon began closing of their own volition. Within seconds, she was fast asleep.

Several hours later, the respiratory tech was paged. One of the recently serviced ventilators was back from repairs and was ready to return to service. A stat request had come from the NICU for a respiratory treatment on one of the newborns. The tech thought that odd; she'd treated Benjamin Hartman many times before, and he was already on her list for ten P.M. No matter, she decided. A reconditioned unit was fine by her.

In the lobby, Jennifer awoke with a start. She hadn't intended to fall asleep. Blinking, she pushed herself upright and quickly looked up at the clock. It was ten-fifteen. She was suddenly seized with an ominous foreboding. Her immediate thought was about her son. Benjamin!

Something wasn't right; she could just *feel* it. Why had she ever let them talk her into taking a break? Overcome by fear, Jen dashed for the elevators and repeatedly jabbed the UP button. It took a full and infuriating minute for the elevator door to open, and another sixty seconds for her to reach the NICU. When she raced

through the door, she could already see the crowd form-
ing around Benjamin's isolette. One of the nurses was
furiously performing CPR.

The cry rose in Jennifer's throat even before she
could see what was happening, a tortured scream of suffering. One of the nurses rushed toward Jennifer, restraining her and trying to lead her away. But despite
her leaden legs, Jennifer tried to push past her, to where
Benjamin's gray body lay limp and unmoving.

CHAPTER FOURTEEN

Thirty miles east of University Hospital, the huge black cauldron finished simmering. Enough flesh had flaked off to make the anencephalic cadaver sink to the bottom. The man used a large wooden paddle to stir the broth, and after several strokes, the emerging skeleton rose to the surface, where bits of rubbery skin and tissue dislodged and drifted to the cauldron's rim. The man skimmed these pieces off, along with the accumulated fat. He placed the boiled flesh and greasy skimmings into a bucket and took it outside.

He carried the residue to a pit a hundred yards into the woods. At his approach, a large, dark flock of crows took off and alighted, cawing and screeching, in nearby trees. Once the man poured the slops and disappeared, the crows quickly descended into the pit, pecking at each other as they competed for the choicest morsels.

When the stewing was complete, the man turned off the heat and removed the glistening skeleton. Over the next several hours, the skeleton dripped onto paper towels. Every so often he'd change the towels and rotate the bones to facilitate drying.

The unusual specimen intrigued him. Before stewing,

the head's most prominent feature had been its protuberant, frog-like eyes. But after they'd boiled away, all that remained of the skull was half a cranium: small mastoid bones, a flattened occiput, a full mandible, and a misshapen maxilla, beneath irregular orbits.

Once the stripped cadaver was completely dry, it was time for the beetles.

When the man lifted their box, he could feel them stir. The beetles knew what awaited them. The lacquered box vibrated in a frenzied oscillation. When the man finally opened the lid, the unrestrained beetles burst forth.

Scent was their beacon. The hundreds of small, massed creatures resembled an inky spill. Its leading edge seemed to ripple. Then, all at once, the wave surged forward, streaming across the stainless steel. As soon as the insects reached the cadaver, they streamed upward, scurrying across bare bone in search of sinew and gristle.

While the beetles gorged themselves, the man went into his specimen room. It had been a long and hectic day, and he felt he'd earned a reward. Sinking into a recliner, he took out his stash of marijuana and lit up. When he drew in his first lungful of smoke, he closed his eyes and leaned back, fulfilled.

He'd assured Dr. Britten that he'd make delivery before midnight. A little more than an hour later, heady and intoxicated, he returned to the preparation room. The beetles had finished their work, leaving a glistening, immaculate skeleton. Using a piece of fresh meat, the man enticed them back into their box. Finally, he put the bony remains into a small, felt-lined casket.

Somewhat unsteadily, he carried the box to his van, depositing it on the floor just inside the rear door. In the driver's seat, he gunned the engine and drove down the lonesome back road to the highway. His night vision was poor, and he squinted through red-rimmed eyes. Once he was on, the Expressway, he turned on the radio, crooning childlike ballads against a background of jazz. Despite his intoxication, he had sense enough to keep the van's speed to sixty-five miles per hour.

He drove in the right-hand lane. But the long, straight highway dulled his already distorted senses. As he passed Exit Fifty-eight, an unexpected volume of incoming traffic forced him to merge left. He wasn't prepared. He stepped on the accelerator, but his reflexes weren't sharp enough.

His van rear-ended the car in front of him. Although the impact was light, it was enough to make the van skid sideways, tires smoking. Miraculously, none of the oncoming vehicles hit his van. Caught in a spin, it did a nerve-racking three-sixty before screeching backward off the right-hand shoulder of the road. Its rear fender smashed into a stanchion.

The rear cargo doors jolted open, and the small casket was hurled through the air. The van's driver, though dazed, quickly collected his senses. A hundred yards away, the car he'd struck was pulling to the side of the road, and several other nearby vehicles were slowing down. He couldn't afford to be caught. He'd been in drug trouble with the law before. Without hesitation, he stomped on the gas and accelerated down the highway, leaving behind him a swirling cloud of dust and a tiny casket.

Everything had happened too fast, and everyone involved felt lucky to be alive. No one got the van's license number. But neither did anyone see the felt-lined box. It wasn't until nearly an hour later that a police officer literally stumbled upon the small casket.

In his flashlight's yellow beam, the scuffed, nailed-together wood was still intact, although the lid had fallen off. The cop's light slowly played over the small white skeleton that spilled out. At first, he couldn't tell what it was, although he thought it might be a monkey. But when he stooped over to examine it more closely, the skeletal remains seemed more and more human. When the police officer finally straightened up, his hands were shaking.

He radioed headquarters and described what he'd found. He was told to pack everything up and bring it in. The officer did so, making sure he first put on latex gloves. When he finally dropped his find off at the Fourth Precinct, it was midnight. Not sure how to proceed, the desk sergeant on duty called the ME's office.

Early the following morning, one of the senior investigators for the Suffolk County Medical Examiner's office arrived. He carefully examined the small skeleton. It was human, he concluded, probably with some sort of birth defect. Uncertain what to do next, he contacted his Hauppauge office and spoke with the Assistant ME, who told him to bring the skeleton in. The investigator signed for it and wrapped the specimen in sterile plastic.

An hour later, the Assistant Medical Examiner bent over a stainless steel dissection table. The tiny skeleton was obviously quite fresh, and also very young. It showed no signs of weathering. Based on its total weight, length, and extent of long bone ossification, his best guess was that it was the skeleton of a recent female newborn, or perhaps even a third-trimester fetus. Someone had gone to great lengths to expertly skeletonize the carcass.

An even greater surprise came when he examined the unusual head. At first, he thought the skull had been dissected, and its calivarium, or skullcap, removed. But on closer inspection, he saw that the skeleton was developmentally abnormal. Not an expert in embryology, he opened a textbook and leafed through the chapter on skeletal malformations. The illustrations made it clear that he was dealing with an anencephalic.

He put on a pair of magnifying loupes and scrutinized the peculiar bone structure. He'd never seen an anencephalic before. Fascinated, he slowly went over the facial bones, then the temporal area, using a penlight to peer into the ear canal. There, something caught his eye. Looking closer, he saw that a tiny object seemed wedged into the inner canal near the internal auditory meatus. Using a jeweler's forceps, he plucked it out and held it up to the light.

It resembled some sort of bug. A tick, perhaps? It was dead, although not decomposed. He put the insect on a glass slide and placed it under his microscope. The bug was striking, with beautiful, but unidentifiable, markings. An hour later, when the ME arrived, they reviewed the slide together.

"I think it's a beetle," the ME said.

"A beetle? What's a beetle doing in an anencephalic's ear canal?"

"I don't know," the ME admitted. "Maybe it crawled in when the skeleton was on the ground. A lot of those things are scavengers. Maybe it got in there before it was boxed up, who knows?"

His assistant was shaking his head. "What kind of guy drives around with an anencephalic skeleton in a coffin?"

"I haven't the faintest idea. But as far as insects go, there is someone who might." He returned to his own office to look up the phone number for Dr. Simon Crandall.

* * *

Jennifer had to be sedated. By the time her husband and Morgan arrived, Jennifer, who was alternately wailing or babbling incoherently, was being evaluated by one of the senior psychiatric residents in the ER. Clearly, she was on the verge of collapse. Finally, the sedative kicked in, and Morgan drove them home.

Richard was shell-shocked. The NICU staff had been assuring him that Ben was getting better, though a pessimistic part of him always doubted it. Now, his worst nightmare had come true. Until then, he'd thought his wife's preoccupation was a sign of serious mental imbalance. Now it appeared she'd been right.

Between exhaustion and the medication, Jen was nearly out on her feet. Morgan helped Richard put her to bed. Then she encouraged Richard to talk. After an hour of tears and soul-searching, he, too, had had enough. He crawled into bed beside his wife. Retreating to the living room, Morgan spent the rest of the night on their couch.

She slept fitfully, getting up every hour or so to listen for her sister. Additionally, Morgan worried about her niece, Courtney, even though she was being well cared-for by the NICU nurses. Courtney was in excellent clinical condition, but she only weighed a little over three pounds. She would have to remain in the unit until she gained another pound. When Morgan finally fell back to sleep, she had nightmares of being pursued by Hugh Britten. She quivered and tossed on the couch, finally getting up at six-thirty.

Morgan puttered around the apartment until her sister woke at nine. Steeped in grief, Jennifer refused to take any more medication or get out of bed. Morgan decided it was best to let her rest. Once Richard seemed to have the situation reasonably in hand, Morgan left for the hospital.

It had been two days since her morning with Brad. He'd sent her roses and called twice; but she hadn't been home to take his call. Still savoring the warm afterglow of their lovemaking, she longed to see him again. As soon as she reached a hospital phone, she had him paged. He relayed word through a nurse that he'd come down to the cafeteria. Morgan ordered coffee and sat down to wait. Ten minutes later, he bent over and kissed her warmly on the cheek, taking her hand as he sat down.

"I'm sorry to hear about your nephew," he said. "By the time the resident let me know, you'd already left the hospital."

"Thanks. There's really not much you could've done."

"How's she coping?"

"Not well," Morgan said. "Last night was the worst, I hope. But Jen's a trouper. She should pull through it."

"Did you get my flowers?"

Morgan nodded, and her face grew radiant. "They're beautiful, Brad. And thank you for your hospitality the other day."

"Least I could do. The welcome mat's always out, Morgan." He paused and frowned. "Wish I could say the same for the state."

"Now what?"

"A state inspection team from Albany showed up yesterday," he said. "Even before Benjamin died. I guess it was inevitable. When there's a death, someone's bound to complain."

"About what? We both reviewed the other charts. There wasn't any negligence."

"No, and if it was just one or two babies, there'd be no problem. But the Health Department's looking for unusual patterns of care. If they find three or four deaths with exactly the same M. O., you're not going to keep them out."

"What's the worst that could happen?" she asked.

"The hospital could lose accreditation. Or it could lose funding—Medicaid and Medicare. If that happens, forget it."

"I suppose you heard that Ben's death was just like the others."

"I did," he said. "I realize this isn't the best time to ask, but is there any chance they'll agree to an autopsy?"

"God, an autopsy. . . . Didn't the poor kid suffer enough in his life? I really don't like the thought of his being cut up."

"Come on, Morgan," Brad said, "an autopsy isn't cutting someone up, and you know it. It's just another operation."

"How important is it?"

"I don't see that there's anything to lose." He shrugged. "And something just might turn up."

Morgan thought for a moment, then slowly nodded her head. "I hope so. I just wish they'd found something wrong with the other babies. If only they had, Benjamin might still be alive. All right," she said. "I'll run it by them."

Brad looked at his watch. "Gotta get back to the ward. Any word from Hugh?"

"No," she said. "You know, I'm starting to think you're right. Finally he might've gotten the message."

Simon Crandall was busy at work when the overnight Fed Ex delivery arrived. He quickly opened the letter-size package and found that it contained a small, clear plastic envelope. He read the accompanying letter from the Long Island ME, squeezed the plastic open, and used a forceps to extract the thumbnail-size piece of white filter paper, the backdrop for a small insect.

It was a beetle, a five-millimeter-long member of the *Coleoptera*. What immediately struck him was its beauty. A shiny jet black, it had a striking purple stripe across its shortened wing case, and prominent green pseudo-eyes to threaten potential aggressors. Simon couldn't remember ever running across anything like it.

Almost certainly, it was a carrion beetle, but of what precise family? It shared characteristics of the *Silphidae*, the *Staphylindae*, and the *Carabidae*. Using a microscope-mounted Nikon, he took several photos before turning to his reference texts. Fifteen minutes later, he had possibilities, but no definite answers.

Crandall suspected that what he was looking for would be found overseas. The British, in particular, were fastidious about cataloging the insect inhabitants of their former empire. Half an hour later, using primarily U.K. websites and a tome called *Beetles of the African Continent*, Simon located what he was looking for.

The beetle was quite rare, native to Equatorial East Africa. It had never been described outside of that area. Known as *Silpha Necrophila Tanzaniensis*, it had unusual feeding habits, consuming either decomposing flesh, dung, or maggots, depending on its stage of maturity. Ecologically, it was quite useful. Crandall downloaded and printed the information.

He logged off, puzzled. Beetles were very particular in their feeding habits. Those native to certain climates didn't take well to relocation. The *Silphae*, accustomed to the tropical warmth of Africa, weren't likely to thrive in the temperate climate of the eastern United States.

What, then, was it doing in a small skeleton found along the Long Island Expressway?

* * *

Someone had to make a decision about the disposition of Benjamin's body. Morgan had promised Brad to inquire about an autopsy. Although Richard was at the hospital with his daughter, when Morgan arrived at her sister's place, Jennifer still hadn't gotten out of bed.

She lay on her side, staring vacantly at the wall. Her hair fell across the pillow in matted, unkempt strands. It looked as if she hadn't bathed in days. An uneaten Whopper lay in its greasy Burger King wrapper on the night table. Jennifer's expression had a distant, defeated look. Morgan sat down on the bed and brushed back her sister's hair.

"You've got to eat something, Sis."

"I don't have to do anything."

"What about Courtney?" Morgan said. "Aren't you going to take care of her?"

"I don't really care. I don't care about anything anymore."

"Dammit, *I* care!" Morgan said. Then she caught herself. "Look, I'm sorry. I didn't mean to snap at you. It's just that . . . you've always been my little sister, and I always tried to do what was right by you. Sometimes I stuck up for you, sometimes I told you when you were wrong. But most of the time, you wound up doing what was right. Now, this is . . . It isn't *you*."

"Nothing I do right now will change anything, can't you understand that?"

"What I understand is that you're not the person I thought I knew! For God's sake, Jen, what happened to you and Richard was horrible, but it's over now! Where's the trouper that used to be my sister? You can't go on like this, lying in bed, not eating, and feeling sorry for yourself. You've got to think of your daughter!"

Jennifer closed her eyes. "I don't need this guilt trip, Morgan. I'm so tired."

Morgan's hands were trembling, and she was sick with concern. "Let me tell you something. I am scared, absolutely scared to death, that something's going to happen to Courtney, too. I'll do *anything* to keep her safe, and the Jennifer I used to know would, too."

Her sister lay there in stony silence.

"For the love of God, Jen, at least let me take you to see a doctor. I know you're depressed right now, but there are medications that can help!"

"What for? Will they bring Benjamin back?"

"No, but they'll help you get out of bed and put one foot in front of the other! If you keep on like this, you're of no use to anyone, not even yourself."

Again, her sister didn't answer. Morgan felt frightened, worried, and helpless.

"You want to know about an autopsy," Jennifer suddenly said.

Morgan was stunned. How did . . . ? Not that it mattered; perhaps Richard or some well-intentioned nurse had already brought up the subject. Or maybe Jennifer had just guessed. Morgan was certain that, because her sister had left the baby alone, Jen felt responsible for what happened. Morgan desperately wanted to dispel that belief.

"It's important, Jen. Not so much for Ben anymore, but for your own peace of mind. It might even help some other child. And deep down inside, I know it'll help me, too. Because I can't help feeling that when we find out what *really* happened to Benjamin and the others, I'm going to get back the kid sister I know and love."

Jennifer's voice was subdued. "What difference does it make? He's dead, isn't he? If someone wants to cut him open, I don't give a damn."

* * *

Brad had asked the pathologist to notify him when they started the post. For some reason the request hadn't been relayed up the chain of command to Dr. Kornheiser until early that evening: Brad was having a pizza with Mikey when he was beeped. When he answered the page, Brad realized that he didn't have enough time to take Michael home and decided to bring him along.

He was preparing to drop his son off at the medical library when they ran into Nbele. When he saw Michael, the tall man lapsed into his characteristic gleaming smile.

"Hello, my young friend!" he called out. "Have you come all this way to kick my tired butt in soccer?"

"When are you coming to my house again?" Michael asked.

"But I will!" he said, chuckling. "I have to wait for the right opportunity!"

"Nbele," Brad said, "could I impose on you for a little while?" He explained about the autopsy. "Think Mikey could tag along with you?"

"Certainly, Doctor. Take as long as you like. Just page me when you're done. Come, Michael," he said, taking the boy's hand. "I have something interesting to show you."

As Brad headed for the morgue, Nbele led the way to his office. Inside, on his desk, was a small skeleton that immediately caught Michael's eye.

"Wow," he said excitedly. "Is that a bird?"

"You have a good eye," said Nbele. "This is a very rare bird, from the Usambara Mountains, in Tanzania."

"Where's that?"

"In East Africa, near my homeland. The bird is called a Narina Trogon. Here, let me show you."

From a desk drawer, he withdrew an old photo. The picture depicted a bird resembling a large parakeet, with a short yellow bill, long gray tail feathers, and a flaming orange breast. The green feathers on its back glittered like emeralds. Michael took the picture and stared at it.

"I'd really like to have one of these."

"They're not easy to find," said Nbele. "When they're seen, you usually spot them around dusk. They are rumored to fly near graveyards, and my ancestors believed they carried away the spirits of the dead."

"Can they really do that?"

"Let me tell you a story," Nbele replied. For the next half hour, he captivated the boy with tales of birds and wildlife, of spirits and curses, of *mindumugu* and rituals. He brought Africa alive in all its mysterious richness, and Michael listened, spellbound. The pulse of Africa was beating loudly in his brain when his father finally called and said it was time to go.

Brad had been hoping that the autopsy would explain what went wrong with Benjamin. When they examined the child's lungs, they found congestion and edema similar to that found in the other infant. It was consistent with the profound hypoxia that preceded death, but because it was expected, it was a clinically insignificant finding. When he finished the visual exam, the pathologist removed tissue sections to be made into microscope slides.

That night, Brad spoke with Morgan on the phone. The sound of her voice had an unusually calming effect on him. A verbal connection, even over the phone, helped relieve the loneliness he felt when she was gone. He pictured her hair, her face, her body. He didn't want to rush into anything, but he wanted to be with her. After six years, he thought he was finally ready for a relationship.

Morgan wasn't surprised that the autopsy results were negative. Whatever had killed Ben and the other babies

wasn't likely to show up in a preliminary anatomic diagnosis. But she was definitely interested in seeing the
slides.

Morgan hadn't yet returned to work. Her nephew's
death and Hugh Britten's attack had left her mind in
emotional overdrive, unable to face the demands of a
nine-to-five day. The next morning, Brad picked her up
at seven. They arrived at the pathology department early,
well before Kornheiser. The slides had been processed
during the night. Brad took them from the technician
and went over to a twin-headed scope. Then they both
bent over the oculars.

"What do you think?" he asked after a moment's concentration.

"Are we playing 'name that organ'? Hmmm . . ." She
paused. "This is lung tissue, right?"

"Yep."

"Well, to begin with, it's filled with edema. There's
a fair amount of extra-lumenal mucus, and significant
inflammation. How's that so far?"

They went on bouncing verbal observations off one
another, moving from slide to slide, from low power to
high power, occasionally using oil immersion. What
struck them was the intensity of the inflammatory reaction. It was as if some unknown substance had provoked
a massive outpouring of pulmonary fluids, a natural protective response so exaggerated it suffocated the victim.
But a response to what? So far, all tests intended to
identify the offending substance had proved negative,
and there was no described stimulus that could cause
this extreme a reaction.

"Back up a minute," Morgan said, peering into the
eyepiece. "Is that a piece of dirt?"

Brad centered the image and adjusted the focus.
Something resembling a microscopic insect came into

view, looking suspiciously like the one Morgan had noticed on the autopsy slide at Brad's house.

"Jesus," he said, "here's another one. It really *does* look like a crab. Must be a contaminant."

"A contaminant?" Morgan said. "How often do you find that kind of microscopic contaminant?"

"More often than you'd think," said a voice from behind them.

They both looked up into the face of Bernie Kornheiser. Brad introduced him to Morgan, and then the pathologist took a look at the slide.

"Just a dust mite," he said. "It seems pretty impressive at this magnification, but it's tiny. You could fit seven thousand of them on a dime."

"What makes you so sure they're not a contaminant?" Morgan asked.

"Because we see them from time to time. We also see hair, pollen, and all sorts of little particles floating around in room air, things that would scare the bejesus out of the average person if he knew about them."

"Could this little thing cause a serious inflammation?" Brad asked.

"Not really. Dust mites are everywhere. They're little arachnids, and they live off human skin cells. We breathe them by the millions every day without even being aware of it."

"But aren't they related to asthma?" Morgan persisted.

"Sometimes. In people who are susceptible, mite feces or their exoskeletons can set off a severe allergic reaction."

"Isn't what we're seeing here an exaggerated allergic reaction?" Brad asked. "The swelling, the edema, the eosinophils?"

"Well, yes and no," said Kornheiser. "Yes, it has

some components of an allergic response, but no, it's not caused by dust mites."

Brad and Morgan stared at one another, deep in thought.

"Is it possible," said Brad, "that this is some variant of the dust mite? A different species, one that provokes a more intense allergy?"

"I doubt it," said the pathologist. "Nothing like that's ever been described."

"But it is possible, right?"

"Brad, Brad," Kornheiser said patiently, "*anything*'s possible. But we've got to be realistic."

Hawkins shrugged. "Mind if I borrow this slide?"

Outside, Morgan gave him a questioning look. "What're you doing now?"

"Maybe I *am* reaching a little," he said. "Bernie's probably right, but I'm going to show this slide to an old buddy of mine."

"Good," she said emphatically. "Dr. Kornheiser bothers me. He just doesn't seem to care. I have a gut feeling that we're in a race against time here, Brad. You know, and I know, that something damn well killed those babies. Unless we can find out what, I'm scared to death for my niece Courtney and all the other NICU babies."

Her voice trailed off. "There's more, isn't there?" he asked.

Morgan nodded. "Jennifer feels responsible for Benjamin's death. I'm doing my damnedest, but I can't convince her otherwise. She's so close to the edge right now, and I'm afraid to think about what might happen to her if we can't find the answer."

CHAPTER FIFTEEN

Britten was true to his word about reapportioning the abortion load. Less than a week after their conversation, AmeriCare referrals to Dr. Schubert for mid-trimester abortions dwindled to a trickle. This was fine with Schubert. He still did a booming business, but without the extra stress. What's more, if Britten was to be believed about their financial relationship, Schubert could continue to meet his wife's financial demands.

What Arnold Schubert didn't count on, and what he could never fully appreciate, was Hugh Britten's single-minded perfectionism. Britten was not one to suffer fools gladly or permit snags in his carefully orchestrated plans. Nor was he someone who tolerated loose ends. And now, to Britten's way of thinking, Schubert was both a loose end and a loose cannon.

When Schubert returned home that day, he began his nightly ritual. The two things he appreciated as much as opera were his pipe and his scotch. After putting on a new CD of *Teatro Alla Scala*'s performance of *La Traviata*, he poured several ounces of single malt scotch into a whiskey glass and took it to his leather recliner. Leaning back into the recliner, he raised its footrest and plucked a wide-bowl pipe from the rack holding his pipe collection. It was his favorite meerschaum. He took a pinch of moistened cavendish from an expensive cedar tobacco humidor.

Schubert rolled the moist, aromatic shreds between thumb and forefinger, then held it up to his nose. For some reason, it didn't smell as appealing as usual. No matter; he needed it. He filled the bowl with a generous amount of tobacco, tamped it down, and struck a match. Then he lit up and sucked deeply on the pipe stem. Soon the room was filled with thick clouds of fragrant smoke.

Closing his eyes, Schubert lost himself in the music. He hoped he was finished with Britten and with the hold the man had on him. Starting to relax, his thoughts returned to his internship thirty years ago, and to the colossal blunder he'd made. Not that it seemed so at the time; as a young, idealistic physician on the oncology service, he truly believed that what he did was right.

A woman with two advanced cancers had been admitted comatose to the ward. She quickly developed a severe infection and couldn't be weaned from the respirator. At first, her family visited every day; but as the hopelessness of the situation became apparent, they came less often. As time went by, the medical staff also seemed to lose interest. When it reached the point where nobody seemed to give a damn, Schubert decided to take matters into his own hands.

It wasn't particularly complicated to administer the overdose of insulin one night, and soon the patient's vital signs were deteriorating. For Schubert, what proved far more difficult was coping with his emotions. Despite the compassion of his act, he felt unaccountably guilty, and his guilt led him to scribble incriminating remarks in the patient's chart. Inasmuch as the woman soon died, these remarks were overlooked—until decades later, when Hugh Britten stumbled upon them during his research. From then on, Schubert was a marked man.

That was ancient history now, Schubert thought. Between the smoke and the heady liquor, he was becoming pleasantly mellow. Every so often he would suck on the pipe, occasionally drawing the smoke deep into his lungs. Between the music, the smoke, and the alcohol, the day's cares drifted away. His finances, his wife, and his problems with Hugh Britten were quickly forgotten.

It started as a tickle in his pharynx. Schubert opened his eyes and cleared his throat. The tickle grew to an annoyance. He sat up straight and, wide-eyed, coughed once, then again, forcefully thumping his chest with his closed fist. His lungs were beginning to feel frighteningly tight.

Suddenly he couldn't breathe. He thought a sip of scotch might help, but his hand was shaking so violently that he could barely lift the glass to his lips. He tried to stand up, desperate to relieve his breathlessness. Rising on unsteady feet, he knocked over his pipe rack. His fingers clutched his throat, which felt as if it were caught in a vise. He could see his horribly pale face reflected in the mirror. Flecks of spittle covered his lips. Eyes wide, lips bared, Schubert staggered across the room.

He made it as far as the doorway when his legs gave way. Knees buckling, he fell to the floor, clutching his throat as he rolled heavily onto his side. It felt as if he were drowning, and he gasped for air. Fluid and a rising tide of froth rose in his throat, and he heard a gurgling sound from his oxygen-starved lungs. As he stared around helplessly, Arnold Schubert's last conscious thought was that he couldn't believe this was happening to him.

On the CD player, the mellifluous strains of Verdi played on unheard for the next ninety-four minutes.

* * *

Brad had met Simon Crandall when they were both biology majors at Yale. Since graduation, the two saw one another several times a year and regularly kept in touch via e-mail. That night Simon Crandall logged onto his p.c. and found an interesting request from Brad. He was sending an autopsy slide for review.

The package arrived at Crandall's office the next morning. Along with the slide, Brad had enclosed a clinical synopsis. The case intrigued Crandall. Familiar with all types of insects that invaded a cadaver after death, he found the notion that a microscopic parasite might be present antemortem decidedly unusual.

Crandall inspected the slide closely under the high power of his Zeiss. Indeed, to the untrained eye, it probably did resemble a dust mite, because it was roughly the same size, and had the same outward appearance. But on closer inspection, it clearly wasn't. The arrangement of its legs was different. It had unusual elytra, and its cephalothorax was too small. Its most intriguing aspect, however, was its mouthparts: the small, pincer-like jaws were firmly embedded in a human epithelial cell. Dust mites, Simon knew, were purely adventitious invaders, just going along for the pulmonary ride.

But Simon couldn't identify the insect. He was certain he'd never run across it before. He showed the slide to several other curators, none of whom knew what it was, which wasn't unusual, because the arachnids numbered in the hundreds of thousands, and most species weren't native to North America.

Simon called Brad, who gave him a quick overview of the NICU deaths and explained his involvement with the case. Then he went over the pathologist's gross and microscopic autopsy findings.

"Do you think it's a dust mite?" Brad asked.

"No, and neither do any of my colleagues. Unfortunately, we're not sure *what* it is. I'll have to make some calls. Just how badly do you need this?"

"*Real* bad," said Brad. "The babies out here are dying horrible deaths. Nobody knows what's causing it, and we don't have a clue—except for the mite—where to go from here. We need some answers, Simon—fast. Who're you going to call?"

"Some British contacts," said Crandall. "The boys in the U.K. love these little arachnids."

As he rang off, Simon wondered what in the world was going on. First, he'd been asked by a Long Island medical examiner to identify a rare beetle, and then this unusual mite appeared. Not that the two could be related, but it was a puzzle he'd have to bounce off his friend.

Benjamin's funeral was the next morning. The day started out overcast, gray and leaden. Richard, Jennifer, Morgan, and Brad rode together in the limo behind the hearse. It was an abbreviated procession. Fortunately, the media hadn't yet discovered that there had been another death.

By the time they reached the gravesite, rain was falling. The intense, cold deluge caught the mourners unprepared, and they were soaked. Barely able to walk, Jennifer had to be supported by her husband and her sister as they stood by the tiny grave. Her hair was matted into wet, unkempt strands. Her face was gaunt and her complexion pale, nearly that of death itself.

The service was mercifully short. Once the prayer books were closed, everyone beat a hasty retreat to their nearby cars. Nearly unable to move, Jennifer shuffled listlessly back to the limo. Beyond grief, numb and unfeeling, she concentrated only on the suddenly difficult task of putting one foot in front of the other.

*   *   *

In Manhattan, it was noon when the rain stopped and Dr. Crandall finished the call he'd begun at eight in the morning. His initial inquiries went to a colleague at Oxford, who directed him to the British Entomological and Natural History Society. From there he was referred to the Royal Entomological Society in London.

The Society's secretary, a Dr. Colin Halstead, was a devotee of the *Coleoptera*, the beetles. Halstead was so enthusiastic that Simon could hardly get a word in. Did he know, Halstead asked, that *Coleoptera* were the dominant form of life on earth, and that one out of every five living species was a beetle? Was he aware that beetles appeared before the existence of dinosaurs, and that they were revered by the ancient Egyptians?

Simon didn't have the heart to tell the Englishman that he already knew. Finally, after listening dutifully, he asked his question.

"Hmmm, interesting," said Halstead. "A mite, you say? What's that got to do with beetles?"

"Probably nothing. I'm calling to see if you can direct me to someone in the Society who might know something about some of the more unusual species."

"Right . . . Now that you mention it, someone *does* come to mind. Fielding's boy, Neville. Bright chap. I'll ring him up and get back to you straightaway."

Crandall had heard about Fielding. Richard Fielding, widely published and even more widely read in the insect world, was a Cambridge-based entomologist who had died two decades earlier. Crandall wasn't aware that Fielding had a son who was an insect expert, but he would gratefully accept the younger man's help.

The next morning, Simon was awakened at six A.M. by the ringing of his bedside phone. He sleepily said "Hello" and was greeted by a British accent.

"Terribly sorry to wake you," said the caller. "This is Neville Fielding, in Cambridge. I got a call from Colin Halstead at the Coleopterists' Society, and he said what you needed was rather urgent. So I took the liberty of ringing you up bright and early."

"Thanks, don't worry about it," said Simon. "I was just getting up. Did you find anything?"

"Oh, yes. Colin's call jogged my memory. I recalled something my father said years ago, just before he died. You see, he'd just returned from a year in Africa—"

"Africa? Where in Africa?"

"The Nairobi area," said Fielding. "I was in university then, home on holiday when father mentioned something about an unusually predaceous mite he'd discovered. Didn't pay it much attention, I'm afraid. But Colin's question brought it all back."

Simon sat up in bed, deep in thought. It had been only days ago that he'd identified an unusual East African beetle found in a Suffolk County skeleton, and now the same area came up again. "Go on, I'm listening. What did you find?"

"Father kept a journal of his findings there. Never published, but quite detailed. I went through it earlier this morning. There are several pages of entries I think you'll find interesting. If you'd like, I can make photocopies of them and post them right off to you."

"That'd be great," Simon said. He couldn't wait to see if the mite that Fielding senior had found in Africa two decades earlier looked anything like that which Simon had just identified in the lungs of a small, dead child on Long Island.

Having time on her hands made Morgan edgy. She'd never been able to make good use of "down time." She needed structure to her day. So, much as she dreaded running into Hugh Britten, she decided to return to work.

Janice greeted her warmly. In her office, her desk was piled high with a week's worth of mail, memos, and correspondence. Morgan sat down and immediately dug in.

She'd been working for about half an hour when the flowers arrived, a magnificent summer bouquet. Morgan hoped it was from Brad, but when she opened the enclosed card, her pulse quickened with fear.

"My dear Morgana," it began. "Please accept my heartfelt condolences for your loss. I know what a great tragedy your nephew's passing must be for you and your family. I'm sure you did everything possible, from an administrative standpoint. Fate sometimes plays cruel tricks.

"On a slightly different note, I must apologize for my childish behavior toward you. How boorish I must have seemed! All I can say is that my feelings for you overcame tact and judgment. I hope you realize that isn't the way I normally act toward women. But then, you are no ordinary woman. I trust that whatever animosity you may have felt for me has lessened with passing time. I'm sure you've thought about everything I said, and I know you appreciate my sincerity. I promise to make it up to you the next time we're together. Fondly, Hugh."

Sickened, Morgan let the note fall to her desk. All week, she'd tried to put Britten out of her mind, to chalk up his strange behavior to nothing more than an unpleasant social experience. As the days went by and she didn't hear from him, she was beginning to think that Brad was right, that time would make everyone forget what happened. Clearly, Hugh Britten had other ideas.

What an ego the pompous ass had! Did he actually think that flowers and an apology could make her forget his outrageous behavior? She'd been the object of adolescent crushes before. Usually, she found that if she ignored her pursuer, he'd eventually lose interest and stop bothering her. But she was afraid this went beyond childish infatuation. What if it turned into a *Fatal Attraction* stalking?

She summoned up her courage. Hands trembling, Morgan picked up the phone and dialed his extension. He wasn't there. She got Britten's number at the university from the switchboard operator, but he wasn't there either. Exasperated but determined, she sent an e-mail.

"Dr. Britten," she wrote. "I've tried time and time again to get my point across, but apparently the message isn't sinking in. I am not now, nor have I ever been, the least bit interested in you personally. I insist you leave me alone. Don't call me, write to me, or send me flowers. Stay out of my personal life. Contrary to what you think, we have no future together. If you bother me one more time, I'm going to the police." She signed it simply, "Dr. Robinson."

The message sent, Morgan tried to distract herself in the glut of paperwork. But her thoughts kept straying to the flowers and the note. She dumped the bouquet in the trash, but she couldn't get it out of her mind. Just before noon, she decided to go to the hospital.

Courtney continued to do well. The only thing keeping her in the NICU was her weight; the staff was reluctant to discharge any baby weighing under two thousand grams. Morgan looked at her niece, feeling a swell of emotion. She was a beautiful child, with a head of wispy brown hair just starting to turn red. Morgan's love for her was equaled only by her fear. Was Courtney really safe? How could anybody be sure when no one knew what had killed the other babies?

When she left the nursery, Morgan looked for Brad,

impatient to find out if he'd learned anything about the microscopic bug. It seemed their best, if not only, hope. They were in a race against time, and time was running out. Brad was nowhere to be found, and Morgan went to the cafeteria alone. She bought a yogurt and then, somewhat reluctantly, returned to work.

She couldn't concentrate. Had Britten read her message yet? Would he finally take it seriously? By mid-afternoon, she pushed her papers aside and logged onto her computer.

Accessing her week's worth of e-mail, she was shaken to see that the last posted entry was from Britten, timed two hours ago. Warily, Morgan flagged it with her mouse. When she saw that it began "Dearest Morgana," her heart sank.

"In the days since we were last together," it read, "I know you've gone through a lot. I also know that when you say you don't want to see me, it's hurt and anger talking. Morgana, trust me when I say this is the voice of stress, the result of your being upset about your nephew's death. If I thought for one minute that your words represented your true feelings, I would happily respect your wishes. But the plain fact is, you're in denial. I am a very perceptive man, and I appreciate what your real feelings are toward me, feelings that you keep bottled up inside. I'm determined to convince you of the truth in this matter. So I really must insist. If you refuse, you will regret it. Therefore, I'm coming to your house tonight, at seven. Please don't try to avoid me. You might temporarily succeed, but that will only prolong the inevitable."

Morgan felt her blood run cold. Obviously Britten would stop at nothing to get what he wanted.

And he wanted her.

CHAPTER SIXTEEN

Morgan didn't know what to do. She'd tried politeness, firmness, and threat, and everything had failed miserably. Suddenly she understood the terror of a trapped animal.

Not knowing where to turn, she called Brad at his office. "Brad, thank God you're there! I'm shaking like a leaf!"

"Whoa, calm down. What happened?"

"It's Hugh Britten," she said haltingly. "I really think he's gone off the deep end this time. He won't leave me alone, Brad, and I don't know what to do!"

He could hear the panic in her tone. Her voice quavered, a tremulous, bird-like warble. Slowly, Brad got her to tell him what happened. Gradually Morgan calmed down.

"This has gone way beyond sexual harassment," she said. "I'm worried he might do something to my family! Courtney's still in the hospital. Their bills are piling up. What if he persuaded AmeriCare not to pay them? Do you think it's time to go to the police?"

"No, you don't really have anything to go on yet. They need a lot more than flowers and threatening e-mail."

"I'm not overreacting, am I?"

"The guy's seriously delusional, Morgan. You're entitled to be scared. But in my experience, people like Britten are more bark than bite. Still, I think it was a mistake to e-mail him back."

"I shouldn't have been firm and told him the truth?" she asked.

"Borderline psychotics—and that's what I'm beginning to think he is—don't respond to the direct approach. My advice would've been to keep ignoring him. But it wasn't my call. He knows where you live, right?"

"Unfortunately."

"Then let him come," said Brad. "Because I'll be there, too. Maybe he'll finally take no for an answer when he realizes the odds are against him and that it's not just you he has to deal with."

Brad promised to arrive at her house before she got home, and he was true to his word. He arrived at six-thirty, and Morgan showed up ten minutes later. Despite the late afternoon heat, when he put his arms around her, her skin was cold. Morgan's eyes flitted nervously about. Seeing no sign of Britten, they went inside and locked the door. After a brief strategy session, they decided Brad would do the talking.

The doorbell rang precisely at seven. Brad was sure he could persuade the man to listen to reason. If not, and if things turned physical, he knew he could handle the little nerd.

For Brad, who had never met Britten before, the sight that greeted him at the door was downright peculiar. The man's clothing was not only mismatched, but it also spanned several styles and decades. The bell-bottoms were appropriate to the sixties, the boots to the seventies, the dress tee-shirt to the nineties, and the cardigan to nothing in particular. Brad extended his hand.

"Come in, Dr. Britten. We've been expecting you."

Britten limply returned the handshake. "You are . . . ?"

"Brad Hawkins. I'm a friend of Morgan's."

Britten's smile was prompt. "Ah, Dr. Hawkins. Of course." Morgan stood slightly behind Brad. "Hello, Morgana. I'd hoped we could have this time alone."

"No way," she said firmly.

"I beg your pardon?"

"Look, Doctor," Brad said promptly. "Morgan's told me everything. She doesn't want your flowers and e-mail. Apparently, her feelings are not getting through to you, so let me spell it out for you: she's not interested."

Britten's smile was unwavering. "Thank you for the spelling lesson, but when I want instruction, I ask for it. I certainly doubt you know anything about her wants. Listen to me, Morgana. I—"

"No," Brad loudly insisted, "you listen to *me*. Maybe you're used to walking all over people professionally, but that's not the way it works in a personal relationship. In the real world, 'no' is a simple two-letter word that means just what it says. So keep your e-mail, your flowers, and your hands to yourself!"

"I take it," Britten said smoothly, "there's an 'or else' associated with your statement?"

"Take it any way you want. But I'll tell you this. If you bother her in any way at all, she'll contact an attorney. With all your love notes and our testimony, the court will slap you with a restraining order faster than you can snap your fingers! Believe me, the newspapers eat up a sensational story like this, and I really don't think you want that kind of publicity!"

The smile slowly melted from Britten's face, replaced by a tight-lipped defiance. "You're making a big mistake, Morgana. Both of you are."

"The door's behind you," Brad said abruptly. "Now get the hell out."

For a long moment, Britten glared at them menacingly, his eyes dark and sinister. Then he turned stiffly and let himself out. Brad slammed the door behind him, then slumped against it.

"Christ almighty," he said, "what's *wrong* with me?"

"Nothing," said Morgan, taking his arm. "I thought you were perfect."

"Perfect? I wanted to keep cool. Instead, I lose my temper and fuckin' sledgehammer the guy! Jesus, how could I let him provoke me like that? He was just so smug, so damn complacent! Christ," he said with a sigh, "I really blew it, didn't I?"

Morgan put her arms around him, and leaned her head on his shoulder. "You did what had to be done," she said, rewarding him with a tender kiss on the cheek.

An hour later, once they were sure Britten wouldn't return, Brad left. Morgan immediately armed her alarm and double-checked all doors and window locks. Brad phoned every half hour. Finally, around midnight, she got drowsy, turned off Letterman, and drifted into a fitful slumber.

The following day, rounds and surgery kept Brad busy all morning. It was almost one before he left for the office. No sooner had he arrived than his receptionist told him he had a call.

"Hello there, Bradford."

Only one person still called him *Bradford.* "Simon, you rascal," Brad said. "Did you come up with anything yet?"

"I think so. This is the most interesting case I've seen in years. But it took some doing. This little critter is a mite, but not a dust mite. It has some similarities, but even more differences. Your average pathologist wouldn't be able to tell the difference."

"Bernie Kornheiser would hate to hear you call him an average pathologist."

"I'm sure he's good," Crandall continued, "but this is specialty work. Anyway, I called a contact in England, where they're fascinated with this stuff. He put me on to someone else. Ever hear of Richard Fielding?"

"No. Should I have?"

"Not really," said Simon. "Fielding was the reigning guru of the *acari*, the order your lung bug belongs to. He died twenty years ago, but he was compulsive. Took damn good notes. I lucked onto a copy of a journal he wrote before he died. And Jesus, there it was, same as on your slide."

"Did he suggest anything about a relationship to human disease?"

"Matter of fact, he did," Crandall said. "He described a Kenyan case of an intense allergic pulmonary reaction, which he thought was due to some toxin or foreign protein secreted by the mite."

Brad listened intently. "Is it possible that this mite's just a contaminant?"

"A contaminant? All the way from East Africa? Not very likely."

"Do you think it's related to what happened to this baby? I mean, clinically speaking, is it causative?"

"I can't say for certain," said Crandall, "but that'd be my guess. You're onto something pretty unusual here, Bradford. Ever think about writing this up?"

"That's the *last* thing I have in mind. Right now, I'm more concerned with trying to keep babies alive, and I think you just helped me out in a big way."

"My pleasure. Tell you what, I'll fax you Fielding's journal notes. Take a look at them yourself, see if they help you." Crandall paused. "Say, what the heck is going on out there?" he asked. "The other day, the county ME sent me another insect for identification. He removed it from the ear canal of an anencephalic newborn skeleton. Turns out it was a very rare beetle, from guess where?"

"Don't tell me, East Africa."

"You got it. In forensic entomology, two unusual findings like that don't happen by coincidence."

Brad felt a prickling at the base of his neck. "You think they're related?"

"You need the CDC to determine that."

Although a mite-related condition wasn't their usual fare, the Centers for Disease Control were better equipped than any other agency for disease investigation. Yet Brad had worked with them before. By the time the bureaucrats got around to sending field investigators, and by the time they finished their report, it might be too late.

Brad rang off with thanks and a promise to keep Simon posted. He sat back in his desk chair, brow furrowed. Something very, very peculiar was happening. Something that, as Simon implied, went way beyond coincidence. At some point he probably would get in touch with the CDC, but right now, he needed to do some intense brainstorming with Morgan.

The more he thought about the case, the more fears flashed through his brain, converging like fireflies. All the dead newborns insured by the same HMO. Drastic changes in that company's abortion and birth rates following modification in HMO policies, with the suggestion of a possible profit motive. A frightening etiology for what happened to the babies . . . The questions were increasing exponentially, but the answers were still missing. Simon Crandall's answer only posed another question: what in the world were African mites doing in the lungs of dead newborns?

Then he had an even more frightening thought: could someone have deliberately placed them there?

Hugh Britten licked his psychological wounds, stewing and simmering, replaying the confrontation at Morgan's house over and over in his head. The encounter underscored his abiding sense of inadequacy. Britten was torn between a superior ego and overriding self-doubt. Uncertain of his own worth, he struggled to succeed the only way he knew how—through his intellect.

Despite being an academic overachiever, when it came to interpersonal relationships, he was a dismal failure. One-on-one interactions always left him weak-kneed and hopelessly outgunned. People easily intimidated him. When he was growing up, any heated give-and-take led him to run away, making him feel like a weakling. Physically, he thought of himself as a loser, the perpetual wimp. Now Brad Hawkins had become the hated symbol of his shortcomings, the man he would never become.

What a fool he was for ever becoming interested in that woman! Certainly she was pretty enough, but his interest in her went beyond physical attraction. It was her keen mind that sparked his desire. She was an M.D., although that in itself didn't mean much. He knew many physicians he didn't even consider smart. Dr. Robinson, however, had the gift of intellectual curiosity. He'd learned that by monitoring her work. She had a facile mind and a clever wit. She was as close a match for him as any woman could be.

Britten couldn't deal with his anger. Normal coping skills eluded him. Unable to properly vent his rage, he internalized it. The little games he played in his head became endless fantasies of revenge. Earlier in his life, whenever he felt humiliated, he would retreat, storing away the hurt and anger. Now he had both wealth and power, and he could act decisively against the people who wronged him.

The list of his adversaries was long and growing. At the top was the university. The Trustees had played with him, teased him with the provost nomination, and used him. Now it was their turn to discover what it was like to be humiliated. It was only a matter of time before the State Health Department shut down the NICU. The negative publicity would produce many patient complaints—some real; some imaginary. Before long, HCFA, the Health Care Finance Administration, would cut the hospital's public funding.

As for his relationship with AmeriCare, that had been a stroke of genius. Daniel Morrison was a pompous buffoon without an iota of fiscal intelligence. Any fourth-rate economist would have made the suggestions Britten had, but he could never have commanded the same financial reward: the stock options, the performance guarantees. Provided the company's rebound was as robust as he projected, Britten would soon be a multimillionaire.

It wasn't always necessary to get personal, as he'd done with Dr. Schubert. God, there was a man destined to self-destruct, if ever there was one! What in the world had possessed the young intern Schubert to pen that incriminating mea culpa in the cancer patient's chart three decades ago? And how had it been overlooked for so long?

But as for Morgana Robinson and that pretentious Dr. Hawkins . . . They both obviously considered him a laughing-stock. For them, he had a special punishment in mind, something a little more protracted. The woman seemed to enjoy poking fun at him, and the man had relished his macho one-upmanship. Well, they'd find out who got the last laugh! First, he was determined to tease them, to make them suffer. He knew everything about them, especially the ways in which they were most vulnerable.

And he knew precisely where to start.

CHAPTER SEVENTEEN

When Melissa Alexander went into labor, she felt alone and frightened. She was unmarried, and she didn't want the man who had fathered her child to be present for the delivery. Although Melissa had gone through natural childbirth classes with several support people, none of them would be there for the actual birth. She was doing that alone.

No matter. She realized that her fears were normal. She had always liked control, and that was one of the many reasons she'd chosen nurse-midwives for her care. But Melissa realized that things weren't going precisely her way when the midwife told her to come to University Hospital.

University wasn't Melissa's hospital of choice. She'd gone to one of its infertility specialists because she needed high-tech, innovative techniques in order to conceive. She did not, however, think she needed them for labor and delivery—a perfectly natural, low-tech phenomenon. Her hospital of choice had been a second-rate, but patient-friendly, Episcopally run community hospital. But the midwife explained that since she already had a patient in labor at University, Melissa had to come there.

Melissa mulled it over, but only briefly. She was fast losing any semblance of control. The labor pains were intensifying, and for the next hour, Melissa endured them stoically at home. Then she called the midwife back and asked her to reconsider. She begged, wheedled, and cajoled, and in the end, she pleaded. But the midwife was firm about her commitments. Ultimately, Melissa relented and took a taxi to University.

Things went progressively downhill from the moment she was admitted. First, her blood pressure was up. The midwife suggested they start an IV "as a precaution," but Melissa refused, antagonizing a nursing staff that was all too familiar with outspoken patients like Melissa. They were considered a nuisance. Then the nurses insisted on a short fetal monitor tracing.

Melissa was equally vehement in her refusal. It was precisely because of invasive techniques like IVs and monitors that she hadn't wanted to give birth at University. And although University had what it called birthing rooms, they weren't the earthy, home-and-hearth units she was expecting. She looked to her midwife for support, but the woman simply shrugged. "Hospital policy," she said, explaining that some things were out of her hands. Melissa acquiesced with frosty annoyance.

Once the fetal monitor straps were in place, things quickly went from bad to worse. Perhaps it was her blood pressure, they said. Or maybe it was because she was overdue. Whatever the case, although the fetal heartbeat was in the proper range at one hundred forty beats per minute, the tracing looked flat, lacking what they termed beat-to-beat variability. The nurse explained that it could be a sign of fetal distress.

Melissa's fears escalated, and she struggled to remain in control. When she asked the midwife what would happen next, the woman was evasive, murmuring something about this no longer being a low-risk labor. It was time, she said, to call in one of the doctors for consultation. Melissa groaned in pain and frustration.

Dr. Richard Summers was the physician on call for the practice. At forty, Summers was the senior M.D. in the group. Melissa hadn't met him, but she knew he had a reputation for insensitivity and bawdy jokes. Half an hour later, Summers, short and rotund, with curly hair starting to go gray, strolled into the labor room.

Summers ignored Melissa and went directly to the midwife. She called him "Ricky," which Melissa thought too cute for a man approaching middle age. Then he studied the fetal monitor tracing. Its volume was low, but the beep was steady. Still feeling neglected, Melissa grew more insulted by the moment.

Finally, he looked her way. "Having a little problem, huh?" he said, flashing a smile.

"I'm Melissa Alexander," she said matter-of-factly. "You are . . . ?"

"I think you know who I am," he said. "Your baby might be in distress, so I'm going to put in an internal monitor lead."

She frowned. "The wire that screws into the baby's head?"

"Look, if you want to be adversarial, that's your business. I'm trying to do my job. And it doesn't 'screw into the baby's head.' It just attaches to the scalp."

Melissa shook her head forcefully. "I've heard all the horror stories. I want to do what's best for my baby, but I'm not going to agree to anything without a damn good explanation."

"Melissa, please," said the midwife.

"Please, what? This man barges into my room with a big smile on his face and just ignores me. He doesn't even *introduce* himself, and then he announces he wants to stick a wire onto my baby's head. And you think I'm being *unreasonable*?"

"Look, Miss Alexander," Summers said, with a growing edge to his voice, "you're not in charge here, *we* are. I'd be happy to let you sign a waiver and then find another doctor, but it's a little late for that. If your baby has fetal distress, we've got to find out and do a C-section. No ifs, ands, or buts. If you really want to do what's best for your baby, you'll let me attach this lead." He paused. "How does that sound?"

"Sound? Frankly, I don't like the sound of your voice."

"You don't like the *sound?*" he said, his face growing livid. Summers marched over to the fetal monitor and turned up the volume. The heartbeat boomed, loud and ominous. "How's that for sound, Miss Alexander? That's the sound of your baby dying!"

After work, Brad met Morgan for sushi. He was late. Brad apologized and explained that he'd gotten a call from a colleague. Arnold Schubert hadn't been attending to his hospitalized patients. His office staff hadn't been able to locate him. When the police ultimately entered his apartment, they found him dead.

"Heart attack?" Morgan asked.

"Looks that way. He was a damn good candidate. He smoked, drank a fair amount, and never got any exercise. Still, I feel bad for the poor guy. But I've got something even more interesting to tell you."

He went on to explain that Simon Crandall had discovered that the tiny insect Morgan had noticed on the slides was a deadly East African mite, unreported in the world's medical literature. But he had no explanation for what it was doing in the lungs of Long Island newborns.

Morgan was incredulous. "Is he implying this mite killed Benjamin and the other babies?"

"That's what he thinks. What bothers me is that he has no idea what the vector is, or how it was introduced."

"Then we have to figure it out," she said, frowning as she stared off into the distance. "Could it be some kind of insect migration, like those Central American fire ants that crossed the Rio Grande into Texas?"

"I doubt it," he said, lifting a California roll. "According to Simon, this mite could be a hybrid of one that exists almost exclusively in marijuana, of all things. At some point, it seems to have mutated and become pathogenic to humans."

"This just gets crazier and crazier," she said with a shake of her head. "Babies and pot. Have you mentioned this to anyone else, like Dr. Harrington?"

"Actually, I wanted to talk to you first. I don't relish getting laughed out of his office."

Morgan reflected as she daubed a piece of tuna with *wasabi*. "Maybe it's not as preposterous as it first sounds. Obviously, the mite would have to be isolated and tested to be certain. For discussion's sake, let's say that someone isolates it, and it proves to be virulent. How'd it get there?"

"That's precisely the problem," Brad admitted. "When Simon told me what he suspected, my first inclination was to call the NICU and warn them. But what would I tell them to look for? It can't be in the air or come through the ventilating system, or else *everyone* would have gotten it. So, what does that leave, something in the baby's formula, or the oxygen tubing? It seems far-fetched."

"What if someone squirted it in?" Morgan said.

"You think some disgruntled nurse *shpritzed* these kids with a mite-filled spray bottle?"

Morgan looked sheepish. "I guess we'd better have a little more to go on before we mention this to the authorities."

"I suppose . . ." Brad took a sip of green tea, then removed several pages of fax paper from his pocket. "I want to run this by you. Simon got all his information from the log of a British researcher named Richard Fielding, who was on sabbatical from Cambridge in Kenya twenty years ago. This Fielding was one of the world's foremost entomologists. Simon sent me copies, fascinating stuff.

" 'The hemp plant grows abundantly around Nairobi, especially in the more temperate hillside regions,' " Brad said. " 'Young Kenyans are increasingly involved in the drug subculture.

" 'According to the local police,' " Brad continued, " 'one of these young people was a tall chap named Makkede. The police surmise that this Makkede stumbled upon a cache of marijuana hidden in an acacia thicket. There were several dried bales of marijuana that were either lost or abandoned. At the edge of the tarp was a nearly decomposed human cadaver, clothing in tatters and flesh nearly mummified.' "

"My God," said Morgan.

" 'Later,' " Brad read, " 'Makkede's friends surmised that the poor fellow was so astonished by the discovery that he decided to celebrate before they arrived. When his friends caught up with him about ten minutes later, Makkede appeared intoxicated.

" 'Ten minutes after that, however, he became short of breath, and his lips turned cyanotic. Young Makkede began gasping for air, and before his friends could render assistance, he developed a frothy gurgle and died.' "

"This is sounding horribly familiar, Brad."

"Isn't it? Anyway, it seems that Dr. Fielding was visiting a biologist friend at the University of Nairobi when a specimen of this marijuana cache came in. The cops had sent samples to local experts hoping to pin down what it was that killed this Makkede character. Fortunately, the biologist asked Fielding to help examine the product, so he puts it under the microscope." Brad scanned the pages and read, " 'I quickly spotted the mites. Since numerous kinds of mites feed on decaying matter and stored foods, finding them in marijuana is not uncommon. Among the *acari*, the predaceous mite *macroheles muscado mesticae* is most frequently found.' "

"Where's all this heading?" Morgan asked.

"Just listen," said Brad, continuing. " 'But as I examined the mites under higher magnification, I grew curious. Indeed, the species had some characteristics of *macroheles*, but its mouthparts were similar to those of the genus *dermatophagoides*, the dust mite. On the other hand, the shape of its cephalothorax resembled *demodex*, the hair-follicle mite host-specific to man. After lengthy study, I must conclude that, under proper conditions in this area, the cannabis mite and human mites have somehow cross-bred, and mutated.' "

Morgan shook her head in stunned amazement.

"Fielding thought the mite he'd discovered had particularly aggressive characteristics," Brad continued. "He thought it might play a role in human disease, like what happened to that Makkede fellow."

"Wasn't that just speculation?"

"Yes and no," Brad said. "When he mentioned his suspicions to the local authorities, the coroner re-examined slides of the nineteen-year-old's lungs, and guess what? Here and there, the mutated mites were attached to Makkede's respiratory epithelium."

"But why doesn't anyone know about this?" Morgan asked.

"Because Fielding never reported it. He'd taken samples of the mites, but they were lost in transit on the way back to England. Apparently he intended to collect some more and publish his findings, but he died before he got around to it."

"Incredible," Morgan murmured. "But that still doesn't explain what they're doing in this country."

"No," Brad agreed, "but Fielding's final few sentences mentioned that some of the marijuana cache was missing. Seems that someone helped himself to a generous portion. If that person managed to keep the mites alive and smuggle them over here, well . . ."

Dumbfounded, Morgan could only shake her head. "It looks like your friend Crandall's come up with some incredible information."

"Along with a further tidbit," Brad said. "Simon had another interesting story involving East Africa. A few nights ago, there was a fender bender on the LIE, and an anencephalic skeleton comes flying out of someone's car. The driver took off. The skeleton had a bug in its ear canal, and the local ME sent it to Simon for identification. Turned out to be a rare African beetle."

"And he thinks the two things are related?" Morgan asked.

"That's what he asked me."

"Do you know anyone familiar with East Africa? What about that friend of yours, the one I met at your house?"

"Nbele? Yes, but I don't think he's into bugs. I guess I could ask."

"Hmmm," Morgan muttered, brow knitted. "I wonder. . . . Britten was trying to locate an anencephalic for his collection. Let's say he's involved with this African beetle," she slowly continued. "Would it be reaching to think he might also be involved with the mite?"

"I doubt it, Morgan. The guy's certainly a nut case, but what would his motive be? Sick as he is, I can't picture him inserting deadly insects into the lungs of newborns. Besides, he's not a doctor. Even if he had the skill, he doesn't have access to the NICU."

"I don't mean him personally," she said, "but I'm sure he could persuade someone else. He admitted that he's very goal-directed, and I wouldn't put anything past him. As for motive, what about helping to fulfill his economic plan for AmeriCare? Caring for those newborns is very expensive."

"You really think he's that ruthless?"

"I'm sure he wouldn't let *anything* get between him and what he wants."

"But what'd be in it for him, specifically?" he asked. "Isn't it enough to be academically successful?"

"Maybe for normal people, but I got the impression that Britten, in addition to his other problems, is money-hungry. Even though he's well off for someone his age, I imagine AmeriCare's making it financially attractive for him."

"I hope to hell you're wrong, Morgan. Is there any way you can find out for sure about the money angle?"

"In fact," she said, "there just might be."

It was the housekeeper's night off, and Brad wanted to get home to his son. As they left the restaurant, Morgan kissed him on the cheek. She wished they had more time to spend together. In time, she hoped, that would come.

She drove directly to AmeriCare, carefully scanning the parking lot for Britten's car. The lot was nearly empty. Morgan parked and let herself into the building.

She felt uncomfortable as she walked through the nearly deserted halls. She could no longer work for them, so now it was just a question of the best time to submit her resignation.

She unlocked her office, turned on the light, sat down at her computer, entered her password, and quickly logged on. What she wanted was a breakdown of AmeriCare stock shares—specifically, an itemization of insider equity, of which Directors owned what. She didn't recall seeing it in the Annual Report, but it might be in unpublished statistics known as Notes to Consolidated Financial Statements. The information wouldn't be easy to find: it would probably be obscured by the in-house software. But Morgan had minored in computer science in college, and she was quite adept at winding her way through computer systems.

Ten minutes later, Morgan persuaded the computer to reveal the information she wanted. The file, called "Directorial Positions," showed who in the company owned large blocks of shares. It was a long list. As expected, CEO Daniel Morrison had a substantial position, as did other board members. There were also quite a few silent shareholders, whose names Morgan didn't recognize. To her anger and astonishment, Morgan saw that the Medical Director, her colleague Dr. Martin Hunt, held an enormous equity position, which seemed way out of proportion.

"Marty, you mercenary bastard," she mumbled.

Non-board members were near the end of the list, and that was where she found Britten, Hugh. When she saw that her guess had been correct, her heart started beating faster. Although it was normal for directors to own large stock holdings, Britten, a relative newcomer to the company, held what currently amounted to two million dollars in common stock. Moreover, he also owned a significant quantity of stock options and what Morgan interpreted to be a performance guarantee. She did the mental calculations. Britten's stake in AmeriCare was worth upwards of twenty million dollars.

Morgan whistled softly to herself, dumbstruck. There was no legitimate way AmeriCare shareholders would pay that much for even the best consultant. Here was the concrete data she was looking for: Hugh Britten's motive. If Britten somehow had a hand in large-scale patient mismanagement, he would be killing two birds with one stone—discrediting the university that spurned him, while lining his own pockets. Morgan shivered at the nightmarish idea.

Morgan suddenly realized that she'd better take notes while everything was still fresh and clear in her mind. Splitting the monitor screen, she immediately typed in her thoughts, listing what she knew, and what she suspected. Fifteen minutes later, she e-mailed the material to Brad. Then, after a few more minutes of perusing the files, she logged off.

"Find what you wanted, Dr. Robinson?"

Morgan whirled around, startled. She was surprised to see Morrison, but more than a little relieved that it wasn't Britten. Although being caught snooping in secret company files by the CEO was embarrassing, she could probably explain her way out of it.

"Yes, thank you," she said. "I was just catching up on a little work."

"You don't say? Since when does your work involve investigating the company's confidential finances?"

"Why would you think I'd do something like that?"

His eyes went wide, and he looked at her menacingly. "Whenever someone accesses certain documents, I get notified. I just happened to be in my office tonight when you decided to peek at them. I want to know why that information is so important to you."

Morgan refused to be cowed. Squaring her jaw, she turned off the power, got out of her chair, and gathered up her things. "Good night, Mr. Morrison. I think it's time I left."

"Now just one minute . . ." he protested. But Morgan continued on her way. Morrison grew livid. "You insolent bleeding heart!" he thundered. "Damn right you're leaving! I expect you out of this office and your resignation on my desk by the end of the week!"

Morgan thought of a thousand things to say, but she held her tongue. Eyeing him resolutely, she simply gave a polite smile and left the office.

Morrison was furious, and more than a little worried. He'd told the damned systems analyst to encrypt that file, but the programmer had talked him out of it. Idiot! As he stalked back to his own office, he wondered again why Morgan had accessed the information. Would her discovery come back to haunt them?

As long as she kept the information to herself, their exposure was limited. But that was the key, making sure what she learned didn't go further. They could deal with her, by extreme methods, if need be. But what if she spread the information further? If word got out, they'd be ruined. And *he* might wind up in jail.

Back in his office, Morrison sat down and stared at his computer screen. The consultants who'd installed their system had inserted sophisticated security measures. Access to certain files, as he'd told Morgan, was strictly limited. What he hadn't told her was that not only was he notified about unauthorized access, but the information gleaned by the cyber-intruder showed up simultaneously on his screen. Thus, when Morgan called up the Directorial Positions file, Morrison knew about it immediately. But now, as he returned to his own monitor, Morgan's e-mail was also there.

Morrison read it and paled. He didn't know who the addressee was, but he could easily find out. The question now was what to do about it. He picked up the phone and hit a speed-dial.

"Hugh," he said, "we've got a problem."

Brad was in the kitchen when the call came through from senior resident Mei Mei Chang. "Summers walked out of the unit?" he asked, incredulous. "Who's taking care of the patient?"

"The nurse-midwife is around, but that's about it. There's no other attending here. I'm worried about the tracing, Dr. Hawkins. It's pretty flat, and she's starting to get late decelerations. I realize you're not on call tonight, but I didn't know where to turn!"

"Where's Dr. Summers now?"

"He said he was going home." She paused. "I really think the patient's got to be sectioned right away, Dr. Hawkins. We called Summers' house and beeped him a couple times, but we can't find him anywhere!"

Brad was disappointed, but not surprised. Though a relatively competent doctor, Summers had a decidedly juvenile personality. This wasn't the first time he'd pulled a disappearing act in the middle of an emergency.

Chang was starting to sound frantic. "Okay, Mei Mei, listen up. You've got a section consent? Are anesthesia and peds around?"

"We're ready to go, Dr. Hawkins."

"Then take her back and get started. I'll be right over."

His son looked up at him. "Dad?"

"Put your sneaks on, Mikey. We're going to the hospital. It shouldn't take long. We'll stop for pizza on the way back."

His son didn't object. His TV show wouldn't come on for another two hours. From past experience, Michael knew that his father worked fast. He was sure they'd be home in plenty of time, even if they stopped for Italian.

En route, Brad called the delivery room from his car phone. The patient, an overly outspoken woman named Melissa, had been demanding lengthy explanations for everything. But shortly after Dr. Summers stormed out, her baby's heartbeat had plummeted, and Melissa suddenly became tractable. She readily signed the operative consent and had been quickly zipped off to the OR. According to the nurse, the patient had been anesthetized, and Dr. Chang had begun surgery without delay. The baby would be delivered shortly.

Brad reached the doctors' parking lot five minutes later. He always gave the senior resident tacit approval to commence emergency surgery once he was on his way. After all, the resident was only months away from becoming an attending, and at some point, the young physician's judgment had to be proven. If the resident couldn't handle the situation, Brad would soon be there to step in.

He wasn't sure what to do with Michael. When they were leaving the house, his son had grabbed a Game Boy, which would keep him occupied for at least an hour. Once they arrived in the DR, Brad planned to turn Michael over to one of the nurses. There were TVs available in vacant labor and on-call rooms. Alternatively, Mikey could simply sit in the nurses' work area and play his computer game.

After hurrying past the ER, Brad and his son reached the fourth-floor elevator banks. Visitors crowded the hospital at that time of day, and it took a long time for the elevator to arrive. While he waited, Brad drummed his fingers impatiently on the wall. Finally the doors opened, and Brad immediately punched the button for eight. Predictably, the elevator stopped again on five and filled with visitors going to upper floors. It seemed to take forever to reach eight.

Once there, they were the last ones to get off. To Brad's surprise, Nbele was waiting to get on. Michael looked up and grinned from ear to ear.

"Nbele!" he called.

"Michael, my friend," Nbele said, his smile almost incandescent. "We make a habit of meeting here!"

"Working late, Nbele?" Brad asked.

"No, Doctor. Tonight I'm just visiting a friend."

"Could I go with him, Dad?" Michael asked, suddenly animated.

"I've got emergency surgery," Brad explained, nodding toward the DR doors. "Had to drag Michael along, but he'll be fine with one of the nurses."

"I'd be happy to have him tag along, Doctor."

"Dad, *please*!"

"Well . . . if you're sure it's not an imposition."

"You know I'd tell you if it were," said Nbele. "He'll be fine with me, Dr. Hawkins. Call my office when you're done?"

"Okay. I'll check in with you guys later."

"Yes!" Michael said.

Brad waved a hurried farewell and ducked through the DR doors. He quickly donned a pair of scrubs and headed for the delivery room. Through the glass, he could see Dr. Chang and another resident busy at work. He stuck his head in and announced his arrival.

"Everything okay, Mei Mei?"

"Hi, Dr. Hawkins. I'm glad you're here. The baby's out, but we have a little bleeding."

"How's the baby?"

"One minute apgar of five," she said, "but he's perking up."

There was an edge of uncertainty in her voice. Brad knew she was a good resident, but emergencies sometimes tied her in knots. He quickly put on paper booties, a cap, and a mask, then did an abbreviated scrub. Soon, uplifted arms dripping soap bubbles, he walked backward into the OR. He was gowned and gloved within seconds.

Brad stepped to the left-hand side of the OR table, across from Dr. Chang, who was busy sopping up blood with laparotomy pads, while the junior resident beside her used a plastic suction device. But the blood flow continued unabated. Looking at the uterus, he saw that it lacked the mottled gray appearance associated with a well-contracted organ. Soft and mushy, it bled freely in a condition called uterine atony.

"Forget the lap pads, Mei Mei," he said. "You've gotta get the uterus to contract. Grab it in both hands and massage the hell out of it."

"I tried that, Dr. Hawkins."

"Try it again," he said, with a slight edge to his voice. "You've got six hundred ccs per minute of blood going through that thing, and unless you control it, the patient's going to bleed out on you!"

He watched Dr. Chang tentatively take the uterine fundus in her hands to begin compression. Without hesitation, Brad placed his hands atop hers and showed her how to knead the muscle more forcefully in rhythmic, determined strokes. "Much better," he said. "Keep that up, but have a plan ready in case it doesn't work. What'll you do next?"

"Prostaglandin?"

"Good choice, but try the simpler drugs first." He

looked at the nearby IV. "What've you got running?"

"Lactated Ringer's, with an amp of Pitocin."

"Open it up wide," Brad directed the anesthesiologist. "And throw in another twenty units, okay? How're her vitals?"

"Pressure's okay," said the anesthesiologist, "but she's getting a little tachy."

"You have blood ready?"

"She's typed and screened for two units."

"Better cross-match her for another two," Brad said to the anesthesiologist. "And have them send it up stat. Did you give her Methergine?"

"Not yet."

"How about giving her two tenths of a milligram I.M.?"

"You got it," the anesthesiologist said.

Brad watched closely. Despite her improved technique, the blood flow was unchecked. He estimated that the patient had already lost a thousand ccs. "All right, Mei Mei," he said. "You've got Pit and Methergine in. Do you have that prostaglandin available?"

"I didn't call for it yet," she admitted sheepishly.

Brad turned to the circulating nurse. "See if you can round up some fifteen-methyl prostaglandin F-2 alpha. We'll need point two-five in a syringe, on the field."

As the nurse hurried away, Brad considered his options. Persistent postpartum hemorrhage from uterine atony was life-threatening. Usually, it responded to simple measures, like drugs and massage; but when it didn't, a competent surgeon proceeded in a stepwise fashion. "Think it through, Mei Mei," he patiently continued. "Give that Prostin as soon as it's drawn up, but be ready just in case."

Soon the scrub nurse had the injection ready. Brad showed Chang how to inject it directly into the uterine muscle. When she resumed massage, everyone watched the uterus for signs of firming up.

"How much time do I give it?" she asked.

"Five minutes, max," Brad said. "How's it feel?"

"I can't detect any difference."

Indeed, the purplish mass appeared soft as fish flesh, and the blood continued to fill the pelvis. By now, the patient had lost another five hundred ccs. The donor blood wasn't yet available for transfusion, and unless they stopped the bleeding soon, the patient would go into shock. "Okay, Mei Mei, Plan B," he said. "What're you going to do now?"

"Hypogastric artery ligation?" she ventured.

"That's the standard board exam answer," he agreed. "But I saw one patient die after the surgeon lacerated the hypogastric vein. It's not an easy procedure, and you have to perform a lot of them to feel comfortable doing it. Why not try uterine packing first?"

Dr. Chang's voice warbled with uncertainty. "I thought that didn't work?"

"Nothing works if you don't try it. Let's give it a shot."

He looked over at the senior resident. He could tell that she, too, was shaken by the incessant hemorrhage. It was at times like this that the diffident surgeon opted for the easy way out, moving directly to hysterectomy. But that had a cruel finality to someone with only one pregnancy. It was far preferable, he thought, to explore treatment options one by one, provided the patient's clinical state warranted it.

While the residents watched, Brad tied two laparotomy packs together and inserted them into the uterine cavity. He hoped that with the cloth packs providing pressure from within, and by massaging from without, the blood flow could be stanched. Once everything was in place, he vigorously kneaded the flaccid muscle. But after another two minutes, it was apparent that this maneuver didn't work, either. The laparotomy packs were a saturated, scarlet mass.

"It was worth a try," he said gamely. "Now, on to Plan C. How's her pressure?"

"Down to ninety systolic," the anesthesiologist said. "I can't get the fluids in as fast as she's losing it."

"What about uterine artery embolization?" asked Dr. Chang.

"Good thought," Brad said, "and it can be effective, when you've got the time. But we don't. We could suture the uterine arteries, but there's an alternative technique. Ever heard of the B-Lynch suture?"

She shook her head. Brad quickly discarded the blood-soaked packs and asked the scrub nurse to prepare a special suture. Using a seventy-millimeter, blunt-tipped, round-bodied free needle, he had her mount a number-two chromic catgut suture. Glancing around the OR, Brad could tell that all eyes were upon him, and several people were holding their breath. It was now or never.

Once the needle holder was ready, he deftly placed the first stitch beneath the lower uterine incision. He had Dr. Chang continue compression while he sewed. It was a long, continuous stitch, in and out, over the dome of the uterus and back again. Its purpose was obviously to encircle the uterus in a snare of tight suture material, thereby uniformly and continuously compressing it. Soon Hawkins brought the two ends of the suture together in front and tied them with several throws of secure surgeon's knots. When he was done, the uterus resembled a round package neatly constricted with tight twine. Then he stopped to see what would happen.

Slowly but perceptibly, the compressed uterus began

to firm up. The muscle became tight, and its once-purplish fibers turned gray and corrugated as the blood flow diminished. Brad allowed himself a deep breath. Looking across the OR table, he could see the relief in Dr. Chang's eyes.

"About time," he said.

"Nice going, Dr. Hawkins," said the anesthesiologist. "I was getting worried there. Everything under control now?"

"Just about. Do a stat 'crit to see where we stand with blood replacement, okay? Mei Mei, you want to close?"

Still trembling, she managed a grateful nod. She held out a shaking hand for the first stitch with which to bring a standard uterine closure. With Brad's assistance, she sewed slowly and deliberately, first suturing the uterus, then the fascia. They closed the skin with a row of stainless steel staples. In all, the surgical team had been at work for forty-five minutes.

Taking the chart from the anesthesiologist, Brad left to scribble a brief note. At the nursing station, one of the nurses told him they'd finally gotten Dr. Summers on the phone and asked if Brad wanted him to come in. For a moment, Brad was tempted to pick up the phone and give the other attending a piece of his mind. But he told the nurse to forget it. Since Summers was a man of limited skills, it was probably better for the patient that he'd walked out.

Finished with the chart, Brad picked up the phone and asked the operator to connect him with Nbele's office. The phone rang three times, then four. There was no answer. Strange, Brad thought. Perhaps they were visiting someone, or else roaming the hospital corridors. In any event, he still had a few instructions to go over with Dr. Chang.

In the OR, the nurses were applying sterile dressings

to the patient's abdominal incision. Soon, the endotracheal tube was removed from Melissa Alexander's throat. As soon as she was breathing satisfactorily on her own, she was transferred to a stretcher and wheeled to the recovery room. The baby's condition had improved considerably, and the child was now in the nursery.

Brad reviewed the post-op orders with Dr. Chang. The patient's pre-op hematocrit of thirty-six had fallen to twenty-three; but since her vital signs were reasonably stable, and she was receiving plenty of fluids, it would be best to hold off on blood transfusions. He ordered coagulation studies. If they came back normal, it would probably be smooth sailing for the remainder of the night.

Fifteen minutes later, Brad tried Nbele's extension again. It had been an hour since he dropped off his son, and Brad half expected them to come marching past the DR doors at any moment. But as before, his call went unanswered. Concerned, he decided to check things out for himself.

Brad knew Nbele's office was near the morgue. At that time of the evening, the halls were cool and deserted. Brad quickly located the office. He knocked on the closed door but got no reply. Trying the knob, he found it unlocked.

To his surprise, the room was dark. He located the switch on the wall, and the overhead fluorescents flickered to life, revealing an empty room. Worried, Brad looked around. Where in the world could they be? He knew one of Mikey's favorite TV shows would soon be on, and it wasn't like his son to miss it. Brad calmly surveyed the small, neat office until he noticed his son's Game Boy under the desk.

His heart started to pound. Michael never let the

game out of his sight. Something peculiar was going on. He tore a piece of paper from Nbele's desktop calendar. "Nbele," he scribbled, "please page me or call me in the DR as soon as you get back!" He signed the note and scribbled down the time on the bottom. Then he taped the note conspicuously to the door.

Brad took a deep breath. Calm down, he told himself. They've got to be in the hospital somewhere. Right now, they're probably cruising the corridors sharing tales of aliens on the African veldt.

He took the elevator back to eight, hoping to find them there—Michael eager to get home, and Nbele apologetic. Bursting through the swinging doors, Brad quickly looked around. The only thing he saw was a sea of inquisitive faces looking his way. He quickly asked the nurses, but no one had seen either his son or Nbele.

Brad half ran back to the elevators and impatiently jabbed the call button. First he tried the lobby, then the cafeteria, and then Nbele's office. His note was still there, untouched. He was getting frantic. "*For God's sake, Michael, I am really going to let you have it!*" he muttered under his breath.

Visiting hours were over, and most people had gone home. He raced outside into the descending darkness, hoping to find the pair staring up at the stars. But he couldn't find them anywhere. Could they have gone to his car? Of course, that was it! He ran across the helipad into the doctors' parking lot. His pace slowed when he neared his car. There was no one in sight.

"Mikey!" he called at the top of his lungs. "Mikey, where the hell are you?"

"Can I help you, Dr. Hawkins?" a voice called out of the darkness.

Brad whirled around to see Sue Frankel, one of the university police and a longtime patient. "Sue, I'm losing it!" he said, running his fingers through his hair. "I can't find my son. I left him over an hour ago with Nbele—"

"The African guy who works in pathology?"

"Right," Brad nodded. "Nbele was watching him while I finished an emergency cesarean. But that was over an hour ago, and I can't find them anywhere, and—"

"Hold on, Doc, take it easy," she said, raising her palms. ".Everybody turns up eventually. Did you try Nbele's office?"

"Yeah, a couple of times. All I found was Mikey's Game Boy. The kid *never* lets it out of his sight!"

"All right, here's what we'll do," she said calmly. "Let's you and me go back to his office, okay? Then we'll start a walking tour of the hospital, top to bottom."

Brad followed her, annoyed at his own impatience and struggling to fight his rising panic. He explained to Sue that he'd never known his son to be inconsiderate. And Nbele? He should definitely have known better! Brad realized that he was babbling. They hurried through the deserted corridors. Nbele's office was still vacant, and the note on the door remained untouched. Brad grabbed the phone and quickly dialed the DR. They still hadn't seen Mikey.

Officer Frankel spoke into her mobile phone. Soon, every security officer in the hospital had been alerted. Within seconds, they heard the hospital PA system paging both Nbele and Michael Hawkins, asking them to call the security office. Then Sue took Brad up to the nineteenth floor, where they began covering every square foot of hospital hallway, one floor at a time.

It took them over an hour. Michael and Nbele were still nowhere to be found. By now, Brad was beside himself. Heartsick, he had a vision of his son hurt, need-

ing his help. He felt a sickening impotence, and while
he knew it was likely untrue, he couldn't get the image
out of his mind.

Every few minutes, they called the DR, Nbele's office, and the security chief. Finally, it occurred to one
of the security officers to search for Nbele's car. Ten
minutes later, they found it parked where expected, its
hood cold.

"He wouldn't have taken your son somewhere, would
he?" asked Sue.

"Nbele? No, he's trustworthy as hell!" At his wits'
end, Brad rubbed his aching forehead. "At least, I *think*
he is."

"Does your son have a house key? Maybe they took
a cab home."

Why hadn't he thought of that? Brad cursed his stu-
pidity as he grabbed the nearest phone and dialed an
outside line. His white-knuckled fingers held the receiver
tight to his ear. He waited three rings, then four, before
his answering machine clicked on. Could they have left
word? He impatiently punched in the code to retrieve
his messages.

There was only one message. His face turned white,
and the phone slowly fell away from his ear. His hand
was trembling, and his voice was weak with fear.

"They've taken my son," he said in a quavering
voice.

CHAPTER EIGHTEEN

Morgan immediately drove to Brad's house when she got his call. The minute she walked in the door, she put her arms around him and held him, comforting and soothing him, just as he'd done for her.

At the kitchen table, Brad explained the nightmarish situation. The message had been simple and specific: if he ever wanted to see his son alive, he had to stop nosing around in AmeriCare business. The caller said he'd get back to him, then hung up.

"Did you recognize the voice?" Morgan asked.

"No, it was a foreign accent." He paused. "But I'm sure I've heard it before."

"It wasn't Nbele?"

"Definitely not," Brad said with a shake of his head. "It sounded a little like him, but it was different. He's not that kind of guy, Morgan. At least I don't think he is. I trusted Mikey with him."

"How well do you really know him?"

"As well as anyone else does, I guess," he said with a shrug. "He's basically a loner."

"So who else might have made the call?"

His expression turned defiant. "Isn't it obvious? It's

that son of a bitch Britten, disguising his voice! He's a malicious bastard."

"But *kidnapping*? I realize he's peculiar, but not *this* desperate."

"No? You said yourself that he's ruthless! Right now, he's burning with resentment. On top of that, he's delusional. Remember how angry he was about being snubbed for university provost? Believe me, they haven't heard the last of him yet either!"

"But that's got nothing to do with you."

"No," Brad said, "but *you* do. That little scene at your place must have knocked a few more of his screws loose. When he had to turn tail and run off like that, it was the ultimate humiliation. And now, he's getting even!"

"Then you don't believe it's about your interfering with AmeriCare?"

"No, this is personal, Morgan, between him and me."

"So what're you going to do now? What did the police say?"

He looked away sheepishly. "I haven't told them yet."

"*What?*" she said incredulously. "Brad, you can't keep them out of this!"

"I don't intend to. But it's too early to get them involved. The cops don't look into missing persons reports until at least—"

"This isn't missing persons, it's kidnapping!"

"I realize that, but what am I going to tell them? That some lovesick maniac, who just happens to be a world-renowned economist, is trying to get even with me? Christ, they might lock me up, instead of him!" Brad breathed deeply, trying to calm himself. "Morgan, you know damn well I'm just as angry as you are, maybe

more so. It's my son. But I have to do this my own
way!"

"You told Officer Frankel, didn't you?"

"The security people agreed not to notify the police
until morning."

"I think you're being foolish," Morgan said, "but it's
your call. I hope you have a game plan."

"First we'll track down Nbele, then find that cretin
Britten. One way or another, I'm going to get my son
back!"

"But you need professionals to deal with kidnapping,"
Morgan argued. "Well-intentioned amateurs only make
the situation worse." As she said it, Morgan realized that
it was Brad's son's life that was at stake. She wanted to
be supportive, so ultimately, she extracted the same
promise he'd made to Sue Frankel: if Brad hadn't found
Mikey by morning, they'd call the police.

Brad thumbed through the Rolodex until he found
Nbele's phone number and address. Although he'd tried
the number several times in the hospital, he gave it another shot. The phone went unanswered. Then, exasperated, he took the tape out of his answering machine and
got in the car with Morgan.

It was nearing midnight. Brad drove east, toward a
rural, wooded area on the North Shore. Beside him,
Morgan used a Hagstrom atlas to pinpoint the street.
Finally reaching Nbele's block, they found themselves
on a poorly lit cul-de-sac. Brad parked in front of the
house.

They slowly got out of the car and proceeded cautiously. The wood-shingle house was completely dark,
and they crept up the walkway in silence. When they
got to the front door, Brad tried the doorknob. To his
surprise, it was open. He gave the door a firm push.

"Nbele?" he called. "Anybody home? Mikey, it's Dad!"

No one answered. Morgan followed in Brad's foot-steps, feeling along the wall until she found a light switch. Suddenly the area was bathed in a pale, yellow-ish light, and they discovered themselves in a small, sparsely furnished living room. Brad strode through a narrow hall to an empty dining room and impatiently pushed through a swinging door.

The unlit room before him was black and featureless. Brad suspected it was the kitchen. The slightly pungent odor of marijuana hung in the air. He walked cautiously ahead, trying to get his bearings. Suddenly he stepped onto something wet and slick. His feet slipped out from under him, and he began sliding.

Brad fell heavily on his side and felt the air go out of him. As he struggled to catch his breath, Morgan found the light switch. Stunned by the fall, it took him several seconds to regain his bearings. What jolted him back to reality was Morgan's blood-curdling scream.

Morgan's face was pale, her eyes wide with fear. One of her trembling fingers pointed to something behind Brad. He pushed himself into a sitting position and turned. Then he, too, inhaled sharply.

What he'd slipped in was a pool of blood, the con-gealing spill as slippery as oil. The blood had oozed wet and sticky from its source, a man's head.

The man lay on his stomach, hands crudely bound behind his back with rough twine. The back of his head had been split open with a heavy knife, whose metal blade was still embedded in the skull. Blood from the massive wound had spilled across his cheek and run down his neck to pool on the floor tile. As Brad strug-gled to his knees, he saw that it was Nbele.

Nbele's eyes were half-open, and his gaze was fixed

on the floor. Brad could see that the whites of his eyes were already dry. The pulse in his neck was absent, and his chest was still.

Energized by the adrenaline rush of fear, Brad jumped up and dashed out of the kitchen, Morgan close on his heels. He tore through the house from room to room, calling his son's name over and over, afraid of what he might find. But every room was empty. Finally he came to a halt beside the front door. His lungs were heaving, and his heart raced. He realized that he had to collect his wits. Taking a deep breath, he put his hand on Morgan's shoulder and gave it an encouraging squeeze. But he couldn't hide the anguish in his voice.

"Where the hell *is* he?"

"We'll find him, don't worry. But we've got to work in a logical fashion."

Brad reluctantly nodded. They couldn't keep running around aimlessly. "First, we call the police anonymously and tell them about poor Nbele," he said with deliberation.

"You want me to do that?" Morgan asked.

"Good idea. I'd rather they didn't have my voice on the dispatcher's tape. After that, we track down that sonofabitch Britten. I'm sure he's responsible for what happened here. We've got a lot of questions. I know he's got the answers." He paused. "And I hope to God he's got my son."

Within minutes, Brad and Morgan were on the road again, trying to figure out the horrific situation.

"In Britten's unbalanced mind," Brad said, "I'm the guy who took his girl and showed him up. All he can think of is getting even, and he can't see beyond that."

"True," Morgan said. "But I keep looking at the bigger picture."

"There is no bigger picture, Morgan. It's simply revenge."

"I know, but what about the possible connection between the newborn deaths and AmeriCare?"

"What's that got to do with Michael?"

"Didn't you get my e-mail?"

Brad shook his head. It had begun to rain, and Brad put on the wipers. Morgan stared through the streaked windshield, concentrating on the road ahead while she filled him in on her earlier confrontation with Daniel Morrison and how protective the CEO had been about insider financial equity.

"Obviously this information was never intended to be seen by anyone outside the loop," she said. "He went bonkers, Brad. Now we know that Britten's got all the motive in the world for killing those babies, all written in dollar signs."

"Fine, but why would he take my son?"

"I wouldn't be surprised if Morrison and Britten were in cahoots," Morgan said. "Britten knows I accessed the financial projections, and Morrison knows I discovered their financial stake."

"You're saying that, because they know about our relationship and realize we've discovered a possible financial motive to the murders, that this is their way of silencing us *both*? And if we agree to keep our mouths shut, I get Michael back?"

"I know it sounds far-fetched, but that's precisely how I felt when you first suggested the AmeriCare link."

He remembered indeed. Morgan had been just as skeptical then as he was now. "But still, the notion of kidnapping . . ." he persisted. "After all, these are intelligent, wealthy, highly educated professional people, not street criminals."

For a few minutes, neither of them spoke, and the

only sound was the squeaking of the wipers. "What about Nbele?" Brad suddenly demanded. "Does he play a role in any of this? The fact that he was killed suggested he doesn't, but . . . Is it possible that Britten and Nbele knew one another? Did Nbele take Michael on orders from Britten?"

Unwanted mental pictures of Michael flitted through Brad's brain—Michael lying cold, still, and abandoned somewhere, crying for his father's help. He shut his eyes tightly and shook his head.

Too many questions, he thought. They desperately needed answers on this dark and dreary night, but all they had was one riddle on top of another.

It was after midnight, and Nuru Milawe drove like a wild man, heading for Manhattan. He drove a rented Ford Taurus, since his van was still in the shop for repairs, and he was determined to be on time for his one A.M. appointment in the East Village.

He was under a lot of pressure. Too many things were happening too quickly. It was a Friday, and he normally worked the three-to-eleven respiratory shift at North Shore University Hospital as a service man. But tonight he called in sick, because Britten had called him for a special job.

He looked forward to Britten's unusual requests because they paid so well. The simple business of putting the mites in Dr. Schubert's tobacco—child's play, really—had earned him a quick ten thousand dollars. His current task of snatching a physician's son had come off without a hitch. Assuming everything came off as planned, he'd soon be twenty-five thousand dollars richer.

But, ah—this job had provided an unintended bonus. For almost forty-eight hours, he'd followed Dr. Hawkins and the boy. Covert stalking came naturally to him, for it was a simple extension of the hunting skills he'd refined as a boy in Africa. After he was told to go into action, the opportunity had presented itself almost immediately when the doctor brought his son to the hospital, leaving him in the company of Nbele.

Nbele! His cousin's name aroused both fear and hatred. They'd both been reared in the same Masai clan. Nbele was two years Nuru's senior and enjoyed the role of the older, more responsible family member, always telling his younger cousin to do this, avoid that, mind his manners.

How self-righteous he was, how sanctimonious! His incessant sermonizing against Nuru's drug use was unnecessarily humiliating. And how, so holier-than-thou, he carped about Nuru's occasional intoxication, saying that he was no better than an American street junkie. As if that weren't enough, he never let Nuru forget his indebtedness for the job at University which Nbele had found for him.

That was all history now. Nbele had a *simi* in his head and would never humiliate him again.

As he crossed the city line, still under a slight marijuana high, Nuru smiled to himself. Everything had been rather easy. When he found his cousin and the boy together in Nbele's office, all he had to do was pull out his *simi* and hold it to the boy's throat. The look on Nbele's face was priceless. No preaching now, the man had turned to putty.

Initially, Nuru didn't have a plan beyond snatching the boy. But once he saw the fear in his cousin's eyes, the means toward accomplishing two goals became clear in his mind. He kept the boy at knifepoint in the car, forcing Nbele to drive home. Then, after making the pious hypocrite grovel, he dispatched him to the land of their ancestors. Finally, he dragged Michael off to his own house.

There, thanks to his endless supply of African botanical drugs, he could keep the boy as long as necessary. Michael fell sound asleep and would remain so for several hours. Thus far, Nuru thought, it had been a very successful night. He had only one more bit of unrelated business before returning home in triumph.

With Morgan directing him, Brad made the final turn onto Britten's street. He extinguished his headlights and slowly drove the last hundred yards in darkness. After he turned off the ignition, he and Morgan sat silently staring at the house. Two cars were parked in the driveway. Morgan recognized one as Britten's, but she didn't know who owned the large Mercedes. Despite the late hour, the house was brightly lit. Determined to get answers, Brad reached for the door handle.

Morgan grabbed his arm. "Let's think this through, Brad."

"Think what through? I want my son back!"

"Do you think you'll get him by barging through the front door and saying, 'Thanks for babysitting'?" Her tone was patient, controlled. "Britten's not stupid enough to have Michael sitting on the couch beside him."

"I'm not just going to sit here while my son's in danger!"

"All I'm saying is, don't go in like a bull in a china shop. I know you want to break Britten's neck, but right now he holds all the cards."

Brad realized that she was right. Besides, Britten wasn't alone. "Who do you suppose his visitor is?"

"There's only one way to find out. Ready?"

Brad took a deep breath, nodded, and opened the car

door. He and Morgan marched purposefully up the walk to the front door. He was about to ring the doorbell when he saw that the door was ajar. He pushed it open and walked in.

Morgan recognized the foyer from her previous visit, but then she hadn't noticed much except his bizarre collection. Now, to her left, she saw a spacious, brightly lit living room. Britten and Morrison were sitting on a sofa, staring smugly their way.

Startled but not surprised, she and Brad halted. Britten and Morrison: wasn't that what they suspected?

"Come in, please," Britten said with exaggerated cheerfulness. "We've been expecting you. Care for a drink?"

"Don't screw with me, you bastard!" Brad shouted. "Where's my son?"

The smile left Britten's face, and he leaned forward, intent. "*Bastard*, you say? Well, this bastard—"

"Hold on, Hugh," Morrison cautioned. "Don't you see he's trying to provoke you?"

"Who the hell are you?" Brad demanded.

"Daniel Morrison. I'm CEO of AmeriCare."

"So you're Morrison, huh?" Brad said slowly. "Murdering babies isn't enough for you? Thought you'd try your hand at kidnapping, too?"

"Hugh told me you and Dr. Robinson would probably stop by, Dr. Hawkins," Morrison said smoothly. "Now that you're here, I see no point in exchanging allegations. Just tell us what you know."

"We know everything!" Brad spat. "But we're not going to tell you a damn thing until I get Michael back!"

Morrison refused to be provoked. "For the record, I won't for a minute admit I have the faintest idea what you're talking about."

"Look, you sick—"

"Brad," Morgan urged, "take it easy."

"An excellent suggestion," said Morrison. "Would that you were equally cautious with your dealings with our company, Dr. Robinson. But if, as Dr. Hawkins alleges, his son is missing, there may be ways of getting him back. Hypothetically speaking, of course."

"Go on," said Morgan.

"As I said before," Morrison continued, "I want you to tell me what you know, or suspect. You can start with what Dr. Hawkins refers to as 'murdering babies.' "

"And if we do?" Brad asked.

"Then I have a strong suspicion that at some point, your son might reappear unharmed."

Brad was seething, but it was a restrained, impotent rage. Looking slowly around the room, he realized that Morgan was right. His son was anywhere but here. And Britten and Morrison *did* have the upper hand. Brad didn't see that they had much choice. Turning to Morgan, he forced down the bile rising in his throat and slowly nodded.

Denials were pointless. Morgan told Morrison what he wanted to know. The CEO listened thoughtfully, lips pursed and eyes narrowed.

"Very interesting," he said at length. "I won't deny that some of us may have played a role in shaping abortion and term pregnancy rates. In fact, I think you'd have a hard case proving there's anything wrong with that. Whether they admit it or not, managed care companies do it all the time. Some would argue it's incumbent on a well-run HMO to manage costs by altering health care policy. Still, it's not the sort of thing we'd want to make public, would we?"

"I doubt you'd want them to know you killed helpless newborns, either," said Morgan.

Morrison slowly shook his head. "This is an entirely

different matter. Microscopic insects and respiratory arrests, ridiculous! We don't know anything about that. I admit, the deaths of these children has worked to the company's financial benefit, but that's only a coincidence. God's will, if you prefer."

"You're a goddamn liar," Brad said through clenched teeth.

"I suppose you have proof?" Morrison calmly continued. "One of you witnessed Dr. Britten or me or someone in our employ placing these African bugs in newborn airways?"

Brad and Morgan exchanged silent stares. Although she'd outlined the generalities of what they'd learned about AmeriCare, Morgan hadn't mentioned Simon Crandall or their East African suspicions.

"No? I thought not. It's a preposterous allegation, and I'm truly offended by it. But the press adores that kind of sensational story. So it will come as no surprise to you that the moment Dr. Robinson left company headquarters this evening, the file known as Directorial Positions ceased to exist. Other than what the SEC already knows, there is no longer a record of precisely who stands to benefit from AmeriCare's financial reversals. But what *may* surprise you is that each of you is now the proud owner of one hundred thousand shares of AmeriCare stock."

"*What?*" Morgan said.

"Yes, I have a document here," Morrison went on, "that confirms equity purchases you both made a year ago. You see, you both thought the stock price had hit bottom then. Unfortunately, the shares continued to tumble, and this disturbed you greatly. So, desperate lovers that you were—"

"You bastard!" Brad snarled.

"—you hit upon a scheme to help improve the company's bottom line," Morrison smoothly continued. "In fact you, Dr. Hawkins, wrote your lover a letter implicating you both." He held up a sheet of paper. "Nasty business, that. Unfortunately, you neglected to sign it, but I'm sure you'll rectify that oversight before you leave."

Fists clenched, Brad took a threatening step forward. "I'm not going anywhere without my son!"

"I think you are," Morrison calmly said. "If you do, your son will probably turn up, in time. His fate is entirely up to you."

Hawkins fumed in tense silence. Finally, Morgan took Brad's arm and turned him away.

"Sign it, Brad," she whispered. "We have no alternative."

"I'm not signing anything!"

"Look, the most important thing was getting Michael back, so play along with them and sign it! We both know they can't make a coerced confession stick, so what difference does it make? We need to buy some time."

Lips pressed into a tight line, Brad turned back to Morrison. "If I sign it, what guarantee do I have of getting Michael back?"

"That's just it," said Morrison, holding out a pen, "you don't. But sign this now, and you just might hear from us tomorrow."

Brad glared at him. God, the man was infuriating! But Morrison and Britten had clearly won the skirmish. Fighting down his rage, Brad stepped forward and reached for the proffered ballpoint. He signed the typewritten statement without reading it and disgustedly threw down the pen.

"Let's get out of here," he said, taking Morgan by the hand.

As he drew her toward the front door, Britten, who had been strangely silent, arose from his seat. "There is one more thing, Dr. Hawkins."

"*Now* what?" Brad said, exasperated.

Britten smiled. "Morgana stays."

"You're out of your mind!" he said.

"Perhaps, but her staying here is part of the deal. Take it or leave it."

"And how long is she supposed to stay?"

"Tonight, at least," Britten said, unruffled. "I'll play the perfect host. And tomorrow, it wouldn't surprise me if she remained voluntarily."

"With *you*?" Brad's fists clenched. "Not very likely!"

"Brad, please!" Morgan said, afraid that he might turn violent. In truth, she was frightened; the last thing she wanted was to be alone with Britten and Morrison. Yet a physical confrontation would do them no good. "Don't worry, I'll be okay," she said. "Just go! I'll talk to you tomorrow."

Brad hesitated, afraid of leaving her there alone, but equally terrified of doing anything that would jeopardize Michael's safety. Finally, squaring his jaw, he said, "If you touch one hair on her head, or Mikey's, you'll regret it!"

"Yes, of course," Morrison said. Smiling smugly, he pointed toward the door. "Now, if you don't mind?"

Morgan forced a courageous smile, but her chin quivered as she fought back the tears. With one last forlorn look her way, Brad Hawkins turned and stormed out into the night.

Nuru took the East River Drive south, eventually working his way to the Lower East Side. His destination was a small, newly opened bone shop called The Spinal Process. Nuru was a major player in the "naturalist" trade, and through the grapevine, he'd learned that the shop was looking for inventory. He made a few calls, indicating what he had for sale. Much of the preliminary discussions were through a go-between, to get a feel for the level of the buyer's interest and price range. The final negotiations would be in person, with the merchandise available for inspection.

He hadn't brought any of his better specimens. In the beginning, it was important to establish his reputation and integrity as a reliable source. To that end, he was bringing quality, though not terribly unusual, stock: an American Indian child's skeleton, a pygmy warrior with skeletal knife wounds, and selected Cambodian skulls from the Killing Fields, everything carefully boxed and labeled. Later, depending on the purchaser's budget, he might offer more exotic items.

Nuru located the store at a quarter after one, fifteen minutes past his scheduled appointment. The street lighting was poor, and it seemed unusually dark. Nuru parked the Taurus and scanned the neighborhood. Nothing appeared out of place. He estimated that it would take half an hour to consummate the deal, leaving ample time for him to return home before the boy woke up. He locked the car, opened the trunk, and removed the box with the Indian child's remains.

Inside the shop, just beyond the darkened storefront window, a man cautiously peered into the street. He wore a baseball cap and a blue windbreaker, both with large yellow block letters reading NYPD.

"We've got a visitor, Kev," he cautiously called toward the rear of the shop. "Black male, solo."

"Has he got merchandise?" asked Detective Riley.

"Looks like it. Hands are full."

"Let him get as far as the counter, Johnny," Riley said. "Then we'll take him down."

Earlier that evening, the New York City Police had been asked by the federal government to assist in serving a warrant. There was a suggestion of Mafia involvement in the shop. Through an informant, they'd learned of a possible transaction at the shop after midnight. Seizing an opportunity to satisfy themselves and the feds, the cops raided the shop at twelve A.M. and arrested the owner.

The shop owner was alone and nervous, and had an unusually large quantity of cash on hand. Once he was cuffed, he immediately clammed up. Although it was late, Riley decided to keep his men there to see who might turn up. Now Riley hovered in the shadows, readying his Glock by thumbing off the strap on his Mitch Rosen leather.

Outside the shop, the box tucked under his right arm, Nuru took out his wallet with his left hand. He was starting to get a funny feeling about this place. Before he left home, he'd scribbled down the address and put it in his wallet. After checking it once more, he placed his wallet on top of the box. Then he tried the doorknob with his free hand. Finding it unlocked, he pushed the door open.

As Nuru walked forward in the near darkness, a sixth sense alerted him. It was an old but familiar feeling, a sensation he'd felt as a child, the sudden awareness of an animal presence. The hairs on his neck bristled. He stopped in the middle of the room. Eyes adjusting to the dark, he slowly looked around.

A man leaped out of the shadows, something in his hand. "Police, freeze!" he shouted. "Keep your hands where we can—"

Nuru instinctively knew that the man was holding a gun. He acted without thinking. Even before the gun was leveled at him, he swung the box toward the man. The wooden container whipped around in an upward arc. The force of the swing knocked the gun from the man's hand, but not before it exploded with a thunderous roar. A second later, the wooden box smashed into the man's face.

Kevin Riley saw everything in a blur—a blinding flash, and a whizzing past his ear. In the fraction of a second that it took for his vision to clear, he saw one of his men tumbling backward. The object that had hit the officer slowly cartwheeled across the room. Almost simultaneously, the assailant pivoted and sprinted for the door. Before Riley could reach the butt of his Glock, the man was gone.

"Johnny!" Riley shouted, rushing forward, his ears ringing. "Johnny, you okay?" The cop was unconscious. "Officer down!" Riley shouted into his lapel mike. "Subject is a black male heading north on Allen!" With his radio crackling in the background, Riley bent down to help the officer.

Fifteen minutes later, with six squad cars and an ambulance assembled in the street, the EMTs carefully assisted the injured officer onto a stretcher. Although he'd regained consciousness, he had a fractured jaw and a severe concussion. The assailant had gotten away cleanly. As soon as the ambulance sped away, Riley went inside to inspect the intruder's makeshift weapon.

Next to a splintered wooden box, a small child's skeleton lay in a twisted heap of weathered bones. Riley knew he'd need Dr. Crandall's help with this one. But even more interesting was the assailant's wallet, which lay in the midst of the pile of odd remains. Riley pulled out the driver's license.

"Nuru Milawe," he read slowly. "Nuru, good buddy, your ass is mine."

*　　　*　　　*

Brad sped away from Britten's house in a poorly controlled fury. He was seething with rage at Morrison, Britten, and most of all, his own predicament. He'd always considered himself a man of action, but now, there was virtually nothing he could do except wait. He followed the road home blinded by hatred.

He tried reassuring himself that Morgan could protect herself, at least physically. But what about Michael, for God's sake? His son was only a boy, a child who'd led a sheltered life. He'd seldom been alone, so what could Michael *possibly* know about taking care of himself? The poor kid probably had no idea what was happening to him. He must be scared and confused and . . . Brad gritted his teeth, trying to dispel the frightening images.

Keeping his mind on his driving, Brad finally pulled his car into his garage. For a moment he hoped Michael might be home, but the house remained as empty as when he'd left it. Afraid of what he might, or might not, hear, he checked for messages on his answering machine. The newly inserted tape was blank. Brad smashed his fist on the wall and screamed at the empty house.

He pictured Michael on their boat, a broad smile on his face, his blond hair fluttering in the breeze. He saw him sprinting after a soccer ball, or intently bent over his Game Boy. He would do *anything* to get his son back.

What he would *not* do was simply sit around and wait. If only he had a weapon . . . but he didn't own a firearm. Then, he had a sudden flash of memory and headed for the cellar.

In one of his summer college jobs, Brad had been an assistant animal warden for a local municipality. Essentially a glorified dogcatcher, he accumulated a lot of experience during his brief tenure, as well as some specialized equipment like an animal tranquilizer gun.

Now the glimmer of a plan began to emerge.

The gun was basically a break-open, breech-loading, pump-action air rifle. Inexpensive and underpowered, it was intended for small animals at distances under twenty feet. Brad still had a handful of tranquilizer darts, which were plastic hypodermic syringes with a needle on one end and plastic fins on the other. Once the dart struck its target, the tranquilizer was driven home by a small primer.

Brad picked up one of the darts and inspected it. Both the darts and the rifle still seemed to be working. Pocketing several darts, he picked up the air rifle and dashed up the basement stairs. A minute later, he was in his car speeding toward his office.

He kept a variety of injectable controlled drugs in a locked office cabinet, medications he occasionally administered during minor surgery. Most often, he used Valium and Demerol, although what he now wanted was ketamine, an injectable anesthetic popular for illegal snorting. He rarely used ketamine because of its long duration and tendency to produce hallucinations.

Reaching his office, he let himself in and unlocked the medicine cabinet. The vial of ketamine had an expiration date of two months previously, but he thought it would still be potent. Using a separate hypodermic syringe, he filled the barrel of each dart with four ccs of the drug, then capped the needles. He found an old doctor's bag he hadn't used in years and carefully stacked the darts on the bottom. Almost as an afterthought, he packed some Brevital, sterile saline, and a few other drugs.

He suddenly felt foolish. What he needed was a real gun, not one of these toys. He wasn't even sure his equipment would function. Moreover, ketamine worked best when given intravenously; the air rifle was intended for intramuscular administration. Nor did he have any idea how long the drug would take to work. His arsenal was decidedly meager, but it was the best he could muster.

Preparation had been the easy part. The hard part began now, when he had nothing to do but wait.

CHAPTER NINETEEN

In emergencies, Simon Crandall had an "as needed" arrangement with the city police and medical examiner's office. Although he was never officially on call during off hours, it was expected that he would respond to a crime scene when requested, circumstances permitting. Since it was understood that his presence would be requested only when absolutely necessary, when the two A.M. phone call came from Detective Riley, Crandall agreed to come to the shop on the Lower East Side.

He arrived somewhat bleary-eyed twenty minutes later. Riley greeted him with a cup of coffee.

"Thanks for coming down, Dr. Crandall. Glad I didn't pull you away from anything important."

"She'll be waiting when I get back, Detective," said Crandall, sipping his coffee. He looked around the empty shop. "Where's the body?"

"See that?" Riley said, pointing to a hole in the wall beyond a display case. "Nine-millimeter hollowpoint. Remington's hundred-fifteen grain plus-P-plus round goes at thirteen hundred feet per second. Follow me." He led Crandall on a path that matched the course of the bullet, into a back room, past a rear wall, and into a darkened alley beyond. He opened the back door and shined his flashlight's beam on a dark shape.

Crandall stepped forward and looked down. A disheveled-looking man was slumped against a brick wall. Eyes closed, he still clutched a half-pint of Georgi vodka. A neat hole had been punched in his right ear.

"Tough break," said Crandall. "Talk about being in the wrong place. At least it looks like he died happy. But he's not why you called me, right?"

"No, he's the justification. But the *reason* is this way."

Riley led Crandall back inside and turned on the light. The area was primarily a showroom, and its walls were lined with cheap metal shelves filled with boxes of bones, and, occasionally, a complete skeleton.

"Cheap stuff," Crandall said after a quick look around. "He couldn't expect to make a bundle off these."

"The business was just getting started," said Riley, heading back into the front room. He pointed toward the small skeleton and broken box. "What do you make of this?"

Simon knelt beside the debris and lifted out a card which said, "Nakoda Sioux, ca. 1874." Then he removed a hand lens and examined several bones. "Now, this is quality. Definitely a higher grade. Looks old enough, but I'd have to show it to someone else to see if it's an Indian. What's it doing here?"

Riley described the intended sale and the bust gone awry. Simon listened intently.

"Did you run the guy through your computer?"

"Yeah," Riley replied, "but it's a dead end. He was on a narcotics probation a long time ago, but nothing recently. The Manhattan address on his license is a phony. One of my guys thinks the name's African, like from Kenya."

At that, Simon's ears perked up. Anything involving East Africans and small skeletons now interested him greatly. "You have that ID?"

Riley handed him the wallet, which had already been dusted for fingerprints. As Crandall opened it, a small slip of paper fell out. He snatched it up before it reached the floor. When he saw the name scrawled on the paper, his jaw dropped.

"Oh, *shit*," he said. "I *know* this guy!"

For Brad Hawkins, biding his time took a Herculean effort. All he could do was pace back and forth through the empty house, strung out on worry, agonizing over his son. Occasionally he stopped pacing long enough to stare at the phone, as if the force of his gaze could induce it to ring. But the phone remained silent. Finally, at three o'clock, he couldn't stand it any longer. He picked up his bag and left for Britten's house.

The problem was that he had no plan. He suspected that Britten was using the time to try charming Morgan; and, failing that, to woo her by threat, extortion, or whatever means necessary. Brad didn't doubt that Britten would fail, but that wasn't the issue. He had to do *something* to stop Britten and Morrison and save Mikey. But what? He couldn't just barge in, brandish the dart gun, and expect them to give up. He wouldn't be surprised if they had guns of their own, *real* guns.

How could this happen? his anguished mind demanded. Here he was, enjoying a comfortable little suburban practice, raising his son, when suddenly his life had become a nightmare. All he had ever wanted was to take care of his patients, watch his boy grow up, and maybe do a little sailing. Certainly that wasn't asking too much of life. Then, to his surprise and delight, he'd also become romantically involved. But just as suddenly, he was thrown into the midst of murder and kidnapping.

And all of this was related to managed care, in some perverse way. Despite his comments when he'd first met Morgan, he had no conceptual quarrel with HMOs. The problem was that the reality of the HMO system didn't live up to its dream. He supposed it was inevitable that managing care would ultimately take a back seat to managing finances. HMOs were a big business, but they were a business that had lost its luster as an answer to the nation's health care needs.

There had been a time when traditional third-party payers were semi-benevolent organizations that, while they strived to remain in the black, had the best interests of the patient at heart. Now, when HMOs were large public corporations, the bottom line meant everything. It wasn't so much that they wanted to make a profit as that they were profit-driven: if a method of treatment wasn't positively reflected in a quarterly statement, it was abandoned, and the patient be damned. This inherently bred excesses. In a system where dollars were chum, sharks like Britten and Morrison were circling in the water.

He was just about to turn into Britten's street when his beeper went off. Jesus, what an idiot he was! Why not have a brass band announce his arrival? He was sure the damn thing's chirping could be heard a football field away. Brad jabbed its button and glanced at the LED screen. He expected his answering service's number to appear in the small window, but instead, it showed a Manhattan area code. After a moment, he recognized the number as Crandall's.

Why in the world was Simon calling him at this hour? Brad quickly pulled over, switched off his lights, and dialed the number on his car phone.

"Simon? What's—"

"Hate to bother you, Bradford, but it's important."

"Simon, I'm up to my neck in trouble right now. What gives?"

Crandall heard the strain in his friend's voice. "Maybe first you'd better tell me what's happening over there."

Brad had a lot on his mind, and close as he was with Simon, he couldn't be bothered to . . . then he caught himself in mid-thought. Why should he be reluctant to confide his fears to a friend? Brad inhaled deeply and launched into his story.

When he was finished, he felt a little relieved. "You still there, Simon?" he asked.

"God almighty, you've got some serious troubles, my man. You call the cops yet?"

"No, and I'd rather not," said Brad, "at least for now. I think all these guys really want is my silence. If I can somehow convince them of that, I think they'll return my son."

"And Morgan?"

"I haven't figured that out yet," Brad said. "I'm worried as hell about her, but I think she'll be okay. Now, what gives with you?"

Crandall got right to the point. He'd just returned from a crime scene where something frightening had turned up. A piece of paper with Brad's name on it had fallen from an intruder's wallet. He relayed the cops' description of the man who'd escaped.

Brad felt his blood run cold. Simon might just as easily have been describing Nbele. "Nuru Milawe," he repeated to himself.

"So you know the guy? Who is he, and what's he want with you?"

"I can't say for sure, but my friend Nbele who was

murdered mentioned a cousin around here, and unless I miss my guess, it's this Nuru. What's his address?"

"It's a phony. Now don't do anything stupid, Bradford. Remember what I said about no coincidences? I'm starting to see how all this—the beetles, the mites, the dead man, the bones—are related. Want my advice? Let me bring the cops in on this, and . . . Bradford? Brad!"

But Brad had already hung up, smiling to himself. The very last thing he needed right now was to take the time to explain the situation to the police. The puzzle was slowly coming together. Now he knew why Morrison and Britten were so smug: *they* weren't holding Michael. Someone else was. And if Hawkins played his cards right, he'd find both that person and his son.

First he had to find Milawe's correct address. The county police might have him on record. There was the small, local East African community, whose members probably knew of one another. Then there were the NICU murders. The ease with which they'd been committed suggested someone familiar with the hospital.

Brad quickly called the university and asked for the night-shift administrator. After he explained what he wanted, the administrator said that he *did* know Mr. Milawe, but not well. Milawe worked days and some evenings as a service man in respiratory, and he had a reputation for being surly. "That'd be him," Brad said, his heart beating faster. Minutes later, the administrator pulled Milawe's address from the computer. Brad thanked him, hung a U, and sped toward the Expressway.

When Nuru got home, the boy was still asleep in the front room. Milawe decided to keep him that way because he had a lot to do. First, he lit the cauldron. Several refrigerated specimens needed rendering. He briefly toyed with the notion of getting some sleep himself, but neither his schedule nor his mental state would permit it.

His nerves were jangling. The near-arrest was still fresh in his mind, sending residual shots of adrenaline through his body. How close he'd come to being captured! He'd been at this business for years, but he'd never looked down a gun barrel before. It was only through an ingrained sixth sense, and a lot of luck, that he'd reacted as quickly as he had.

In the future, he'd have to be much more careful. The precautions he'd taken were obviously inadequate. Next time he'd be more certain of his contacts, especially the new buyers. He'd insist on neutral territory for the first buy. Perhaps more important, despite his mistrust of firearms, he might have to be armed.

The business with the wallet bothered him. It wasn't the three hundred dollars he'd lost, or the credit cards, all of which were stolen. Rather, it was the driver's license photo ID. Despite the phony address, the police now had a name to go with his picture. He doubted they'd locate him, but he'd have to take steps to ensure they wouldn't.

Frazzled, he desperately needed release. It was time for his usual reward—the succor, the relief, the oblivion, that only high-grade cannabis could provide. How he craved it! He needed to smoke the way other people needed food or water.

While the cauldron was heating, he went to check on the boy. He shook Michael's shoulder. The boy stirred, struggling briefly to open his eyes before once more falling limp. Nuru lifted one of his eyelids. The pupils were still dilated, though less than before. He'd have to repeat the dose of sedative within the hour. By now, with everything in place, it was time to relax. He slumped into his recliner.

As he filled his pipe with marijuana, he hesitated. One of the problems with this kind of gratification was its tendency to make him sleepy, and though his body craved rest, he didn't have time for it. Still, that was no reason to defer smoking.

For every narcotic problem, there was a pharmacological solution. At present, the answer lay in stimulants. Although he wasn't a big fan of uppers, they had a place in his current predicament. They would cut the effect of the marijuana, like diluting wine. But not caffeine or nicotine; they were too weak. And not methylphenidate or amphetamines, either. Rather, what he decided on was more natural—the unadulterated leaves of *erythroxolon coca*, the plant that produced cocaine.

Nuru took several leaves from a humidified bag, stuffed them into his mouth, and began to chew. The bitter-tasting cocaine and other alkaloids were quickly absorbed by his oral mucosa, their anesthetic effect numbing his throat and soft palate. It was time to light up before they sent his pulse soaring. Nuru struck a match and held the flame to the bowl, sucking deeply on the pipe stem. Within seconds, molecules of THC bound with the receptors in his brain.

The effect was immediate, and deeply soothing. Serotonin and endorphins flowed liberally through his brain stem. The drug's soft fingers gently caressed his soul, calming him, keeping his worries at bay. At the same time, the coca worked its magic on other cerebral sites. The overall effect was that of a tasty pharmacological stew in which stimulation was married to sedation. With an intoxicated sigh, Nuru inhaled great draughts of smoke. Leaning contentedly back in his recliner, he was alert, carefree, and stupid.

* * *

To convince Morgan of his incalculable worth as a life partner, Britten had made a video entitled, "The Economist: A Bachelor's Life and Times." While he fiddled with his VCR, Morgan quietly took stock of the house, searching for exits and possible escape routes. Not a passive person, she didn't relish the prospect of meekly cooperating with her captors. Yet outright defiance might jeopardize Michael, and so, for the time being, she decided to humor them.

The tape was professionally produced by a well-known documentary filmmaker. In the voice-over, the narrator described the collage of old snapshots arranged in chronological order: baby Hugh; Britten the dedicated student; Britten as award-winning professor. At the end of the hour-long presentation, Britten made a personal on-screen appeal to Morgan, speaking directly into the camera. His lengthy monologue was a rehash of everything he'd already told her—how they were suited for one another, how they'd make an ideal couple, and on, and on. He pranced before the camera with all the sincerity of a used car salesman. Morgan found it extraordinary that someone had actually paid a great deal of money to create such an egotistical testimonial.

The tape was only an affirmation of the profound depths of his delusion. Sadly, to Britten, the presentation was a perfectly reasonable way to win the heart of the woman he wanted. Measured, logical, and precise, the video was more business proposition than marriage proposal. But it was not without its dark side: threat and innuendo were an integral part of Britten's message. It left Morgan firmly convinced that Britten didn't need a wife as much as he needed medication and a long hospitalization.

During the video, Britten sat by her side, casually

drinking Sauternes while eating foie gras, as if munching on popcorn at a movie. But when the video was over and he turned on the lights, she saw that his smiling ebullience had returned.

"What do you think, my dear? We belong together, don't we?"

"Very, very impressive, Hugh," she said. "World-class video. It must have cost you a small fortune to make it."

"The money's not important. All that matters is whether you've been persuaded."

"You've given me a lot to think about," she said, trying to sound sincere. "You have qualities I never noticed before."

He actually blushed. "Thank you. I do my best. Now, if—"

"Hugh," Morrison interrupted, barging into the room, "come here a second."

"Do you mind?" Britten said, glaring. "I'd like a little privacy."

"This can't wait. I just got a call from one of our contacts in the NYPD. The name Nuru Milawe just turned up on the police computer."

"*What?*" Britten's smile vanished. "There's got to be a mistake. He's supposed to be at home with the boy!"

"Maybe he is now, but at one-thirty he was in the city trying to unload one of those ridiculous skeletons."

"Was there any mention of the boy? Did he get caught?"

Morrison shook his head. "He got away. Barely. And he was alone."

"I see," Britten said. "Then the fool may be home by now! As far as I know, the police have no idea where he lives. Or so he assured me."

"Then let's find that out."

' "Yes, of course." Britten turned to Morgan. "Excuse me for a moment, my dear? We have an important call to make."

It took Brad three quarters of an hour to find Nuru's back road, a remote, rutted lane. During the drive, he kept agonizing over Michael, whose face appeared unbidden in his thoughts. It was drizzling, and the road was unlit and forbidding. He parked a safe distance from Milawe's home and removed the air rifle and medical bag from the back seat. Taking pains to remain quiet, he gently closed the door. Then, bending into a crouch, he slowly jogged down the dark, muddy road.

The building was a low, ramshackle wooden structure, more like an old, abandoned barn than a home. There was a faint glow from somewhere within. Thinking of his son held captive inside strengthened his already-fierce determination. Squaring his shoulders, he pushed ahead, his face damp with rain.

Brad hoped to find Nuru alone. Given his adrenaline level, if things got physical, Brad knew he had an even chance of winning. Still, he couldn't forget how easily Nuru had apparently killed the physically fit Nbele.

Undaunted, Brad crept toward the building. There came a distant rumble of thunder. Twenty feet from the front door, he hid behind a stout tree trunk. His heart was racing, and he had to inhale deeply to catch his breath. He carefully studied the door and then scanned the windows. Overhead, he could make out a slender black cord dancing in the wind, a telephone wire.

He doubted he'd need a phone, but he didn't want Milawe to use one, either. He knelt on the wet earth and rummaged through his bag. Finding a disposable scalpel, he quickly removed the plastic blade guard, reached up, and neatly severed the phone line.

*   *   *

Britten leafed through his address book until he found the appropriate listing, then punched up the numbers on his phone. He listened carefully, hung up, and dialed again. There was a click-over, but no ring. A frown creased his forehead.

"That's odd. I can't get through."

"No answer?"

"No," said Britten, "it's not ringing. Let me try the operator."

After an abbreviated conversation, Britten hung up again. "She says there's a problem with the line, maybe from the storm."

"That doesn't help us much."

"We can't afford not to know. Come on, we're going out there."

"What about the girl?" Morrison asked.

"She's coming with us."

The thunder grew louder with the approach of the storm. Brad's mood was as dark and brooding as the sky. After several anxious minutes, he emerged from the shadows and stole to the side of the house, clutching the tranquilizer gun and doctor's bag.

His destination was a shuttered window twenty feet away. Brad thought he had detected a pale light beyond the window's glass. Hunkering down, he crept through the wet undergrowth. A sudden cold rain pelted his shoulders and quickly saturated his clothes. Behind him, the rising wind howled through the swaying trees like a wounded animal.

He reached the window and stopped, breathing heavily. With luck, the storm would hide the sound of his approach. The worn wooden shutters left a wide vertical gap in the middle of the window. Pressing himself against the rough wood, Brad inched his face toward the patch of uncovered glass.

It was hard to see through the rain-streaked pane, but Brad had the impression that he was looking into a large, almost empty room. He thought he detected the pungent odor of marijuana. A sudden, sharp gust sent wet leaves swirling, peppering his face with debris. He wiped his eyes and squinted through the glass.

The pale glow came from a small night-light across the room. Brad pawed at the glass, trying to wipe away rain streaks and condensation. A dark rectangular shape slowly came into focus, about ten feet away. Brad's heart stopped until he saw that it was the upright back of an easy chair. A faint wisp of smoke hovered above it. The recliner swiveled several inches to the left. A pipe-smoking head emerged from the shadows. Even in the dark, the sharp, angular features and strong neck were reminiscent of Nbele.

Brad's pulse quickened, and he hastily ducked down. Marijuana smoker or not, Milawe appeared every inch a formidable, powerful opponent. At least, Brad reassured himself, the element of surprise was his.

As the heavy rain continued to fall, Brad carefully unlocked the receiver of his tranquilizer rifle and canted it forward, exposing the barrel's throat. Removing the safety guard from one of his darts, he gingerly inserted it into the breech point-first, then closed the receiver. He quietly cycled the pump three times, generating enough air pressure to propel the dart at five hundred feet per second. Masked by the sounds of the storm, the pump action's noise was a muted clack. The rifle was ready to fire.

The approaching thunder boomed like artillery. Ever so slowly, Brad chanced another look past the shutters. The recliner had swiveled back to its original position, shielding Milawe from view. Brad now turned to the left, where the night-light's glow was stronger. In its pale luminescence, he could make out a small cot next to the wall. His eyes widened. Lying on the cot was his son, mouth bound with duct tape.

Michael was staring up at him.

Brad longed to scream out his son's name. But that would be insanity. He quickly jerked his head back, wondering if Michael recognized him. Given the storm's conditions, the darkness was undoubtedly impenetrable. At least, Brad thought with relief, the boy was alive and appeared unharmed.

Even if Michael *had* recognized him, Brad doubted that his son would make any noise. Michael was too bright to tip his hand. But Brad realized he couldn't procrastinate any longer. Mikey was okay, but there was no telling how long that would last.

Yet what should he do? He could try entering through the front door, but it'd probably be locked. Still, if he could creep up unseen from the rear and hit Milawe on the head with the rifle butt . . .

Overhead, the storm raged fiercely. Brad's clothing was soaked through to the skin. A heavy, damp wind whistled through the trees, and waves of torrential rain danced along the rooftop. Resting the muzzle of his rifle against the windowsill, Brad put down his bag. As carefully as possible, he pushed up the window.

Michael had been awake for a few minutes, lying perfectly still with his eyes closed when the big man was near him. He'd seen firsthand what the man had done to Nbele, and he was terrified that it might happen to him. If he just played dead, the man might leave him alone.

Something tight and sticky held his lips closed. At least he could breathe okay. And then he smelled something—a strange, yet slightly familiar scent, something he had occasionally smelled on the playground when he was around big kids. Ever so slowly, Michael opened his eyes. The man was sitting in a chair nearby, lighting a pipe. Michael cautiously looked around the room, taking everything in. His gaze fixed on an object mounted on the wall beyond the man's chair. Concentrating, Michael could slowly make it out. When he did, his eyes went wide.

It was a skeleton, and one of its bony fingers was pointing right at him.

Michael's eyes widened in horror, and his heart started to pound furiously. He couldn't take his eyes off the skeleton's pitch-black eye sockets, which seemed to glare straight at him. The skeleton was about four feet tall, and it had been partially crucified. Its feet overlapped, and a thick spike had been driven through them, while another nailed the bones of its left hand to a rough wooden cross. But its right arm was free, and a thin forefinger seemed to point at him in unspoken accusation.

For several terrifying minutes, Michael couldn't take his eyes off it. Finally, however, when he convinced himself that it was dead, he looked away, toward the window.

Staring through the sheets of rain cascading down the glass, Michael saw the unmistakable outline of a man's head come into view. As he watched, it became a familiar silhouette, the features clearly recognizable, just as they had been countless times before, when it had hovered near his bedside.

It was the face of his father.

Then, just as suddenly as it had appeared, the face vanished. Michael didn't know what to do. Part of him wanted to jump up and run from his captor to his father.

But a little voice within cautioned him to stay where he was.

Michael momentarily closed his eyes. Was it all a dream? He listened to the powerful melody of the storm, the wind whistling through the rafters, the incessant pounding of rain, the booming crack of thunder. Seconds later, he re-opened his eyes. All he could see was the ever-downward swirling of rain. And then, suddenly, the outline reappeared.

Trembling with fear, Michael watched his father try to push the window up. It didn't budge, though it did make a strident sound. Then came an extremely bright flash of lightning, followed almost immediately by an ear-splitting boom of thunder. For a long moment, Michael could see his father's brilliantly backlit figure struggling with the window.

Nuru heard it, too. Despite the driving rain, he heard the unmistakable screech of wood on wood. Cocking his head to one side, he put down his pipe. As he listened, there came a brilliant burst of lightning, immediately followed by a thunderous roar that made him wince. Out of the corner of his eye, he detected movement. Turning, he spotted the boy's upraised head, staring at the window. Nuru followed his gaze.

Outside, Brad's ears rang from the thunder. He worked on the window with both hands, but it wouldn't give. The frame and the wood were obviously warped. He tried to see if it was stuck at one particular point, but the incessant rain washed down his forehead and into his eyes, nearly blinding him. He was worried about making too much noise, but he knew it was too late to turn back.

Brad spread his hands wide, onto the stoutest part of the frame, and pushed for all he was worth. At first, the window wouldn't move, but then there was the tiniest bit of play. Encouraged, he strained even harder, closing his eyes, growing red-faced, until—

The crashing of glass coincided with a razor-sharp stinging on his face. His face was peppered by needles of glass. And then came a sudden, vise-like pressure around his neck. He felt his body being lifted off the ground. In spite of the mounting pressure within his head, Brad managed to force his eyes open. He found himself looking into those of Nuru Milawe.

The window had two gaping, jagged holes through which Milawe had punched both fists. The powerful, intoxicated man had him around the neck and was strangling him with both hands. His dark face was contorted by rage, his lips drawn back in a silent snarl. Through blurring vision, Brad could see the whites of the man's eyes, laced with tiny red vessels.

Brad struggled, unable to breathe. Milawe's sinewy fingers had closed off his windpipe. He felt the first pang of oxygen deprivation as his brain began to scream for air. Brad's body danced like a marionette. Every so often, his shoe tips touched the ground as he bobbed up and down. With both his hands, Brad tried to pry away Milawe's fingers, but the man's grasp was incredibly strong.

Brad's vision was going fast, taking on a gun barrel look, central clarity with a darkening around the edges. Unexpectedly, he thought of Michael. There were so many things he wanted to say to his son, but there was no time. He could still see Milawe's malevolent face. Then the ringing started in his ears, caused by the cessation of blood flow through the carotid arteries. As he dangled there helplessly in the driving rain, darkness was descending on him.

Suddenly there was a blood-curdling scream. Through the pinpoints of his remaining vision, Brad saw

Milawe's profile and bared teeth. All at once, one of Milawe's hands released his neck, and Brad's shoes touched the moist earth. Tottering, he struggled to regain his balance. He still couldn't breathe. Even one-handed, Milawe's grip was unrelenting, and his thumb pressed painfully into the notch above Brad's sternum. Everything began to go black.

In desperation, Brad remembered the tranquilizer gun. Ignoring Milawe's crushing fingers, he quickly swept both hands downward. His fingers fumbled, and for a moment, he thought he'd knocked the gun over. And then, just as he was giving up hope, his fingers found the rifle's muzzle.

Brain screaming for oxygen, Brad yanked the rifle up by its barrel. He raised it hand-over-hand until his right fist closed around the pistol grip, and his left hand was on the stock. With the last vestiges of his strength, Brad rammed the muzzle through the glass toward Milawe's head. His leaden forefinger found the trigger, which he yanked without hesitation.

And then, as unexpectedly as it had appeared, the suffocating pressure was gone. Brad tumbled backward, nearly unconscious, falling heavily onto his shoulder. Through slitted eyelids, he looked up through the window, but his face was awash with rain, and his retinas were flashing with a thousand tiny dots of oxygen deprivation.

Then came another prolonged flash of lightning. The storm-riven skies turned blue-white, and for a brief moment, Milawe's stark image was illuminated. His expression was a curious mixture of anger and astonishment as he tried to pluck the dart from his neck. Then the sky went dark again, and thunder boomed.

Brad lay gasping for air. He breathed in hungrily, past burning throat and bruised larynx. For several seconds, until his thoughts and fears returned, he wasn't sure where he was. He forced himself up on his elbows as he tried to regain his senses. Milawe was still out there somewhere. He might be wounded, but that would make him an even greater threat. Brad thought of his son and was terror-stricken.

"Michael!" he screamed, but his weak and raspy voice was drowned out by the sounds of the storm. "Michael!"

Had he put Michael in greater danger? He'd forced Milawe's hand. The man was a vengeful killer. For all Brad knew, Nuru could at that very moment be attacking his son.

Insane with fear, Brad struggled to his knees and forced himself to his feet. He staggered ahead, yelling his son's name over and over, his shouts carried away by the howling wind. He clawed at the shattered window, mindless of the broken glass. Pushing against the sash, he strained in desperation.

"Dad!"

Brad looked up at the rain-washed glass, startled. At any minute, he imagined a revitalized Milawe suddenly looming up before him. The sight of his son standing there was completely unexpected. Overcome with emotion, he stood mutely gazing at Michael, his eyes filled with tears.

"I think I have to unlock it," Michael said calmly. He climbed up on something, worked the window latch, and looked down with a smile. "Okay!"

The torrential rain was starting to lessen. Still cautious, Brad looked past his son. "Mikey, are you okay? What happened to that man?"

"He's over there," Michael said, pointing to a spot on the floor. "You really knocked him out, Dad."

Knocked him out? thought Brad, bewildered. Could

the drug possibly work that fast? He pushed up the sash. "Watch out for the glass, Mikey. And don't turn your back on him!"

Unlocked, the window easily glided up. Brad brushed shards of glass off the sill and squeezed through the opening into the warm, dry room. Finally, he swiveled his lower torso around with a wriggle that landed him on his feet.

Milawe was lying on his back, eyes closed, unconscious and breathing deeply. Brad rushed to Michael and lifted him up, crushing him in an embrace of the most profound relief he'd ever felt.

"Thank God, thank God!" he said over and over, pressing his cheek to his son's. "I was so worried!"

"Dad, come on! You're all wet!"

With one final hug, Brad kissed the boy's cheek and put him down. "Did he hurt you, son? Did he do anything to you at all?"

"I'm okay. He made me drink something sweet when we got here. It made me real sleepy, but that's all." He looked at his father's face. "You've got a lot of little cuts. Do they hurt?"

Brad hadn't even been aware of them. "Not really." Then he hunkered down to his son's level and lovingly caressed the boy's face. "Here's what I want you to do, Mikey. Go out the front door," he said, pointing, "and go to the window. There should be a gun and a doctor's bag out there. Bring them both in, okay?"

"A gun?"

"An old air rifle. Now get going." He gave the boy a pat on the rear, and Mikey scampered away. Brad watched him disappear, indescribably relieved that his son was safe.

With another look at the unmoving Milawe, Brad hunted around until he found some paper towels. He dried his face, dabbing at the blood. The tiny cuts had almost stopped bleeding. He looked around and noticed that a second room lay beyond the first. Switching on the light, Brad entered it.

The room was filled with preserved skeletons and wall-mounted stainless steel shelves. At one end sat an enormous black iron kettle, filled with simmering water. Brad paused for a moment, puzzled. Then he closed the door and returned to the man he'd shot.

He found the bloodstained dart on the floor. The projectile had done its job: the plunger was depressed, and the drug was gone. Kneeling by Milawe, Brad immediately saw why the man was unconscious. By sheer luck, the dart had found a vein under the triangle of skin overlying the vessels in the neck. It appeared that the ketamine had gone directly into the internal jugular vein. The drug would have reached Milawe's brain in fifteen seconds, soon rendering him unconscious.

Suddenly the door opened and Michael ran in, clutching the bag and the rifle. "Is this the stuff, Dad?"

"That's it," Brad replied. "Just put it on the floor. When did you wake up?"

"Right after he started smoking pot, and—"

"What do you know about smoking pot, buster?"

"Dad, come on! I smell it every day in school."

"God almighty," his father said, shaking his head. "Go on."

"There was this tape on my mouth, but my hands were tied real loose, you know? When I opened my eyes, he was just sitting there and smoking. I'm sure he didn't see me. Then I saw you at the window."

"I wasn't sure you knew it was me."

"I didn't, until the lightning," said Michael. "But then, I saw him get up. I knew you couldn't see him. I wanted to warn you, but . . ." Michael's voice quivered, and he began to cry. "I'm sorry, Dad."

"Hey, hey! I was scared, too." Brad pulled the boy close. "And now we're both okay, right?"

Michael sniffled and nodded. "I guess. But when he went at you, I got so mad I bit him in the leg."

"You *bit* him?"

"Yeah. It was all I could think of. I got him real good."

An amazed and grateful smile crept over Brad's face. Now he knew why Milawe had screamed and released his death grip. Michael's anger had undoubtedly saved his father's life.

As Brad looked at Milawe, an idea occurred to him. Over the past few weeks, he and Morgan had come up with many unanswered questions. Milawe was the perfect person to answer them. The most likely instrument of Britten's malicious plans, the man undoubtedly knew exactly what had happened at the hospital. After checking Milawe's pulse and pupils, Brad opened his bag.

"What're you going to do, Dad?"

"There's this drug called Brevital." The boy looked puzzled. "Ever hear of truth serum?" he asked.

Mikey shook his head.

"Truth serum can make people talk. If you give a lot, it'll put them to sleep, but if you give just the right amount, they'll answer any question you want."

"Cool. What're you going to ask him?"

"I'm working on that." Brad removed a multi-dose, two-point-five-gram vial of Brevital powder. Normally, the drug was dissolved and then transferred to a larger volume of diluent, usually two hundred fifty ccs. Then the person administering it would slowly inject ten ccs, equivalent to one hundred milligrams of Brevital. But the only diluent Brad had was fifty ccs of sterile water, which would make the drug five times more concentrated than normal. He'd have to inject carefully. If he administered too much or gave it too quickly, Milawe would not only remain asleep, but might stop breathing altogether.

Brad carefully dissolved the powder, diluted it, and filled a ten-cc syringe. Then he paused. Any excess ketamine would have to wear off before he could give the Brevital, and he didn't know how long that would take. His best guess was about an hour, an hour he couldn't spare. Once more he rummaged through his bag.

Brad wished he'd kept up with pharmacology, but right now all he could do was guess. He removed several ampoules and vials and aspirated their contents into a five-cc syringe. When he finished, he had a powerful mixture of Mazicon, ephedrine, and Narcan. He had no idea of the proper doses, or even if the drugs would work.

Michael watched his father wrap a tourniquet around Milawe's biceps. "Can I ask him something, too?"

"What do you have in mind, champ?"

"I want to know why he hurt Nbele."

"I'd like to know that, too," Brad said, feeling his anger return. "But first I have to make him a little more alert."

Michael stepped back, frightened. "Don't wake him up, Dad!"

"Don't worry, he's not going anywhere."

Brad slapped the skin in Milawe's forearm, making the blood vessels distend. He found a prominent vein in the crook of the elbow and started an IV with a butterfly infusion set. Attaching his five-cc syringe, he began injecting very slowly. Every so often he pinched Milawe's skin or slapped him on the cheek. After about three minutes, Milawe began to stir. Brad checked the pulse, which was bounding, and Milawe's pupils, which were starting to constrict. Then, before Milawe could wake up, Brad changed syringes, attaching the Brevital to the butterfly's port.

He began injecting cautiously. Under the effects of the stimulants, Milawe was on the verge of coming around. His lids fluttered open, and his eyes twitched horizontally. His head was starting to turn Brad's way when the Brevital hit. There was the briefest spark of recognition before his eyes dulled again, fixing on nothing. Brad stopped injecting.

"Time to wake up," Brad said, slapping Milawe's cheek. "It's question time."

The man grunted.

Michael kept his distance. "I'm scared, Dad."

"I know, Mikey. But he's not going to get up, believe me. I just want him to come around a little."

By correctly juggling the dose, he could keep his patient in a nether state of consciousness, a twilight corridor between wakefulness and sleep. He watched Milawe's expression closely. In some respects, Brevital was like alcohol. By loosening inhibitions, it also loosened tongues. A euphoric smile usually meant the drug was starting to work. Gradually, some tone returned to the big man's facial muscles, followed by the smile. It was time.

"Can you hear me, Mr. Milawe?"

It took a considerable effort, but his lips finally pursed. "Fuck . . ."

"That's more like it. Now I'm going to ask you some questions, okay?"

"Questions," Milawe slurred.

"What is your name?"

It seemed to require exertion, as if his brain's circuits

were slow to process the inquiry. "Nuru Milawe," he finally managed.

"There you go. Next question. Why did you bring Michael Hawkins here?"

In slow, halting increments, Milawe answered everything he was asked. Brad had to space his injections carefully, adding more Brevital when necessary, withholding it when the man drifted off. The more Milawe revealed, the more furious Brad became. It took all of his will power to resist the temptation to administer a fatal dose of the drug.

Bringing Michael there, Nuru explained, was his own idea. The rest was Britten's doing.

"Just how did you come to know Dr. Britten?"

"Bones," Nuru said. "Britten . . . a collector."

"And it was his idea to kill the babies?"

"Yes," Nuru slurred. "I told him about mites . . . He knew I worked in respiratory. The babies . . . he said they were too expensive."

Nuru's head rolled, and his lids began to lift. Brad cautiously injected more medication. "You do everything he wants, is that it? Why?"

"Good money," Nuru managed. "Also took care of Schubert."

Brad was stunned. "Schubert? You mean Schubert was murdered?"

Nuru grinned and nodded.

"But why did you have to kill your cousin?" Brad asked.

A semi-conscious smile curled Nuru's lips. "Deserved it."

"What about my boy here? How long were you planning to keep him prisoner?"

"Indefinitely . . ."

When he heard that, Michael began crying. Brad

reached out and reassuringly squeezed his hand. He was appalled by the monstrousness of Britten's plan. Milawe was only a well-paid gofer, an admitted murderer with few scruples, but Britten . . . The extent of the conspiracy was mind-boggling.

When he had all the answers, Brad drew his son toward him, wrapping Michael tightly in the warmth and protection of his arms.

"Take these."

Morgan eyed the two green capsules Morrison held out. "What for?"

"Because we don't need your damn interference," he said. "You've gotten in the way too many times. If you've got to come with us, you'll do it on my terms!"

"What are those pills?"

"Something that'll keep you out of our hair for a while." He handed her the medications and poured several ounces of scotch for her to wash them down with.

She'd had quite enough of meekly following their instructions. Once she took the pills, she'd be out of the contest. With a furtive glance toward the door to make sure Britten wasn't lurking, Morgan accepted the glass of whiskey. But no sooner had her fingers closed around it than she tossed its contents in Morrison's face and whirled, heading for the exit.

Morrison had anticipated her defiance. He averted his head, avoiding most of the dousing, and stuck out his foot. Morgan tripped and fell heavily to the floor. With casual dignity, Morrison retrieved the glass and poured another healthy dose of liquor. Then, with a condescending smile, he pulled Morgan to her feet and held out the glass and pills once more.

Smarting over her own clumsiness, Morgan reluctantly accepted the pills. She looked at the capsules closely, rolling them over in her palm. She recognized them as a brand of ethchlorvynol, a powerful hypnotic. Popular with the college crowd, it had been abandoned by most physicians due to its toxicity. Two seven-hundred-fifty-milligram capsules, consumed with alcohol, were a drug cocktail strong enough to knock her out for hours.

Glowering defiantly at Morrison, she took the scotch in one hand and chucked the capsules in her mouth. Deftly Morgan maneuvered the pills into the pouch beside her upper molars. She took a swallow of the whiskey, coughed, and then finished it off, handing Morrison the empty glass.

"Delicious."

Morrison was staring at her. "You wouldn't be trying to pull a fast one, would you?"

"You must think I'm an idiot."

"Open your mouth," he said. "Lift up your tongue."

Morgan complied. "Satisfied?" She shot him a frosty look and quickly moved away before he got other ideas.

"All right, get going." He pushed her roughly in the back.

Morgan marched into the other room, where Britten held out his hand. "Ready, my dear? Daniel gave you something to relax?"

"Relax?" she said. "Those two pills could knock out a horse."

"I'm sure you could use the rest. Come," he said, leading the way. "We'll take my car."

Outside, it was drizzling. Morgan got in the Infiniti's back seat while her captors sat in the front. On an empty stomach, it would ordinarily take about fifteen minutes for the capsules to dissolve and enter her bloodstream. She could already feel the sliminess of the melting gelatin. When she was sure both men were watching the road, Morgan spat the sticky capsules into her palm.

Soon they were on the rain-slickened highway. The car's wipers made a soft *thunk*, and the tires made a slushy hum. Morgan watched the minutes tick by on the lighted dashboard clock. When she thought the drug should be starting to affect her, she yawned loudly. Britten looked at her in the rear-view mirror.

"Tired, Morgana?"

"Tired, hell," she slurred. "I'm gettin' stoned."

"Then you might as well get some sleep. Go ahead, lie down. We'll wake you when it's over."

That was precisely what she wanted to hear. With a sigh, Morgan collapsed theatrically onto her side and yawned again. In her head, she counted off the seconds. When another three minutes had gone by, she started snoring loudly.

As she lay there with her eyes closed, Morgan listened to the sounds around her. Outside, the waning storm punctuated its retreat with a crescendo of thunder. The tires continued their highway song, occasionally interrupted by the bump-de-bump of a concrete spacer. She felt a slight glow from the scotch. It calmed her, soothing her frazzled nerves. Inside her head, her mind was racing.

Whatever hope she had lay in the element of surprise. Once they reached wherever they were going, she presumed they'd leave her in the car, although there was always the possibility they'd try to wake her and drag her along. If not, she'd follow them. If she managed to sneak up on them, she might be of some use.

Morgan continued her resounding snoring. She estimated that another half hour had elapsed before the car started to slow. It left the highway and drove along winding back roads. Through slitted lids, she noticed that Britten had extinguished the headlights. Finally, the car drew to a stop, and he turned off the engine.

"Son of a bitch," she heard Morrison say. "Whose car is that?"

"If I'm not mistaken," Britten said, "it belongs to our friend Dr. Hawkins."

"Christ! Didn't you say no one knew about this place?"

"It looks like I was wrong," Britten calmly continued. "But that's neither here nor there. It appears Hawkins is inside."

"How'd he find out his kid's here?"

"Maybe he didn't," Britten said. "But if he did, that's his problem. He has no idea what he's up against in Mr. Milawe. Come on, let's go."

"And the girl?"

Morgan heard clothing rustle as Britten turned around. Mouth open, she continued her slow, deep breathing.

"She's out of it."

Morgan held her breath and heard the unmistakable metallic *snick* of a magazine being snapped into a pistol, followed by the racking of the slide to chamber a round. Then both car doors were opened and closed with a muffled *thunk*. Morgan thought she detected the soft sound of receding footsteps; but with the car windows shut, it was hard to tell.

After several more minutes, Morgan slowly dared to raise her head and peer out the window. The car was parked in a dense, dark woods, and in the distance, she could see the outline of a ramshackle barn. She thought she detected a flicker of movement in that direction, but it disappeared almost immediately. Her pulse quickened when she spotted Brad's car. Morgan carefully slipped out of the back seat and quietly closed the door.

*　　*　　*

Brad finally got Michael to stop crying. He had no further questions for Nuru Milawe. It was time for the police to begin their interrogation. He was about to reach for the phone when he remembered he'd cut the wires, an act that in retrospect seemed foolish. Fortunately, the county police headquarters wasn't far away. They could drive there in fifteen minutes.

But he didn't want to leave Milawe unguarded. Once more, Brad rummaged through his bag. He quickly popped open ampoules of Fentanyl and diazepam and aspirated the contents into a fresh syringe. He injected both drugs, followed by a large dose of Brevital. Between the barbiturate, sedative, and narcotic, the man should sleep for as long as it took the police to send a car around. Satisfied, he closed his bag and lifted the tranquilizer rifle by its barrel. "Let's get out of here, Mikey."

A voice boomed out from across the room. "Where're you going, gentlemen?"

Brad froze. Daniel Morrison had appeared out of nowhere and was approaching, gun in hand. Britten stood in the doorway behind him. Adrenaline surged through Brad's veins, and he felt a mounting rage. Without thinking, he hurled the rifle at Morrison.

Morrison saw the rifle coming toward his face. He tried averting his head, but it was too late. The wooden stock smashed heavily into his forehead. In an uncontrollable reflex action, his finger tightened on the trigger of his own weapon. The gun roared.

In a microsecond, the hollowpoint bullet whizzed downward through the air, striking Milawe's jaw. Hitting bone, the bullet shed its copper jacket and broke into pieces that deflected upward into the man's brain. The largest fragment severed the middle cerebral artery before lodging inside the temporal bone.

"Run, Mikey!" Brad shouted. But Michael was terrified. Wide-eyed and open-mouthed, he remained rooted in place.

"Get him!" yelled Britten.

Morrison quickly regained his senses. When his vision cleared, he spotted Brad racing through an interior doorway. Without aiming, Morrison raised the gun and fired. The pistol bucked ferociously in his hand, booming twice more. The bullets smashed through the doorframe, sending splinters into the air. But Brad was gone.

"Go after him!" shouted Britten. He grabbed Michael's arm. "I've got the kid!"

Brad was frantic. He looked around in panic. His gaze finally fixed on another door at the back of the room. He ran toward it, desperate to escape. As he dashed past the boiling cauldron, he brushed against its cast-iron rim, burning his arm. Gritting his teeth, he lunged for the doorknob. It was locked. He leaned back, then rocked forward with all his might, smashing his shoulder into the weathered wood. The door gave way with a loud crack. Brad leapt out into the night.

His shoes sloshed through rain-splattered leaves, squishing in the mud. Beyond him lay the forbidding expanse of woods. For a fraction of a second, he was torn. Every fiber of his being told him to stay near Michael, yet he knew that to remain there meant certain death. He had to escape and find help. The woods were his sanctuary; and though his thoughts never left his son, Brad half-slid, half-ran toward the trees' shadowy embrace. Looking back over his shoulder at the house, he saw Morrison's silhouette outlined in the doorway.

"Hawkins, you forgot your kid!" Morrison shouted. "I have a feeling Britten can do some kinky things with little boys, Doc. Don't make me come after you!"

Brad dashed through the leading edge of trees, torn

by Morrison's words. Low-hanging boughs stung his face as he ran. Soon the woods enveloped him like an inky shroud. Finally he slowed, breathing heavily. He could hear Morrison heading his way. Without hesitation, Brad plunged headlong into the oppressive darkness.

CHAPTER TWENTY

Morgan was startled by the sound of gunshots. She stopped momentarily, then ran for the cover of a tree. Heart pounding, she paused to catch her breath. She was sure Brad was in the farmhouse, and maybe Michael, too. If only she had a weapon. Summoning up her courage, she tiptoed toward the house.

Around her, the wind had picked up again, a whistling siren in the treetops. Branches whipsawed and droplets splattered her head and shoulders. Keeping to a crouch, Morgan stole to the nearest window, only to find the panes completely shattered. Hearing a whimpering, Morgan cautiously peered over the windowsill.

On the other side of the dimly lit room, Britten was forcing Michael down on a cot and binding his hands with tape. The whimpering sounds came from Michael, whose tear-streaked face tugged at her heartstrings. Britten's face was livid. When he suddenly turned in her direction, Morgan quickly ducked down.

She didn't think he'd seen her. Keeping to a crouch, Morgan inched along the wall. At the corner, she peered around but saw only blackness. Taking another deep breath, she crept forward, trying to find a way to get into the house without being discovered.

*   *   *

A hundred yards away, Brad stumbled through the woods. Flayed by the branches, his skin was bleeding. His night vision was starting to kick in, and he could make out a small clearing nearby. If he could somehow creep up behind Morrison, he just might be able to take the gun. Then, with luck, he might be able to rescue Michael.

Suddenly, he stopped, his nostrils filling with a stench like death. A warm, moisture-laden breeze over the bog intensified the smell of decaying flesh. It was the pungent odor of a hospital morgue, only a thousand times worse. Brad's nose wrinkled, and he recoiled in disgust.

With his next step, the ground underfoot turned mushy, and his shoes sank into the muck. The mire pulled at his feet. The odor grew even stronger. Brad wrenched his body violently sideways in an effort to free his feet. His shoes came loose with a coarse sucking sound, and he staggered forward, but the footing became even more precarious. In an instant, Brad was up to his knees in the muck and sinking fast.

He felt a surge of panic. Brad struggled violently, trying to find a foothold. But the swamp seemed bottomless. He was sinking ever deeper into the swill, first to his hips, then to his waist. The overpowering, fetid smell surrounded him. Frantic, he flailed his arms, desperately seeking something to grab on to.

He felt the grim approach of death as it pulled him relentlessly into the putrid slime. But Brad wasn't tempted to give up. Thoughts of Michael and Morgan flashed brightly through his mind, giving him strength. Energized once more, he lunged forward.

The quagmire seemed determined to claim him. The muck quickly rose to his neck and sloshed around his ears. Brad tilted his head back, chin stretched skyward, frantically trying to keep above water. His churning arms and legs pumped rapidly. But his body wasn't buoyant enough, and it felt as if he were dog-paddling in molasses.

In the black and fetid night, he found himself gasping for oxygen. As he inhaled the stinking air, little waves of filth sloshed past his lips. Solid bits of what seemed like rancid flesh swirled into his mouth. Brad coughed and spluttered, spitting out the nauseating hunks of decay.

But he still wouldn't give up, and he fought to keep his head above water. With one last, frenzied lurch, he launched himself upward, arms outstretched. Incredibly, his fingers touched something solid. Brad precariously grasped the tree root with a dying man's desperation and hurriedly pulled himself toward it with both hands.

Pulling himself hand over fist, lungs heaving from the strain, Brad managed to keep his head out of the filth, and soon the receding water reached only to his knees. He was glad to be alive. He still had a chance to save himself and his son.

He looked out into the night, scouring the darkness. Suddenly, he was blinded by a dazzlingly bright light. He averted his eyes in pain.

"Taking a little swim, Dr. Hawkins?"

Brad immediately understood that the noise of his watery struggle had drawn his stalker right to him.

"What a stinking mess," Morrison said. "Seems you're up to your neck in this rancid filth."

"You can still get out of this," Brad said defiantly, "unless you're determined to keep acting like an idiot."

Morrison cautiously stooped and put the gun to Brad's head. "You know, I wouldn't mind blowing your brains out. Or I could let you drown in this shit. Same difference. But I'm a man of my word, and I've got to keep my boy Hugh happy. So haul your ass out of that slop!"

Brad didn't see that he had any choice. He'd be of no use to his son as a floating corpse. Morrison switched off the flashlight and backed away. Ever so slowly, Brad pulled himself along the root until he'd dragged himself up and out of the swamp. He lay on the marshy bank, breathless and shivering.

"Jesus, you stink," Morrison said. "Now get up. Walk back to the house, and don't try anything stupid."

Heart pumping, mind racing, Brad rose dejectedly to his feet. All that his desperate escape had succeeded in doing was nearly getting himself drowned. Exhausted and breathless, he plodded heavily back to the farmhouse, dreading to discover what Britten might be doing to Michael.

Morrison followed at a safe distance, staying alert, realizing that Hawkins was desperate and unpredictable. He wouldn't be surprised if the doctor tried to make a run for it, or even attack him. Either way, his finger was ready on the trigger.

Up ahead, the door to Milawe's workroom remained open, and the light inside beckoned. The boiling cauldron made the air in the room warm and humid, and a steamy vapor wafted out the door. Brad hesitated at the doorstep, but Morrison pushed him firmly in the back.

From where she was hidden, a short distance away, Morgan watched, her heart in her mouth. She'd heard Morrison shout at Brad minutes before and then disappear into the dark, forbidding woods. Morgan decided to stay where she was until she could figure out what was happening. But then she saw Brad being marched back to the farmhouse, a look of defeat on his face. Morgan bit her lip, knowing that she had to act.

A thin sliver of light streamed out around the doorframe. Suddenly, a ploy occurred to Morgan. Summoning her courage, she marched up to the door and rapped firmly.

Inside, Morrison tightened his grip on the pistol. "What the hell . . . ?" For a moment he thought Britten might have slipped outside with the boy. He carefully approached the door, gun poised. "Who is it?"

"Lemme in!" Morgan pleaded, slurring her words. "I gotta pee!"

"Morgan!" Brad shouted.

Morrison turned the gun on him. "Don't even think about it." Then he slowly cracked the door open. "When the hell did you wake up?"

Morgan tried for an award-winning performance of drunkenness. "C'mon, I gotta go!"

Morrison's arm shot out. He grabbed her roughly by the shoulder and yanked her inside the doorway. "Get your butt in here!"

Standing before the bubbling cauldron, Brad gaped in astonishment as an apparently stoned Morgan stumbled forward. Morrison pushed her toward him, and Brad caught her in his arms. "Take it easy, for God's sake!" he cried.

Morgan tried to pull away. "My bladder's gonna burst," she slurred. "Lemme go!" Before Brad could react, she slipped out of his embrace and tottered ahead, brushing past Morrison.

"Morgan, don't!" Brad pleaded.

"Where'sa damn toilet?"

"Stupid bitch!" Morrison bellowed, elbowing her mercilessly in the back, catching her in the kidneys.

A bolt of pain shot through Morgan's chest, and she went sprawling to the floor. She lay there in agony, gasping for breath. Yet despite her misery, she realized that she was precisely where she wanted to be: behind Morrison.

At the sight of Morgan being struck, Brad grew enraged. Every ounce of common sense told him not to attack an armed man, but emotion overruled judgment. He raised his arms and leapt at Morrison, going for the throat. But Morrison was ready. With a vicious backhand swipe, he swung his gun hand toward Brad.

The heavy barrel caught Brad in the temple. He winced and bent over, reaching for his head with both hands. But he refused to stop. Even before his head cleared, he rushed at Morrison, trying to tackle him at the waist. But Morrison remained wary, and just before Brad reached him, he brought his knee up sharply, smashing Brad in the chin.

In the next room, Britten knelt by Milawe's side, watching the man's life seep out through a hole in his grotesquely shattered jaw. The African's eyes were glazed, and his lips slowly, silently pursed.

When he heard unexpected voices in the other room, followed by muffled thumps, Britten warily rose. Damn that Morrison! He was far less useful than Milawe, and now the moron had bungled again.

Brad lay on the floor, knocked nearly unconscious. His vision had constricted into little points of light, and his ears were ringing mercilessly. He struggled to right himself but could only rock unsteadily to his hands and knees. He felt blood trickling down his cheek. With Morrison looming over him, Brad shook his head, trying to clear the cobwebs.

"God, you're pathetic," said Morrison. He pointed the gun at Brad's head and snicked off the safety. "But I'll say this for you, you're persistent. I don't think Hugh will mind if I end this right now."

While Morgan had been lying on the floor struggling

for breath, she was surveying the room. Behind Morrison stood an enormous iron kettle. When Morrison's knee downed Brad, Morgan looked around frantically for a weapon. When she saw Morrison level the gun, she couldn't wait any longer. With a high-pitched snarl, she came out of her crouch, springing at Morrison like a sprinter coming out of the blocks.

Hearing her, Morrison whirled around, mouth agape. The streaking blur was nearly upon him. At the last minute he turned his gun toward her, but it was too late. Morgan's head smashed powerfully into his midsection.

The gun was jarred from his hand and sailed across the room. Morrison tumbled backward until his hips collided with the cauldron's rim. Its edge became a fulcrum, and Morrison pivoted head over heels, plunging into the furiously boiling water.

Suddenly there came an unimaginably blood-curdling scream, a horrible wail of pain and anguish. Brad and Morgan got up as quickly as their trembling legs would allow.

As Morrison's head slipped below the bubbling surface, a terrified, choking sound arose. His right arm momentarily remained above water, its fingers wide and quivering, the skin red and blistered. Then it, too, sank beneath the churning bubbles.

"My God, get him!" Morgan screamed. She frantically looked around for some way to save him. Spotting a shock of his hair floating just under the surface, she started to reach for it, but Brad grabbed her wrist.

"Forget it, Morgan," he said. "Didn't you see his skin? He's had it."

A voice spoke up behind them. "Oh, this is priceless."

Caught unawares, Brad and Morgan quickly turned around. Morrison's gun had landed near the door, and

Britten now casually picked it up and pointed it at them. He peered disgustedly into the cauldron.

" 'Had it' is a bit of an understatement," Britten said. "But he *was* becoming a little overbearing. Now you've solved that for me. Dear Morgana, aren't you the clever one! I take it you didn't swallow the pills?"

She simply glared at him.

"Ever resourceful," Britten continued. "Which is one of the reasons I still intend to share my life with you once this unpleasantness is over."

"What'd you do with Michael?" Brad snapped.

"He's safe, no thanks to you. A little tied up at the moment. Look, Morgana," he went on, "let's try to put this experience behind us, okay? I'm really very reasonable, you know. It's time we both thought of the future."

Morgan hesitated. She detested the deranged man with every fiber of her being. His obsession with her was textbook, but it was the kind of mental instability that made someone unpredictable, and that unpredictability worried her. She wasn't afraid for herself, but given his callous reaction toward his partner's death, she was terrified that he might harm Brad or Michael. "That sounds like a good idea, Hugh."

Brad gawked at her. "Morgan, you *can't* be serious! He's a lunatic!"

She shot him a warning look.

"Lunatic, you say?" Britten said, barely missing a beat. "Maybe you're right. Not that your opinions will be much use to you in the future." He took the roll of duct tape from his pocket and tossed it to Morgan. "Tie up the good doctor. Arms behind him, please."

"After that, we're leaving?" she asked.

"Oh, indeed. Just you and me. Everyone else remains here, including poor Mr. Milawe. Remarkable man, a pity about him. He'll be hard to replace, but the work must go on."

"You're one sick bastard," Brad said.

Britten raised the gun. "You're rapidly trying my patience, Doctor. I may not know much about firearms, but I'm sure I can pull the trigger."

His tone carried enough of a threat for Morgan to start tearing the tape. She was impatient to get out of there and leave everyone safely behind. She ripped off several long strips and waited for Brad to put his hands behind his back. Reluctantly, he did. She circled his wrists with several coils of tape, not loose, but not really tight.

There was an old wooden straight-backed chair against the wall. Britten dragged it to the center of the room and beckoned Brad toward it with the gun barrel. Brad took a seat, lips pressed into a defiant line.

"That's a good boy," said Britten. "Tie him to the chair, my dear. At least three times around the chest."

When she was finished, Britten took the tape and removed a pair of handcuffs from his pocket. "Your turn, Morgana. Turn around. Esteem you though I might, I can't say I fully trust you yet."

Morgan felt a shiver of fear. Suddenly everything was going all wrong. Her hopes of resisting depended on remaining free. Her eyes flitted nervously around the room. In the bubbling cauldron, Morrison's body had floated to the surface. His horribly blistered skin had begun to separate from the underlying flesh, and the room was filled with the stench of burned hair. With a mounting sense of hopelessness, she placed her hands behind her back.

"You said Brad and Michael stay here, right?" she said as the handcuffs clicked in place. "When we leave, do I have your word they won't be harmed?"

That brought a chuckle from Britten. "Be honest: I never promised anything about their physical condition, did I?"

Morgan nervously turned around. "What are you saying?"

"What I'm saying," Britten nonchalantly continued, "is that this house is a tinderbox. I warned Nuru about that many times, but he was a stubborn man. Unfortunately, accidents have been known to happen." Smoothly he took out a can of lighter fluid from his pocket. Removing its plastic tip, he began squirting it on the wood walls.

Morgan jumped back, aghast. "No!"

Britten ignored her. He took out a lighter, worked the flint, and tossed it toward the base of the wall. The fluid ignited with an audible *whoosh*, and tongues of flame licked upward. Britten grabbed Morgan and pushed her toward the door.

Morgan's emotions quickly went from incredulity to rage. She'd never thought Britten capable of committing cold-blooded murder himself. Incensed, she tore out of his grasp and kicked him in the shin.

Britten screamed in pain. "You bitch!" He avoided her next kick and tried to grab her by the hair.

Morgan dodged his lunge. She longed to rake his face with her nails, to scratch his eyes out. But handcuffed, the only weapons she had were her feet and her head. She recalled what she'd done to Morrison, and when Britten reached for her again, she sidestepped his grab and rocked forward, launching her head toward his. Her forehead struck the bridge of his nose with a sickening crunch.

The gun went off. The forty-caliber slug shot toward the stainless steel racks, striking the corner of the beetle box. The enamel end-plate shattered, and the awakened beetles streamed out in an instinctive search for food.

Britten staggered backward, moaning, his face in his hands. He gagged on the blood seeping past his fingers. He let his hands fall away, first looking threateningly at Morgan, then at his fingers, incredulous. His crimson palms were wet and sticky, and the blood gushed from his flattened nose. When he turned back to her again, his face was twisted with hate.

The flames were fast consuming the wall. The room quickly filled with acrid smoke, and the smell of gunpowder and burnt flesh. Morgan's head still throbbed from the blow, and her eyes watered. She looked uncertainly at Brad, and he at her. Time was running out.

"Now you've done it!" Britten snarled. "Here, I had such hopes for us. Goodbye, my dear."

Morgan's heart beat wildly. When she saw Britten take aim, she wrenched sideways just as he pulled the trigger. The gun roared, nearly deafening her. The blast seared her cheek, but the bullet sailed harmlessly past her face, striking the steel shelf supports.

Still tied to the chair, Brad leaped to his feet. Before Britten could take aim again, he lurched awkwardly toward him, clearing the intervening space in two strides. When Britten turned to face him, Brad lowered his shoulder like a linebacker, and rammed Britten's midsection, knocking him backward.

Britten reeled into the nearby wall, smashing into the shelf supports. The shelf above him was upended, and the black mass of beetles toppled over in an inky wave. They spilled by the hundreds over Britten's head and shoulders.

Unsophisticated creatures, the beetles reacted largely by reflex. Once set free, their immediate, ingrained response was to begin a quest for food. Now, as they scurried over Britten's face, a new and provocative scent reached them. Accustomed to eating carrion, the lure of fresh blood was provocative. It was tantalizing. It was irresistible.

Stimulated by the smell of blood, the beetles were stirred into a frenzy. They ran in all directions, and Britten's face was soon covered with them. He screamed as thousands of mouthparts bit into his flesh. He tried to swat the beetles away, but they were massed three and four deep.

The tiny creatures were insatiable. Foraging gluttonously toward the food's plentiful source, they scrambled into Britten's fractured nose, clogging his air passages. His shrieks turned to choking. He wheezed and spluttered, slowly sinking to his knees, gasping for breath as the beetles worked their way into his mouth and eyes. His face became a mask of beetles and blood.

Morgan couldn't watch. She turned away and was horrified to see that the room was fast turning into an inferno. She finally turned back to Brad, who'd been knocked over by the force of his collision. Still burdened by the chair, Brad struggled to regain his footing.

"Morgan, get the handcuff key from his pocket. Hurry!"

Hands still behind her back, Morgan crept toward Britten and sank to a sitting position. Her cuffed hands fumbled awkwardly. Managing to get one hand into the jacket, she felt the key at the bottom of the pocket. Just as her fist closed around it, one of Britten's hands shot out and grabbed her by the neck.

His fingers sank painfully into her flesh. Morgan tried wrenching her head away, but he had her in a death grip. She couldn't breathe, and panic quickly set in. Just when she was beginning to see stars, Brad got to his feet and charged toward her.

His foot viciously lashed out, smashing into Britten's

wrist and knocking his hand away. Morgan gasped and
breathed in a lungful of air. Holding fast to the key, she
rocked to her feet. The smoke now swirled thick about
their heads. Their eyes stung, and they couldn't stop
coughing. Above the steady roar of the flames, they
heard a child's muffled cry.

"Mikey!" Brad shouted. "Hold on, I'm coming!"

Brad glanced at Britten one last time. Britten was on
his knees, but he no longer clawed at his face. The struggle was nearly over, and he had lost. His hands fell
limply from his face, Then he slumped to his side and
toppled into the roaring flames.

Morgan led the way. Despite the handcuffs, she managed to get the door open, and she and Brad staggered
into the next room. The choking smoke streamed after
them through the doorway.

"Michael, where are you?" Brad called.

"Dad, over here!"

The voice came from the other end of the room. Brad
spotted him bound to the cot. "Hang on, Michael!"

"Brad, try to uncuff me first," Morgan said. "Careful
with the key."

The flames that raged through the doorway started to
race dangerously across the beamed ceiling. In a short
while, the whole house would be consumed. Brad and
Morgan came together awkwardly, back to back, fum-
bling around the chair between them. Morgan gingerly
dropped the key in his palm, and Brad went to work on
the handcuffs. When he finally manipulated the key into
the lock, the cuffs fell to the floor with a clatter.

"My bag," he prompted. "It's got a scissors!"

While she ran to retrieve it, Brad rushed to his son.
Despite the tape binding him to the cot, Michael had
managed to loosen the strip covering his mouth. By now
he was coughing heavily, and his eyes watered from the

smoke. With the flames licking toward them, Brad sank to his knees.

"Hang on, son. Just another second."

Michael crinkled his nose. "What's that *smell* on you?"

Brad had forgotten that his clothes were wet and putrid. "It's a long story," he said.

Morgan rushed toward their side. First she cut Michael's tape, pulling him to his feet and pushing him toward the door leading outside.

"Get out now," she said. "Run!"

The boy hesitated, looking at his father. "But—"

"Go, go, *go!*" Brad yelled.

As Michael scampered for the exit, a beam crashed down behind them in a fiery cascade. Pillars of golden fire had now consumed half the farmhouse, and searing flames were racing toward them like an unrolling carpet. Morgan's trembling fingers frantically cut Brad's taped wrists loose before setting to work on the strands binding him to the chair. The advancing heat was becoming intolerable, and Morgan struggled with the scissors. Finally, as sparks began to rain down on their shoulders, she cut the last piece of tape.

Just as they began sprinting for the door, there was a creaking groan, and a section of roof above them started to give way. As it tumbled toward them, Brad desperately yanked Morgan's wrist. The glowing beams smashed to the floor behind them with a thunderous crash. A second later they were outside, sucking in the cool night air.

Paralyzed by fear and astonishment, Michael just stood there, until Brad lifted him up and carried him a safe distance away. When they turned around to watch, there was a sudden flashover, and the remainder of the building blazed up with an audible *whump*. In the inferno's bright light, their faces took on an orange glow. They stood there in shocked silence, listening to the howling roar, watching the flames leap toward the heavens.

"It's finally over, isn't it?" Morgan said.

"Yes," Brad replied, putting his arms protectively around his son and then reaching out to her. "It's over."

EPILOGUE

LABOR DAY

Long Island's southeast shore was a Mecca for the rich, the famous, and pretentious wanna-bes. But a secret little-known to the summer's beautiful people was that some of the Island's poorest enclaves were a stone's throw from the Hamptons' golden beaches. A week after a gala political fund-raiser in East Hampton, Brad drove down a potholed street less than a mile from where the President had spent the night.

He pulled up in front of a small white building with new aluminum siding. The office was a work in progress, with an unfinished driveway and a front door in urgent need of paint. Above the door was a block-lettered sign: "LONG ISLAND FREE PEDIATRIC CLINIC." Brad honked the horn and leaned back to wait.

Soon the door opened and a pregnant Hispanic woman emerged holding a baby. She was undoubtedly one of the migrant workers drawn to the local farms during harvest season. Despite the afternoon's heat, the infant was tightly bundled. A minute later, Morgan walked out, waving goodbye to Janice and smiling at Brad. Beneath her white lab jacket, she was casually dressed in jeans and a polo shirt. A gust of wind sent her red hair swirling as she approached the car. She got in the passenger seat and kissed Brad on the cheek.

"So how was your first week?" he asked.

"Fantastic." She was beaming. "I don't recall pediatrics being this much fun."

"Maybe it wasn't. Back then, you were doing what you *had* to do, rather than wanted to do. Everything considered, think you're going to stick with it?"

"At least for now," she said. "It sure beats being in management. I'll stay as long as the money holds out."

Brad pulled away, nodding. The clinic seemed like a great investment for someone re-thinking her professional future. Its start-up funds had arrived courtesy of Britten and Morrison. Although neither Brad nor Morgan wanted the stocks they suddenly found in their brokerage accounts, the electronic transactions were ironclad, and they were unable to divest themselves of their hundred thousand shares apiece. Brad decided that, after what Michael had gone through, he deserved to have the money put aside for his college education; and Morgan felt that the AmeriCare shares might best be used for the kind of health care she'd once dreamed of: working with the most needy. They both sold their stocks immediately.

A few days later, when the AmeriCare scandal hit the papers, the share price plummeted. An incredulous public could not believe what AmeriCare had done to turn a profit. Within a month, unable to survive the investigations and adverse publicity, the company was bankrupt. Ultimately all HMOs suffered by association. The backlash against managed care was swift and far-reaching. Within weeks, people were clamoring for major changes in the industry.

When the police searched Britten's home, they were

as astonished as the public had been. Files in Britten's computer revealed the economist's intention of unleashing his newborn strategy statewide. Other files indicated that the man was considering expanding his methods to other medically unprofitable populations such as AIDS and cancer patients. It was a nightmarish scheme of staggering proportions.

As they headed home, a late afternoon storm rolled in from the west on mountainous gray thunderheads, reminding Brad of that fatal night. It had taken Mikey a full month to cope with the gruesome events, but a child psychologist reported that the boy was very resilient. He'd probably have some lingering night terrors, the doctor said, but they'd subside in time. Equally strong was Jennifer, who eventually discovered that the best antidote for her son's death was the full-time nurturing of her daughter.

Morgan watched the storm approach. A month remained in the sailing season, and they'd planned on picking up Michael for an early evening cruise. She gestured toward the clouds.

"Should we take a chance with that?"

"Probably not," Brad said. "But we should go to the slip and anchor for a blow."

"Think we can sail tomorrow?"

"I'd imagine," he nodded. "After a front like this rolls through, it's usually smooth sailing."

Rather like life itself, Morgan thought. Life's harshest storms were sometimes followed by glorious new beginnings, if one was lucky. She glanced up at the sky, then at Brad. And she smiled.

They had been very lucky indeed.